FEAR AND DESIRE

The Indians moved on and when she realized that her own group was safe she was overcome with a fit of trembling.

She could not control herself. She was so very tired. So very hungry. So very frightened. She felt the security of Connor's arms as they came around her and she burrowed her head into his chest. Her hands clutched at his shirt as she moved closer, pressing her body against the length of his. She could not get close enough.

"Shush, *mo cridhe*," he whispered. His lips touched the top of her head. "They are gone and we should be away whilst we know where they are."

She didn't want to move. She wanted to stay where she was, secure in his arms until this nightmare ended.

She could have remained in Williamsburg, safe with her uncle.

Safe and not knowing if her brother were alive or dead. Or if Connor were alive or dead. Would it have mattered to her then?

He rose, pulling her to her feet as if she weighed nothing. She looked up into his eyes, which were lost in the shadows created by the moonlight. His hand touched her cheek, his thumb moved under her eye and she realized there were tears. Then his hand cupped her chin and tilted her face up.

He was going to kiss her. The fear, the worry, the discomfort, all flew from her mind as her stomach churned with anticipation. The pad of his thumb moved across her lips, and they parted, ready...waiting...

Other *Leisure* books by Cindy Holby:

WHIRLWIND
FORGIVE THE WIND
WINDFALL
CROSSWINDS
WIND OF THE WOLF
CHASE THE WIND

Writing as Colby Hodge:

SHOOTING STAR
STARGAZER

CINDY HOLBY

Rising Wind

LEISURE BOOKS   NEW YORK CITY

For Justin.

A LEISURE BOOK®

August 2007

Dorchester Publishing Co., Inc.
200 Madison Avenue
New York, NY 10016

ISBN-10: 0-8439-5865-0
ISBN-13: 978-0-8439-5865-2

The name "Leisure Books" and the stylized "L" with design are trademarks of Dorchester Publishing Co., Inc.

Printed in the United States of America.

Visit us on the web at www.dorchesterpub.com.

AUTHOR'S NOTE

I was raised on a battlefield. Some of my first memories are of visiting the memorial at Tu-Endie-Wei Park and wondering about the battle fought there and the men who died. The place was full of history and I loved it. The battle I am referring to is The Battle of Point Pleasant, the only battle fought in what was referred to as Dunmore's war. The battle was between the Virginia Militia and the united Indian nations led by Chief Cornstalk. It is of historical significance because after the English victory there was peace on the Frontier along the Ohio River. This peace allowed the colonists to come east and fight in what was to become the Revolutionary War.

I lived in Point Pleasant, West Virginia, as a child so I suppose it was destiny that led me to write this story. The places I knew well, the history, were part of me and the research involved led to many late nights and tired eyes. I used actual people from history and intertwined them with my characters: Connor, Carrie and her father and brother. It was not my intention to make this book into a history lesson but to represent the courage it took to build a nation. So if some of you are history majors and know that General Andrew Lewis was not in a certain place at a certain time, all I can say is—sorry. I loved the image of him as Connor's mentor and placed him in time accordingly.

The accounts of the Shawnee atrocities were taken from actual historical records given by eye witnesses. It was the way of life then. It amazes me to think of the courage our forefathers possessed.

And at last I would like to say Thank You to my mom and dad for taking me to Tu-Endie-Wei and letting me see the history there. Every journey starts with a step and those were the first steps on this journey.

Prologue

"Ye must go." James Connor Duncan placed his hand on the firm swell of his wife's stomach. He felt the hard thrust of a kick against the plaid that she held tightly clutched to her chest. It slipped from her reddish blond hair and he pulled it back into place, tenderly touching her cheek as he arranged the fabric to his satisfaction.

"He wants to fight," Anice MacLachlan Duncan said. Tears filled her bright blue eyes. "He is like his father."

"His father is a fool," James said. He tossed a look over his shoulder to see if anyone was listening, but the sleet that whipped across the boggy marsh sheltered the pair. They might as well be alone. Five thousand Scotsmen stood on the land, each one lost in his own thoughts. There was no sound save the creak of leather and the occasional shifting of one of the few horses that had been kept from the stew pots. "Surrounded by fools, led by a fool, on a mission that is sure to fail."

"If ye believe that, then why are ye here?" Anice said. Her eyes were huge in her face, surrounded as they were by the dark shadows of starvation and exhaustion.

"Because I gave your father my word that I would stand and fight with your clan. Because the alternative is dishonor and slavery, and I will no' have that for the babe."

"Leave with me," Anice begged. "We could go to the new country."

"I must see it through," James said. "I gave my word."

"And what of the word ye gave to me?" Anice, always patient, always sweet, suddenly was overcome with rage. Her hands beat against the heavy linen of his shirt. "Ye promised to stay with me always. Ye promised to take care of me."

"Until death parts us," James said. He grabbed her to him, surrounding her with his arms to silence her. "Do no' let the last words I hear from your sweet lips be those of anger."

"What if I donae want this to be the last words?" Anice cried. She leaned her head under the shelter of his jaw, seeking the warmth of the bare skin where his shirt lay open. His hair, a shade darker than her own, lay in tangles over his shoulder and she pulled her fingers through it, recalling the way it glowed copper in the firelight. "What if ye die?"

"Then I will die wi' the belief that a part of me will survive. I will die wi' the belief that I had the love of a good woman. I will die wi' the belief that ye will go and raise the bairn."

"I donae want to go on without ye."

"Ye must, Anice. Ye must go now." James resisted the urge to shake some sense into her. She seemed so frail. So weak. If only she had stayed home. If only she were safe and warm and surrounded by women who would take care of her when her time came. It would be soon, he knew. He was afraid she would not survive it. Her eyes were sunk into her head with starvation and great dark circles showed up violently on her pale skin. "How can I turn and fight if I donae ken ye are safe?"

"I cannae walk away kenning that ye will surely die." Her voice broke.

"I will surely die if ye are no' safe," James said, more forcefully than he wanted to. His hands gripped her arms, and he knew there would be dark bruises from his fingers on her pale skin by the evening time.

He would never see them.

"Fortis et fidus." Her clan motto: brave and faithful. That she was, and bonnie too. "Please go. Hide. Stay hidden until it is over."

"James!" someone called out to him.

He pulled her close and his lips claimed hers, burning his brand into her. Then he pushed her away.

"Go, Anice. Go. And donae ever forget that I love ye."

James drew his claymore.

"Go." His voice was firm, but his eyes swelled as she gathered the red and blue plaid under her chin and finally turned away.

He watched as she walked away—proud, erect, even though she was weary—until she disappeared into the scrubby brush that grew around the moor. Then he turned and joined the ranks of MacLachlans that stood side by side behind Bonnie Prince Charlie.

It was over within the hour. Anice watched the bloody battle from a rise as she prayed. She knew it was all for naught. God was not on their side this day.

When the sound of the battle was over, she made her way back down the road past her kinsmen and countrymen, who fled, begging her to go with them.

It did not matter. The English, almost double in number and still enraged with battle, turned on the men, women and children who clogged the road toward Inverness.

Yet somehow they missed her. Was it because she was a vapor? She felt hollow inside, as if she were nothing more than a formless spirit left to haunt this moor.

She no longer felt cold or hunger.

She did not even feel the babe inside her.

Without knowing how or why, she went right to the spot where James lay. She walked past the hands that grabbed at her skirts. Past the moans and cries of the dying men, even though she knew some were her kinsmen. Her father and brothers were dead. She didn't even pause when she passed their bodies. They had died in the thick of battle.

Perhaps it was the color of his hair that drew her, although it was hard enough to tell one reddish hue from another among the bodies.

There was so much blood.

James lay on his back, his hand still clenching his claymore. A body lay across him, the sword arm gone. Blood still poured on the ground from the wound, mixing with sleet into a thick, congealed pool.

With great difficulty Anice pushed the body away and ran her hands over her husband's face. His blue eyes, as blue as the autumn sky, stared straight up into the heavens.

Was he dead? How could he be? There wasn't a mark upon him. Her hands followed the trail of her eyes, roaming over the familiar dips and curves of his hard muscles and long limbs.

"James?" she said finally, but there was no response.

She put her hand behind his head, intending to lift his head into her lap. Instead she came away with a bloody mess of gore in her hand.

His brains had been knocked out. He had been struck down from behind.

Anice looked at the mess on her hand and realized she held the essence of her husband in her palm. The parts of him that made him speak, that made him walk, that made his eyes twinkle merrily when he was up to some mischief.

But it wasn't his heart and it wasn't his soul.

Those belonged to her. They would not be scattered upon this desperate place. She would see to that.

She moved to his head and pushed his shoulders up. It was hard and slow work for her. James was a head taller than most, and wide of frame. She managed to get her hands beneath his arm and dragged him backward as she watched over her shoulder so that she would not stumble over the other bodies that littered the battlefield.

Even thought it wrenched her insides, even though her arms felt as if they were being pulled from their sockets, even when she felt warmth trickling down the inside of her legs and knew the babe was on its way, she would not stop.

"You there," a voice called out. She ignored it. "Stop!"

A man rode up, his uniform disheveled, bloody. A piece of torn linen was tied about his upper arm. He was an officer of some rank, she noticed. As if that mattered to the dead men lying about the field.

"I command you to stop," he said. He held his sword at the ready. "That man is a prisoner."

"This man is my husband," Anice said. She let go for a moment, to push her wet hair from her eyes. James fell to the earth with a heavy thunk.

"Even so, madam, he is a prisoner."

Anice looked up at the man. He didn't seem much older than she. He seemed weary.

He could not be as weary as she felt. She felt as if she were thousands of years old and cursed to live forever.

"What use does His Majesty have for dead prisoners?" Anice asked.

The man dismounted quickly and bent to see for himself if she lied.

"I mean to bury him," Anice said determinedly.

"Then he is luckier than most," the man said.

Anice looked at him in confusion. A noise from beyond caught her attention. A scream of pain. A man held up his arm in defense as an English soldier stabbed him with his bayonet.

"We've been told to spare no one," the officer said when he realized what she was looking at. "Not even you."

"Are we such terrors to His Majesty that you must kill the babes in the wombs?" Anice asked. Her hands went unconsciously to her belly, which was contracting in pain.

"There are some that think so," the officer said wearily. "What was his name?" he asked, nodding at James's body.

"James Connor Duncan," Anice said. "He fought under my father's banner. The MacLachlans. I am Anice."

"Then we will bury him with the same," the man said. "If you will allow it."

Anice let out a heavy sigh and looked down at the dear face of her husband. She hoped she would never forget it.

"I will," she said finally. She knew it was a miracle that she was still standing. She had no idea how she would bury James. She just knew she couldn't leave him as he was.

"Would you lay me wi' him then?" she asked.

"I beg your pardon?'

"You said you are to spare no one," she said. "Not even me." She doubled over as a stronger pain hit her. The man caught her arms and held on as she felt the babe pushing down. "I wish to be buried wi' him and my kinsmen."

"Is it your time?" he asked.

"I fear it is," Anice said when she was finally able to breathe.

"We must get you to the physician," he said. He looked around as if in panic.

"A rebel's son born at the hands of an English doctor?" Anice said with a wry smile. "T'would be enough to wake the dead and send them back to battle." She doubled over with another pain.

"We must do something," the man exclaimed.

"A midwife would do," Anice gasped. "If you havnae killed them all."

"At least let me get you to shelter," the man said. He wrapped an arm around her waist and tried to get her to move, but she wouldn't budge.

"I cannae leave him like this," she said finally, looking down at James.

"If you care for his child, then you must," the officer urged. "I will see to him," he promised. He must have seen the doubt in her eyes because he called out to some soldiers who were checking the wounded.

"Take this body and put it with his clansmen," he commanded. "And make sure he remains unmarked and whole."

The soldiers looked confused but smartly saluted and carefully picked up James's body. Anice watched wearily as they carried him back to where her kinsmen lay.

"They can be trusted," the officer assured her. "Your husband and kinsmen will be as you've left them until they can be buried."

Anice took a faltering step at his urging and then stopped again. She looked up at him and saw lines of worry around his eyes.

"Why are ye doing this? Why are ye helping me?"

"I have often thought that this world would be a better place if we would just take the time to be kind," the officer said. "And I admire your spirit. You remind me of my wife."

"James would say I was foolish and headstrong." Anice gasped as another pain gripped her.

"Such are the things great nations are built of," the officer said.

"What is your name?" They were moving now, toward a stone cottage in the distance.

"James," he said with a smile. "James Murray."

"A fine Scottish name," Anice said. Not all had joined the cause. If only her clan had also refrained. "No title?"

"No. I leave that to my younger brother, The fourth Earl of Dunmore. The one who isn't a bastard."

Anice tried to smile but grimaced instead at his dry statement of the facts. She often thought that children were the ones who paid for the crimes of their parents.

"Children?"

"A son. Just walking when I left him."

"Have you sent word to your wife? That you survived?"

He stopped, as if surprised.

"She will be worried for your safety," Anice said.

"You followed your husband? Even onto the battlefield?"

"I would ha' strapped on a sword and stood by his side had I not carried this babe."

"It's a wonder we defeated you."

"It's not hard to defeat starving, exhausted men," Anice said. "It's a wonder they lasted as long as they did."

"This child is your first?"

"Aye. And most likely my last." The burden of her labor was more than she could stand at the moment, and her legs buckled beneath her. She did not have the breath to protest when Murray scooped her up into his arms and carried her to the cottage. The light was getting dim, even though Anice knew it was early afternoon.

The next pain nearly split her in two, and the world grew dark as Murray stooped to enter the cottage.

"You must push, child," someone, a woman, said to her later. She had lost track of the time, consumed as she was with pain.

"I cannae," Anice said. "I havno' the strength. Leave me to die. Bury me with James."

"Would you kill the child too?" a masculine voice said in her ear. "Would you have your husband's name die with you? And with him?"

"Damn the English," Anice said and struggled to rise. She felt sure she was going to die anyway, no matter what Murray said.

She pushed and screamed and pushed again until the midwife caught her son and placed it on her belly.

"James Connor Duncan," Anice said. "After his father." She looked up at Murray, who was smiling at her. "If it pleases ye to think differently, then so be it," she added as she wrapped the bairn in the cloth provided and held him to her chest.

He cried lustily as he nuzzled against her breast.

"I'm glad to see he has his mother's spirit," Murray

said. His touched the swirl of bright red on top of the baby's head.

"And his father's," Anice said. "Another fine warrior. For Scotland."

"If you wish him to survive this day, then you'd best keep that sentiment to yourself," Murray said. "I will check on you tomorrow," he said, and left the cottage.

"I would not have believed it if I had not seen it myself," the midwife commented as she finished the business of the birthing.

"Kindness comes from unexpected places at times," Anice agreed. "There must be a reason for it, but only God can tell what good will come of this day."

"All is not lost, child," the midwife said. "You have a son. And I'm guessing he has the looks of his father."

"Aye, he does," Anice said, looking down at the sweet face. A pair of bright blue eyes looked up at her as if puzzled at the happenings of the day. "I'll never forget him. My dear, sweet James." Her voice broke as she said his name. "I will call my son Connor," she decided.

"Let me give Master Duncan a washing," the midwife said. "Come, young Connor."

"Is it still today?" Anice asked as she watched. Through the window she saw the light of campfires in the distance. Night had fallen, but for when she did not know.

"Today?"

"April sixteenth. The day of the battle."

"Aye, it's evening time."

"It's a good thing, then. That he was born this day. He will never forget what happened on this day."

"I'm afraid that none of us will," the midwife said as she handed Connor back to Anice. "For a very long time."

Chapter One

Connor Duncan realized it was his twenty-eighth birthday when he rode into the great city of Williamsburg at dusk and saw the candles in the windows. The citizens traditionally put candles in the windows to celebrate great English victories. Culloden certainly met that requirement.

It was easy to lose track of the days when you were in the wilderness. Easy to lose track of the years too. Had it really been eighteen years since he'd come to the colonies as a bond servant?

Twenty-eight years since his birth. Twenty-eight years since the death of his father. Eighteen years since his mother's death, and his forced servitude. Eleven years since he was freed. Seven years since his friend, benefactor and former master, Sir Richard Abbington, had died.

April was always the month for happenings in his life. And here it was another April, another birthday, and he carried a summons to the Governor's Palace. What great event could he look forward to now?

The summons had come through his friend and mentor, Andrew Lewis. General Andrew Lewis. It was hard to think of him as an officer in the militia, since Connor had spent so much time with the man on the frontier.

Andrew's letter suggested the two friends meet before Connor answered the summons. He appreciated the caution his friend showed where he was concerned. Perhaps he thought of Connor still as the young bondservant, newly arrived from Scotland and terrified to find himself in the middle of a war with the French and the Indian tribes.

If not for Andrew and Sir Richard, he would not have survived it. There were many who would have taken his scalp because of its bright copper hue. And the idea of killing a ten-year-old boy did not cause those who wanted his scalp any concern at all.

Connor rode his chestnut mare through the bustling streets to the Raleigh Tavern. The populace, a mixture of rich and poor, master and slave, townsman and frontiersman, quickly moved about, in a hurry to conclude their business for the day and find their supper.

Connor found that he was looking forward to a nice meal himself. He had spent most of the day in trade, turning a healthy profit on the furs and skins he'd trapped during the winter. He was suddenly hungry for food, fire and conversation. He spotted Andrew as soon as he entered the tavern. The man was hard to miss because of his stature. Connor was one of the few men who could look him in the eye.

Andrew waved him with a pewter tankard toward a table by the fire.

"I see you survived another winter," he commented as Connor joined him at the table. "With all your hair."

Connor grinned at him. "The Cherokee like my hair upon my head."

"I'm sure the females do," Andrew said, returning his grin. James Southall, the innkeeper, pushed his way through the crowd with ale for Connor and the promise of a roasted chicken. "So all is peaceful on the Blue Ridge?"

"Aye. But no' farther north, I hear?" He rolled his *r*s, as was his wont. Even after all these years in the colonies, his Scots heritage was evident in his speech.

"There's been unrest up around the Greenbrier and New."

"Shawnee?"

"Yes. And there are rumors that they've signed a treaty with some of the other tribes."

"Delawares? Wyandots?"

"Mingoes, Miamis, Ottawas, Illinois and some others," Andrew continued. "It happened last autumn."

A barmaid set two plates of chicken before them, along with a crusty loaf of dark bread. She gave Connor a saucy look before she walked away. Andrew smiled benignly as Connor ignored the woman and dug into his meal.

"Who is the war chief?" Connor asked after swallowing. Sir Richard had been a stickler for proper manners, even on the frontier.

"Keigh-tugh-qua." Andrew carefully pronounced the name.

"Cornstalk," Connor translated for him. "The chief support of his people."

"Do you know him?"

Connor felt the familiar shiver down his spine at the thought of the time he had spent as a hostage of the Shawnee. The never-ending screams of his friend Tom still haunted his dreams. He took a long swallow of his ale. There were things he did not care to remember. He had seen sights he never wanted to see again.

"Aye, I ken him," he said finally. "They chose well for their purpose."

"You're the only one who's spent any amount of time around him and survived to tell the tale," Andrew reminded him. "After his treachery at Muddy Creek, he's become a legend."

"I was a prisoner," Connor said. He pushed away his plate, his appetite suddenly gone. "I was only in his presence twice."

"But you got his measure."

"He is no' one to trifle with."

They sat in silence for a moment. Connor was glad for it. It gave him time to get the fear back under control.

Having to watch your best friend burn alive for what seemed like an eternity was something he'd never thought he'd survive. Especially when he knew the same fate awaited him. If not for Daniel Boone . . .

"Lord Dunmore wants to hear your story," Andrew said quietly.

"It isnae something I like to share," Connor said. "With anyone."

"He needs the measure of the man," Andrew reminded him. "He should know the enemy."

"Boone kens their ways better than I," Connor said.

"Boone's eyes are turned west," Andrew said. "He still mourns James."

Connor nodded. Sixteen-year-old James Boone had been skinned alive by a raiding party just last autumn. They found his body within a few miles of his father's camp. Boone knew the ways of the Indian well.

"Lord Dunmore has sent for Boone too," Andrew said. "But his plans for him lie in Kentucky. Dunmore hopes he can claim the land there before the Governor of Pennsylvania does."

"Politics," Connor said quietly. There was no escaping it. Since the day he was born he had been tossed back and forth by politics. "Ye would think that as vast as this land is, there would be plenty enough for everyone." His tankard was empty and he motioned to the barmaid.

"England does not wish to share with France or Spain. Why should her governors share with each other?"

Connor nodded as another tankard was set before him. He cast his eyes toward a closed door at the back of the common room. It was known far and wide that the House of Burgesses used the room for meetings.

Andrew saw where he looked. "You heard about Boston, then?" he asked.

"Aye," Connor said. Some colonists had dared tweak the nose of Parliament by dumping tea into the harbor this past December.

"It's been a bit hard for the house to meet," Andrew said, referring to the House of Burgesses, which represented the colonists. "Without raising Lord Dunmore's ire."

"I hear that Henry is getting more vocal in his protests about taxation without representation."

"Patrick has been vocal for years," Andrew said. "I think that finally some are willing to listen to him." He looked around to make sure no one was eavesdropping and lowered his voice so that Connor had to lean in to hear. "But until we solve the problem on the frontier, we cannot address the problem closer at hand."

"If we can achieve some sort of peace on the frontier?"

Andrew raised his hand to keep Connor from saying anything that could be perceived as treason by listening ears.

"Lord Dunmore is having a ball tomorrow night to introduce his niece to Williamsburg," he said, quickly changing the subject. "She has recently come from England, where it is rumored that she was widowed thrice before she was married once."

"How can that be?" Connor asked.

"It seems that her bridegrooms have a habit of dying just before the wedding."

Connor burst out laughing. "Is she that terrifying? Perhaps she is hideous and they preferred death to waking up to the sight of her?"

"They call her the Virgin Widow," Andrew said.

"Do the authorities suspect her of harming her intendeds?"

"I do not know," Andrew said. "The rumor is that her father has given up on her marrying in England and hopes that perhaps she will make a marriage here. He is an officer of the king and has been in Boston of late. Her mother died recently, and she traveled here with her brother, who is also an officer in the army."

"And her father sends her to Virginia, where we have a kinder view of the British than those in Boston."

"Do not wear your sentiments on your sleeve, Connor," Andrew advised him. "There are many who would make a profit at your expense by accusing you of treason."

"What could they gain by my imprisonment?" Connor said. "I have naught but a small cabin and a decent horse, which I hope to breed. It is not as if my treasonous thoughts would be a surprise to anyone, especially the British, considering where I come from and how I got here."

Andrew looked at Connor as if taken aback by the hostility in his voice. Then a sudden understanding filled his eyes.

"Culloden," he said. "The anniversary of your birth."

Connor raised his tankard as if in a toast. "To anniversaries," he said, drained it and waved his hand for another. "The good people of this town see fit to celebrate it."

Andrew grabbed his arm. "We have all evening to drink to your health," he said. "Why the rush?"

"I have a lot of anniversaries today," Connor said. He saw the concern in his friend's eyes but was in no mood to be coddled. "And the day is almost done."

The barmaid arched a questioning brow at Connor as she set down another round. Andrew dropped some coin on her tray, then looked at his young friend.

"You've survived more in a few short years than most have in a lifetime," he said. "And you've come through it with strength and intelligence. Yet tonight you sound bitter."

"Why should I nae be bitter?" Connor asked. "Should I be grateful that the English killed my father on the battlefield and hanged my mother ten years later in front of me because she dared to show a bit of the plaid on the anniversary of her husband's death?"

"The men responsible for that were not acting on the king's orders," Andrew said. "They should have been held accountable."

Connor almost laughed. "Yet that did not stop them from chaining me up, throwing me into the hold of a ship where I almost died and selling me as a slave," Connor continued. Why was he bitter on this day? What made this anniversary different from all the others he had observed? He usually let them pass, taking a moment to pay tribute to the courage of both his parents. It would have been easier for both of them to run. But they hadn't. They'd stood their ground. And they'd died.

Leaving him alone. Today of all days the loneliness seemed worse, if that was possible.

"You were luckier than most," Andrew said gently. "Sir Richard cared for you."

Connor raised his tankard. "To Sir Richard," he said. "Although at first I didn't know which was worse, Sir Richard's threats that he would surely beat me to death or the way every Indian we met looked at my scalp."

"You were in a sorry state," Andrew agreed. "When Sir Richard said he was off to get a bondservant to help with his surveying, I expected someone big enough to carry his equipment, not a scrawny lad such as you, with a wild look in his eyes and hair the color of blood. You looked as if a stiff breeze would blow you away."

"That's because I dinnae eat anything the entire time I was on the ship. I couldnae keep anything down," Connor protested. "Then the first thing Sir Richard did was douse me in a trough. He handed me some clothes to put on, which were much too large, and the next thing I knew I was on the road north, walking into the middle of a war."

"It's a good thing the clothes Sir Richard put on you were too large. Once you started eating, we were afraid you were never going to stop."

"Sir Richard did complain that he got the worst of it when he saw me eat," Connor admitted. "He thought he'd gotten a bargain since I was so thin. He figured it would-nae take much to keep me."

"And once you got over your wariness, you were deter-mined to put a knife in the back of General Amhurst be-cause you were sure he commanded the entire British Army. Including the ones patrolling in Scotland." Andrew roared with laughter.

"One red coat looks pretty much like the next," Connor said with an indolent shrug. "And I was anxious to use the knife ye gave me." He pulled the blade from its sheath and placed it on the table. "It has served me well."

"Then it has served its purpose," Andrew said. "I'll never forget the look on Amhurst's face when you said that the army might do better if we hid in the trees and fought like the Indians instead of marching down the middle of the road banging on those drums. We'd been telling him that for years, but the fool wouldn't listen. I was surprised he didn't hang you on the spot."

"Sir Richard got a good laugh out of it," Connor said. "After he beat me for insolence."

"Sir Richard rode with Braddock. As did Washington. Both learned from the experience."

"The problem with the English is that they are so stiff-necked," Connor said.

Andrew once again placed a warning hand on Connor's arm. "I've got a room for you at Christiana Campbell's. It's just across the street. You'll need a bath and a decent coat before you meet with the governor. I've arranged for both."

"Thank you, Andrew," Connor said. "For everything."

"Just mind your manners for me, son," Andrew said. They rose as one and made their way through the press of the crowd to the door. "Especially with the governor." They stepped into the night air. It smelled fresh and clean after the staleness of the tavern. It smelled of spring. "It's easy to speak your mind when there's no one to hear you but the wind," Andrew said as Connor took the reins of his horse to lead it down the street.

"I understand," Connor said. "Will ye be there when I meet the governor?"

"I'll be there," Andrew said. "Sleep well, my friend."

Connor watched as Andrew moved on down the street and disappeared into the darkness. Most of the candles had been extinguished now, leaving nothing but the light spilling out from the taverns located on Duke of Gloucester Street.

In the darkness above, a few stars pricked the night sky. It almost seemed empty. When he was on the Blue Ridge, it seemed as if there were millions of stars, close enough that he could pluck them from the sky. Sometimes he fancied that they were tiny holes in the heavens that his parents could look through. That they were watching over him.

But that was when he was much younger. He was twenty-eight years old now, and the governor expected to hear about one of the more horrible times in his life.

It was April, after all.

Chapter Two

Caroline Murray looked at her reflection in the mirror as a young woman knelt on the floor beside the small platform on which she stood and adjusted the hem of her new gown. The striped blue satin certainly matched her eyes as promised, and the lace of the ruffles was as fine as any she had seen in England. Her mother's pearls would go well with the gown.

Carrie ran her hands down the stomacher and twisted against her stays.

"Please, miss," Abigail said.

Carrie sighed. She was in a new country, and she wanted to see something of it beyond the safe city streets of Williamsburg. But since her arrival a week ago, her uncle had conspired to keep her safely locked away in the governor's mansion or accompanied to fittings like this one, while her brother John was out exploring the countryside. If not for the promise of the ball to be held tonight, she would think they were ashamed of her.

Could she help it if her reputation preceded her?

Could she help it if the men her mother had chosen

for her to marry were clumsy or drunkards or just so plain old that they couldn't survive long enough to speak their vows? Was it her fault that her family had no money because her father was born a bastard and was not entitled to inherit anything? Was it her fault that she had no dowry to offer and therefore had to settle and hope for the best?

It wasn't as if she really wanted to marry. But it was expected of her. *Marry someone so your father doesn't have to support you any longer on his officer's salary. Marry well so your brother can make a good match. Hurry up and marry before your beauty fades and you have nothing left to offer a husband.*

She heard her mother's words as if she were still standing behind her, lacing her stays.

Carrie hated stays. Almost as much as she hated the side hoops that were now the fashion. She had heard that the native women wore nothing under their gowns. And their gowns were nothing more than pieces of hide sewn together, with fringe and bead added.

She had even heard it whispered about that some of the native women wore nothing above the waist.

"Please, miss," Abigail said again. "If you want the gown finished in time, you must stand still."

Carrie hadn't even realized she was fidgeting. It was one of her worst traits, next to her clumsiness, and her mother had boxed her ears for it often enough. Yet neither had abated, despite her mature age of twenty-four.

Long past the age when she should have married.

She decided to will her rebellious mind and body into submission. She would simply think of something else besides the great country to the west that was just begging to be explored.

Think of something depressing . . .

She should think of her mother, only gone this past winter, and her father unable to get home in time because of the weather. The pain was still fresh in her mind, especially hurtful since she felt she'd been a disappointment to her mother.

Instead she thought of the saddest thing she had ever seen. Even after all these years, the sight haunted her. It was pretty close to her first memory. She was certain it was the first time she'd realized that the world was a harsh place outside comfortable little house they lived in due to the good grace of her titled grandfather.

It was the first time her father had been stationed away from home since she was born. She was certain she would never see him again as he prepared to go to the colonies. At the age of six, her father was her entire world. The whole family had gone to the docks to see him off.

"Why can't we get out of the carriage, Mother?" asked John, nearly twelve. "I want to see the ships."

"Your father asked us to wait until they are finished loading," her mother said.

"I'm going with Father," John declared impatiently and jumped out of the carriage

"Stay put," Mother instructed as she went after him.

Carrie, entranced by the sounds, sights and smells of the wharf, rose to her knees on the padded seat of the carriage and peered out the window.

She saw her father's bright red coat standing out among the drab, faded colors worn by the dock workers. His blond hair glistened in the sunlight, and Carrie thought him more magnificent than anyone on the docks. She saw John bobbing and weaving his way toward him and her mother a few paces behind. She kept a hand clutched to her head, as if she were afraid her hat would fly off.

A strange clanking noise drifted to Carrie's ears, and she moved to the opposite side of the carriage to get a look at what was causing the sound.

Chains. A line of men, ten or so, slowly walked by with their ankles chained together. They looked frightening, as if they were dead already. Their clothes hung on them in tatters, and their faces were shrunken and dirty. Carrie imagined they must be horrible criminals of some sort, the type that weren't mentioned in her presence, although she was very good at listening to things she wasn't supposed to hear.

At the end of the line was a boy. He couldn't be any older than John. He looked as tall as her brother, but painfully thin. His feet were bare and bloody, as if he had walked a long way. His hair was a bright reddish color, and even though it was filthy, it still shone brightly in the sun.

Carrie watched with her mouth hanging open in the most unladylike pose. She was sure if her mother caught her hanging out of the carriage window gawking at a line of chained men, she would be beaten until she could not sit down for a week.

Her heart immediately felt pity for the boy. What had he done to be locked in chains? Where were his mother and father? Where was he being taken?

The men walked by with eyes downcast. But the boy looked at her. His eyes blazed the brightest blue she had ever seen. They were fierce. They terrified her, as if his heart and soul cried out to her. She met his eyes with her own and as she did, she said a prayer for the soul of the boy. The chain jerked, and he stumbled in his effort to keep up. He turned and looked at her just as the line disappeared into the crowd.

"Father, where are they taking those men?" she asked as soon as her family returned. She could see them now, slowly making their way up the gangplank of a tall sailing ship. The same ship that would take her father away.

Her father plucked her from the carriage and held her against his side as he looked where her hand was pointing. Her mother, always mindful of proper etiquette, quickly pulled Carrie's hand down to her side.

"They are going to the colonies," her father said. "They are to be bondservants."

"Slaves," John clarified for her.

"No, John," her father corrected. "Not slaves. They will do service to a master for seven years to pay for their passage, and to off their debt to the Crown. They will be free men when their service is over."

"But what if they don't want to live in the colonies?" Carrie asked. "What if their families are here in England?"

"Then they can come home if they wish," her father said.

But Carrie knew he was being less than truthful. If it was so easy to come home to England, why was her father going to be gone for so long?

"I saw a boy," Carrie said. "Will he ever see his mother or father again?"

And her father, who always wanted her to be happy, told her what she wanted to hear. "I'm sure he will, my sweet. Now give your father a kiss that will last him a long while."

"I wonder what happened to that boy," Carrie said.

"I beg your pardon, miss?" Abigail asked.

Carrie blinked and caught her reflection in the mirror. For a moment, she had felt as if she were that child again, a child with a heart breaking for an unknown boy, who she was sure was going to miss his father as much as she knew she would miss hers.

As she grew older, she realized that the boy was more than likely an orphan, and a criminal. But still she never forgot him. And sometimes she even remembered to say a prayer for him, especially when she was lonely and missed her father.

She usually thought about the young bondservant in the mornings, when she looked in the mirror at her own blue eyes and brushed her golden blond hair.

What happened to the boy with the bright red hair and the fierce blue eyes? Did he ever get to go home?

"We're done, miss," Abigail said. "I can have the gown delivered if you wish."

"I'll just take it with me now," Carrie said, "and save you the trouble."

"Thank you, miss."

Carrie was sure she saw the girl sigh with relief. She wondered how many more dresses she would have to hem before the day was over. It seemed like the whole town would be attending the ball.

"I'll help you dress," Abigail said.

Carrie sighed. Dressing should not be so complicated. Abigail unhooked the stomacher and helped Carrie pull off the blue satin creation and the matching petticoat.

"It's a very good color for you," the girl said as she took the gown away through the curtain that protected the small dressing room from the front of the shop.

Carrie put on her silk petticoat over her hoops and underpetticoat and tied the drawstring in the back. She pinned her stomacher to her stays and wondered where Abigail had run off to. She really needed help to get her gown back on.

The sound of whispers and suppressed laughter caught her ears so she opened the curtain a bit to see what was going on.

She saw her blue-striped satin gown lying on a counter. Abigail and another girl stood looking out the window, gossiping about something.

"I've never seen him before, have you?" the other girl asked Abigail.

"I'm sure I would remember if I had," Abigail said. "One doesn't often see hair that color."

"It looks like molten copper," the girl said. "It would be a shame to cover that with a wig."

"And he's so tall," Abigail said. "A head above everyone else on the street. I wonder what he's doing here."

"He's dressed simply enough," the girl said. "Although his coat is made of silk."

Carrie had to see whom they were talking about. She stepped off the platform, tripped and caught the curtain.

"Oh, miss." Abigail ran back to the dressing room. "I am sorry. I was er . . . looking at . . ."

"Hair like molten copper?"

Abigail blushed. "He was a fine-looking man," she said with a slight smile.

"I'm sorry I missed him," Carrie said with a laugh as Abigail helped her fasten her gown.

"Miss?" Abigail said, her voice rising, as if she was appalled at Carrie's behavior.

She was reminded that she wasn't a shop girl. She was one of the gentry. They were supposed to be above things like admiring a handsome man when he walked down the street.

Hair like molten copper . . . She would dearly love to see that. She placed her lace neckerchief around her neck, and settled her hat atop her lace cap.

The other girl had Carrie's dress boxed up for her, along with a pair of matching shoes.

There are some benefits to having the governor of the colony as your uncle, Carrie thought when one of her uncle's slaves immediately came for the boxes and put them in the carriage.

"I would like to walk for a bit," Carrie said to her driver. It was still early, and she knew her uncle had several appointments and John wasn't due back from his explorations until later that afternoon.

It would be nice if her father could arrive in time for the ball, but he was taking the long route down from Boston, all the way west to the frontier to look at the forts there.

If only she could see some of this wild, untamed country.

The carriage followed her as she walked down the row of shops. The street was crowded with horses, oxcarts, wagons, carriages, wandering chickens and what seemed to be stray sheep. The road in itself was close to being a quagmire, and Carrie felt as if a strong rain would make it impassable.

The populace she passed was a mixture of gentry, tradesmen, farmers, frontiersmen and slaves, all wearing various types of dress from fine silk to the coarsest linen.

Carrie disliked the notion of slavery. She knew that some of the people she saw were freemen and able to pursue their own trades. But others were not. How horrible it must be to be torn from your family and the only world you knew and be forced into a life of servitude.

She cast a curious look at the carriage and wondered about the driver and footman. They seemed concerned about her walking alone. Would they be punished because she wished to take a few moments to explore this new place?

Where did they come from? How long had they been here? Had they been auctioned off on the steps of one of the taverns? She'd seen an advertisement for such a sale tacked to the front of a shop. Had the boy she recalled from years before been auctioned off like a slave?

The sight of a man wearing buckskin leggings, a loincloth and moccasins nearly stopped her in her tracks. She didn't mean to stare, but . . .

Hair like molten copper. It wasn't the man in the buckskins. It was a man on the opposite side of the street who saw her staring. He was riding a tall chestnut and wearing a green coat. He took off his plain cocked hat and dipped his head in a slight bow as he rode by. The early morning sunlight caught his hair, and it glowed like molten copper.

He was smiling at her. Or maybe laughing at the way she was gawking at the man in buckskins. And above his practically perfect teeth, she saw dazzling blue eyes that were crinkled up in laugher, or possibly against the sun.

Carrie's hand went to her mouth as she watched the man ride on toward the end of the street where the governor's mansion was situated.

"It couldn't be, could it?"

"Ma'am?" The footman was at her side, eyes downcast as he spoke to her. "Would you like to go home now?"

"Yes," Carrie said. "I would."

The molten copper head disappeared in the crowd. A wagon went by, then a carriage, which delayed her own passage.

Carrie tried not to hang out the window, knowing that it would set the gossips' tongues wagging, but she had to know.

Was it the boy from years gone by?

Chapter Three

Conner wasn't looking forward to his interview with the governor. Not at all. But he had delayed it as long as he could. Andrew was waiting for him to arrive at the mansion so they could meet with Lord Dunmore together.

He had bathed and shaved after a restless night at Christiana Campbell's inn. Andrew lent him a waistcoat and a very nice green silk coat that fit Connor perfectly through the shoulders, although it was a bit wide through the waist. He also supplied Connor with a pair of shoes, since his boots were in desperate need of resoling and his moccasins were not appropriate attire for the governor's mansion.

He was forced to purchase a new pair of stockings since his fine silk ones had been discovered by moths, and then he dropped his boots off to be mended. Only at that point had he realized that the pair of black shoes with the silver buckles that Andrew had lent him was too small.

Painfully so.

Connor rode west on Duke of Gloucester Street. His

stock chafed his neck and his toes throbbed against the
stiff leather of the shoes.

"They're probably too small for Andrew and that is why
he passed them on to me," Connor muttered.

He caught a glimpse of a frontiersman in the crush of
traffic along the street and stood in his stirrups to see if he
recognized the man. He did, but couldn't put a name to
his face at the moment.

Probably someone he had shared a fire with at some-
time in the past. The name would come to him later.

He recalled the young woman, garbed in the fine silks
of the gentry, who had been gawking at the frontiersman.
She'd most likely thought the frontiersman was some sort
of savage.

"What will she do when she first sees a native?" Connor
mused.

As long as she stayed within the confines of Williamsburg, she would be safe. His lips curled into a smile at the
thought of her screaming her lungs out if a savage
showed up on the streets. That thought was enough to
make him laugh out loud.

Connor recalled that she'd been quite pretty, with her
hair of pale gold and her trim figure beneath the fine
gown. And she'd looked positively thunderstruck at the
sight of him.

"It's nice to know the winter hasn't affected your looks,"
Connor said to himself as he rode on. He never had any
trouble attracting women. As a matter of fact, two Cherokee women had fought over him this past winter. Which
had led to his leaving the village earlier than planned;
he did not want to fall out of favor with the men of the
tribe.

He felt the back of his head burning. She must still be
staring at him. Probably branding him for future punishment in the stocks. It was the same feeling he got while in
the deep woods when he knew Indians were about and

possibly stalking him. The feeling had saved his life more than once.

"She's not for the likes of you, Connor Duncan," he said. "Ride on."

She was gentry. He was not. There was nothing more to consider.

Yet he couldn't help thinking about her as he turned north on Palace Street and rode past the long, narrow expanse of lawn called Palace Green that led to the governor's mansion.

It was an impressive building. Its three stories dominated the vista as Connor rode closer. There was a cupola on top that overlooked the city to the south and the gardens behind. Connor could not help staring in wonder at the building.

He recalled Castle MacLachlan from his youth. He and his mother had lived within sight of it for a time, but poverty had dimmed its grandeur. He just remembered being cold, hungry and mindful of the rotting staircases. The clan's coffers were empty. There was no money to maintain the castle.

The Governor's palace was funded by the taxpayers. It was a fine representation of the power of the British government, even in these far reaches.

The gate was guarded by a stone unicorn on one side and a stone lion on the other, so that none would doubt that it was a place for royalty.

A footman stood waiting to take his horse, and Connor grimaced in pain as his foot hit the pavement. His toes screamed in anguish. They were shoved against the front of the shoe and his heels protested as he took a step. He would surely have blisters before the day was over.

A butler opened the door as soon as he mounted the stone steps, and he stepped into a hall that displayed a coat of arms and a collection of bayonet-tipped muskets.

It was nice to know that arms were handy, in case they

were attacked. He supposed it was an impressive show of power, but he would be more impressed if they were actually loaded.

Connor resisted the urge to pull at his stock as the butler instructed him to bide his time while he announced his presence to the governor.

He wanted to look around at the treasures displayed before him, but his feet told him no. If he wished to make a graceful entrance into the governor's presence, it was best that he stand still for the moment.

He sought to make himself as inconspicuous as possible as a steady flow of officers, slaves and servants made their way through the hall.

Surely Andrew had arrived. Connor presumed he was already in with the governor.

Perhaps Andrew could provide Lord Dunmore with enough insight about the Shawnee that Connor's word would not be needed. The thought of reliving those days . . .

Think of something else.

A vision in yellow, bright as the sunshine, filled his mind. He pictured the young woman standing on the side of the street, gawking at that frontiersman.

He framed the image in his mind so he could keep it as a memory, one he would bring out on dark, lonely nights on the frontier. Who was she? Was she newly arrived to the colonies? She was gentry, judging by the way she was dressed. Wouldn't it be nice if she were a shop girl? Someone he could perhaps court?

Connor looked at the ceiling arching above his head and tried to wiggle his toes. He shook his head. He had nothing to offer a wife except a cabin in the wilderness and a dream of breeding horses for racing.

The door opened and a ray of sunshine floated in, followed by a footman laden with boxes. She promptly removed her hat and blinked in the sudden darkness of the hall.

Connor wondered if the floor could open up and swallow him where he stood. If he were in the woods, it would be a simple matter of just fading into the trees and holding perfectly still.

He dared not draw a breath. Perhaps she had not seen him laughing at her on the street. He tried to make himself as inconspicuous as possible, but considering his height and the bright color of his hair, he knew he was fighting a losing battle.

What were the chances that she would show up here? Was she pursuing him because he had dared to laugh at her behavior on the street?

"Lord Dunmore is having a ball to introduce his niece. . . ."

His conversation with Andrew the night before came back to him. Was this Lord Dunmore's niece? The one he had suggested might be so ugly that her bridegrooms preferred death to the marriage bed?

Connor felt a sinking feeling in his gut.

He had laughed at Lord Dunmore's niece on the streets of Williamsburg. Had there been witnesses to his unseemly behavior? Were they lined up to give testimony against him?

Ye are acting a fool, Connor, he told himself. He had done nothing wrong other than laugh at her silliness.

And your mother did nothing more than carry a bit of the plaid and look where it landed her. . . . Ye well know English justice.

She was walking straight toward him. Connor's eyes darted back and forth, seeking an escape route.

Perhaps he should apologize . . .

"You're the one," she said. Her blue eyes swept him from head to toe.

Connor had the presence of mind to sweep into a bow. "I humbly beg your forgiveness," he said, nearly choking on the words.

Why had his voice suddenly failed him? Was it because she was studying him so closely?

"I have often wondered what your crime was," she said.

Connor blinked as he straightened. Had he missed part of the conversation? Or was she a wee bit daft?

"Lord Dunmore will see you now," the butler said as he approached. "If you will follow me."

Connor could not help casting a glance over his shoulder as he cautiously stepped away from the lady. His foot slipped on the first step, and he grabbed awkwardly at the banister.

"Damn these shoes!" he cursed under his breath.

She was laughing at him. She covered her mouth with her mitted hand so no sound issued forth, but her eyes danced with glee.

Connor grimaced and forced his screaming feet to obey. When this meeting was over, he just might thrash Andrew.

Chapter Four

Andrew was waiting for him in the governor's office. The two men were bent over a map that was spread on Lord Dunmore's desk. Andrew's height and girth overshadowed the governor, who was most obviously descended from royalty. His manner plainly stated his importance. Connor estimated his lordship to be somewhere in age between himself and Andrew.

Andrew grinned sheepishly at Connor from behind the governor's back as he was warmly greeted by Lord Dunmore.

"You look well," Andrew said when the introductions were over. Connor was fairly certain he looked miserable and sensed that Andrew was making fun of him.

Connor pulled at his stock and prayed that he would be invited to sit. His feet badly needed a respite.

"Andrew tells me that you have some experience with the Shawnee," Lord Dunmore said pleasantly, as if he were asking about the weather.

Connor stood at attention with his hands clasped firmly

behind his back. "I have," he said. The earl did not waste any time.

"You have been west of the Ohio?"

"No' by choice," Connor said. Andrew gave him a stern look from his position beside the governor's desk. Connor knew he was not being very helpful.

"Please show me," Lord Dunmore said, indicating the map.

Connor took a few painful steps to the desk and looked down at the map. He recognized it as one that Sir Richard had drawn, and memories of their time together ran through him. It wasn't until Sir Richard was gone that he'd realized how lucky he'd been to be bonded to such a man. Sir Richard had cared for him in his own strange way, and Connor appreciated the things the nobleman had taught him.

Connor traced the rivers with the tip of his finger. He started with the New, which flowed northward out of North Carolina into Virginia. From there he traced the Gauley River to Kanawha Falls, then the Kanawha River down to where it flowed into the Ohio. Memories rolled over him, good and bad alike.

"I was taken from here," he said, pointing to where the rivers intersected. "Tu-Endie-Wei," he said, using the Wyandot name for the place. "In late summer," he continued. The map ended at the Ohio, but a few tributaries where drawn in on the opposite bank. His finger moved north to a river. "And taken up this river. The Shawnee called it Muskingum."

"That's where their village is located?" Lord Dunmore asked.

"Nay. They move it constantly. In the winter they break into small groups, in the summer they band together for council. Their village should be on a river, somewhere in this area, but I dinna' ken where. There is another river called Scioto, and there is the Miami. It could be there. I ken that they call wherever it is Chillicothe."

"You were not alone when you were taken."

"Nay," Connor said. "Another was with me."

Tom, who died screaming in agony while I listened and quaked in fear because I was certain I would scream louder and longer.

"And?" Lord Dunmore said. He sat down behind his desk and examined Connor over his steepled fingertips.

"We met up with another band that had taken an English officer. We traveled with them until we reached the main village."

"They killed the officer?"

"Aye. The day after we arrived at the village."

"I've heard tales of their savagery," Lord Dunmore said. "They burn their victims?"

Connor swallowed back the bile that rose in his throat. Was it that simple? They burned their victims?

"Aye," he said finally.

For three days they burn them. They burn them during the day, and at night they care for their wounds so they'll be strong enough to survive another day.

"And what about the gauntlet?" Lord Dunmore asked. "They force everyone to run it? Even children?"

"Sometimes," Connor said. "It depends on their mood. If you do nae make it through the first time, they force you to run it until you do. The other choice is being beaten to death, I suppose."

Which would be better than being burned, tomahawked and scalped while still breathing.

"You were with them for how long?" Dunmore asked.

"Six months," Connor said. "I was ransomed by Boone."

"How is it that you weren't killed? I believe your friend was?"

Connor looked down at his feet. Funny, he had forgotten how much they were hurting.

I was spared. Why was I spared?

"Because of my hair," he said finally. "There was an old woman who had lost her only relative, a grandson, to the

English. She liked the color of my hair, so she took me as a slave to replace him."

Connor wondered what Lord Dunmore was thinking as he explained.

"They called me Mshkwaawi," he continued. "I was bound to her until she died."

Dunmore gave him a skeptical look.

"I was tied to her during the day," Connor said. "With a long rope." He held his arms out to indicate the length. "At night I was tied to a tree. Sometimes they let me hunt for her, but they were always watching me. They would rather kill me than let me escape. I did escape one time and they brought me back." *They stripped me and staked me to the ground, and the women whipped me with switches until I bled, and then insects came with their own torment.* "She gave me a blanket when it got cold. One night she died in her sleep. They couldnae decide what to do with me, so they decided to kill me. By then I understood their language, so I knew what they planned. Before it happened, Boone showed up and ransomed me."

"How was it that Boone was able to walk into their camp?"

"He used an agent. A Wyandot who worked with the French during the war, ransoming English prisoners."

Connor wondered if the fear showed in his eyes. He looked at Andrew for guidance. The man gave him a reassuring smile. "Boone came for Tom, but he was dead, so he ransomed me. The Wyandot did not know the difference."

He swallowed hard as he remembered the look of horror on Tom's father's face when Boone returned to the Blue Ridge. Without Tom.

"Tom had a family," he said. "I had no one."

He did not tell Tom's family how he'd died, just that he was gone. There was no need to give them the details. They knew what happened to the captives that were not made slaves.

Connor had paid them back for the ransom money. It took two seasons of trapping, but he paid them back.

Connor was certain he was going to be sick. He swallowed the bile that threatened at the base of his throat.

This was why he did not want to talk about the past. This was why he chose not to think about it. He was the one who should have died. He had no one to miss him. No one to even know he was gone. No one to mourn his death.

Tom had a father, a mother, brothers and sisters and a sweetheart.

It should have been him.

"Why are they so vicious?" Lord Dunmore asked, jolting Connor back to the present.

"Because the English do nae keep their promises," Connor said.

Andrew raised an eyebrow in warning.

"The English signed a treaty with them, promising they wouldnae cross the Blue Ridge," Connor explained. "Yet settlers crossed it."

"There is plenty of land," the governor began.

"The English continually break their treaties," Connor said, ignoring the interruption. "The Indians are only protecting what they believe is rightfully theirs."

"This land belongs to Britain," Lord Dunmore said, getting to his feet. "And they should be grateful that we allow them to live on it."

"It belonged to them first," Connor said. "And they willnae allow us to live on it if ye continue to ignore their claim."

His voice had risen. He did not realize it until he saw the look of anger on Lord Dunmore's face, and the concern on Andrew's.

"You came here as a bondservant?" Lord Dunmore asked. His eyes bored into Connor as he leaned across his desk. Connor quickly realized that he had overstepped his bounds. "An outlaw, I believe?"

"He was a boy of ten," Andrew said quietly. "Hardly an outlaw. He was sent here after his mother was hanged for wearing the plaid."

"Your father fought at Culloden?" the governor continued.

"Aye," Connor said quietly. He felt the familiar pain in his gut.

"The colonies are full of the regret of Scotland," Lord Dunmore said. "I assume I can count you among those who have not forgotten."

"I was born after my father died," Connor said. "I have no memory of the battle."

But I well remember the murder of my mother . . . .

Connor did not back down, nor did the governor. Andrew cleared his throat.

"You wanted to get the feel of the Indian nation, milord," he said calmly. "I believe Connor has given it to you."

"It appears that we shall have to show the savages the power of Britain," Lord Dunmore said as he sat down once more. He rearranged some of the papers on his desk. "Even as we speak, my brother, General James Murray, is preparing the forts along the frontier for battle." He pointed to the map. "I have already dispatched surveyors here," he said, indicating the area south of the Kanawha. "And we have plans to build a fort here, at Point Pleasant," he concluded.

"Point Pleasant?" Connor asked.

"That is what Washington called it," Andrew explained.

Connor nodded in agreement. It was a beautiful place, in spite of his horrible memories.

"We also have plans for the militia," Lord Dunmore said. "My brother is putting together an army here," he said, pointing to a place on the Greenbrier. "My nephew, Captain Murray, will join him there. I would like you to accompany him. Show him the way."

Connor felt Lord Dunmore's eyes boring into him. It was as if the man was challenging him.

"I am no' a member of the militia," Connor reminded him. "I hold no rank."

"I have designated you as a scout," Lord Dunmore said firmly. "As a subject of the colonies, it is your duty to answer to the king and those who speak in his name. You have knowledge of this wilderness. A knowledge that will aid my brother as he prepares to protect our settlers. You also know the ways of the enemy. I am certain you do not want anyone else to suffer as you have?" The last came as a question, and Connor knew he was trapped.

He wanted nothing more than to return to his cabin, preferably with a foal in his mare's belly, and live his life without the interference of His Majesty's dictates.

He was trapped, and everyone in the room knew it. To walk away would be considered treason. It would also label him a coward. Where the Shawnee were concerned, he *was* a coward. But if he could save someone else from what he'd suffered, then so be it.

"When do we leave?" Connor asked.

"Two days hence," Lord Dunmore said, suddenly returning to the charming man who had greeted Connor upon his arrival. "There is a ball tonight to introduce my niece and nephew to Williamsburg. I would be most honored if you would attend."

Once again Andrew raised a concerned brow at Connor.

Connor bowed low to the governor. "I am honored to accept your invitation," he said. One thing Sir Richard had taught him was not to be rash or impetuous. But it was hard to fight his nature. His mother's blood flowed strong in his veins.

"My wife will be delighted," the governor said. "I look forward to seeing you." He dismissed Connor by going back to the papers gathered on his desk.

"I'll walk you out," Andrew said. "With your permission, sir?"

Lord Dunmore waved an uninterested hand in their direction.

"I donnae have the proper attire for a ball," Connor said when he and Andrew were safely out of earshot. His toes screamed with each step down the staircase.

"What you are wearing is fine," Andrew assured him.

"What I am wearing will probably kill me before the day is out," Connor said. His temper simmered just below the surface, and he felt his jaw tighten as it always did when he was angry. Lord Dunmore had handled him and handled him well. It was an admirable trait, but Connor was not in the mood to be generous to the man at the moment.

"Damn Scottish stubbornness," Andrew said.

"These shoes are too small," Connor complained. "And my boots willnae be ready until tomorrow."

"You will survive," Andrew said. "All of it. You've survived worse than this. Much worse."

"I had no choice then," Connor said.

"And you have no choice now either," Andrew said. The butler held the door open and they stepped outside. Connor took a deep breath of fresh air and frowned at his feet. "Do as the man says and when your job is done, disappear into the wilderness. If he cannot find you, then he cannot give you orders."

"He said I was to be a scout. What if his brother or nephew has an ongoing use for me?"

"Then you will do it. And you will do it to the best of your ability. You never shirked your work, Connor, not when you were bound or when you were free."

"The difference is who I was working for."

"Sir Richard was as English as the earl," Andrew reminded him.

"Sir Richard's head was guided by common sense, not the long reach of king and country."

Once again Andrew saw fit to place a warning hand on Connor's shoulder. The king's soldiers stood guard on the drive, and one was bringing around Connor's mare. "I would hate to see all of Sir Richard's good guidance lost because of a moment of foolishness," he said.

Connor felt his jaw go rigid. He was long past the age of being told what to do. But he also realized that Andrew cared for him and only had his best interests at heart.

"Hold your tongue until you are away from the governor and his relations. If things continue the way they are in the colonies, a break will come, and probably sooner than you think," Andrew advised him.

They stood silent for a moment until the footman was well out of hearing range. Connor's feet throbbed painfully as he placed one in the stirrup to mount.

"Do I have to go to the ball?" he asked. He grinned. He knew he sounded like a petulant child.

"Yes, you do," Andrew said, grinning back at him. "And bring that Scottish charm of yours for the ladies. I want to see what it is that the Cherokee women fight over."

"It could be *that* part of me is not something that I show in gentle company," Connor said mischievously. "But it is worth a tussle or two, or at least so I've been told."

Andrew shook his head.

"My feet are cursing you, my friend," Connor called back as he rode off.

And damn the English.

He gave the soldiers a friendly salute as he rode into the street.

Chapter Five

Her cheeks hurt. Carrie's mother had often told her when she was younger not to make faces at her brother because her features might freeze that way, and then she'd spend the rest of her life with a horrid visage presented to the world.

She wondered if it were possible for her face to freeze into a permanent smile. She wished she could make a face at John. The sight of him enjoying himself, resplendent in his dress uniform and surrounded by a crowd of eligible young women tempted her to do something outrageous.

She also wondered how many times she'd curtsied this evening. She was certain she had met every free person of any means in all of Williamsburg and the outlying counties. Some names she recognized, thanks to her aunt's instructions. There was Randolph, Washington, Jefferson, Wythe. Along with their wives, their sons, their daughters and one very annoying nephew of someone in the peerage back in England. Or so he told her over and over again. Sir Geoffrey Wainscott, nephew of Lord Someone and grandson several times removed of someone else who only he was impressed with. She had heard it all before, when she was in England. And she knew as soon as dear Sir Geoffrey found out that she had an inconsequential dowry, he would go try to impress some of the other young women.

The thought suddenly occurred to Carrie that maybe he had already tried his line on the other available young women and she was his last resort.

"Heaven forbid," she murmured to herself.

"I beg your pardon?" Sir Geoffrey said.

He also had a very annoying habit of sneaking up on her. She'd thought she'd managed to escape him after their last dance.

"I said that last dance nearly did me in," Carrie said quickly. It had been a lively reel, which she normally would have enjoyed, except that her shoes were too big and kept slipping off her heels.

"Would you like to lie down for a bit?" Sir Geoffrey asked, concern evident on his carefully powered face. "I would be happy to escort you to your chamber."

He must have suffered from horrible outbreaks when he was younger. He had scars. And an amazing amount of lace around his neck and wrists.

"No, I'm fine," Carrie said, and wondered if he really thought her that naïve. "Thank you for your concern. I just need to stand here a bit and catch my breath."

"Very well, then," Sir Geoffrey said. He placed his hands behind his back, as if settling himself to await her recovery.

Carrie watched in feigned interest as couples dressed in differing shades of silk and linen moved around the ballroom in another lively dance, John among them with a pretty brunette. It should be time for a minuet soon. She would have to escape Sir Geoffrey before then.

A glint of copper caught her eye against the opposite wall. Maybe he stood out among the crowd because he was one of the few men there not wearing a wig. His hair, neatly tied back with a piece of black ribbon, shone as bright as the candles. Or maybe it was his height that drew her eye, although his companion was as tall and much wider of girth. He was the only one present she had not yet been introduced to. Perhaps that was a good thing. She'd behaved quite foolishly when she'd seen him earlier that day. He must think her quite insane, because he was doing a very good job of staying as far away from her as he could.

She really should watch the way her mind ran on. The chances that the boy from the docks was even still alive were slim, and to think that she would recognize him after all these years was absolutely insane.

But then again, how many men had hair of such a vibrant and rich shade of copper as his? Or eyes so bright a blue that she noticed the color from across the room?

The more Carrie watched him, the more she realized that he was doing a fine job of keeping to himself, in spite of many interested looks sent his way by the young women of the local gentry. She did not see him dance at all, as a matter of fact; he seemed as if he was in a great deal of pain, judging by the look on his face. He had tripped on the stairs this morning. Perhaps he had an injury.

"Oh, how lovely," Sir Geoffrey said. "A minuet."

Carrie rolled her eyes heavenward in a silent prayer as Sir Geoffrey pulled her into the dance. She'd been so wrapped up in watching the man with the copper hair that she'd forgotten to pay attention to the music.

"These military men should stand aside," he said as he assumed the lead position. "This is a dance of refinement and grace." And then he hastily added, "With apologies to your brother, of course."

"Of course," Carrie said, and wondered if there was any way she could escape without causing a scene.

The minuet was supposed to be danced by only one couple at a time. Carrie felt her cheeks pinken at the thought that Sir Geoffrey wanted to perform for the assemblage. She was even more alarmed when she realized that most of the other dancers were making their way from the floor to allow it.

What was she thinking? And more importantly, what was her uncle thinking? Carrie saw her uncle and aunt both beaming at her across the room. Were they already considering a match between her and Sir Geoffrey?

Carrie slipped, almost lost her shoe, and tried to remember what count she should be on.

She couldn't marry Sir Geoffrey. She wanted to see this new country. She wanted to go into the wild, see the rivers, the trees, the wildlife, the Indians. She couldn't imagine Sir Geoffrey even venturing out of Williamsburg, much less into the wilderness.

But isn't that why your father brought you here? To make a match?

She completed her *Z* figure and met Sir Geoffrey diagonally in the middle of the floor. They made the right-hand turn and moved on into the opposite corner.

She had not seen her father in three years. She well knew his concern for her future. Her father could not support her forever. And neither could her brother. But after spending the last four years of her life caring for her ailing mother, and three engagements that had ended with the deaths of her fiancés, she had hoped to experience a bit of this brand-new country before settling down to be a wife.

And above all else, she hoped to have some say in who her husband would be.

She completed her next *Z* and met Sir Geoffrey for the left-hand turn. Apparently her timing was off, because he seemed to be moving in place.

Still he smiled at her. A patient smile.

If only she didn't have to marry. If only she could earn a living somehow.

But how? The only thing she knew how to do was keep house. She was only trained in the art of being a wife. She could serve tea. She knew how to play whist. She could read. She could sew, although sitting still for long bored her. She spoke French, played the harpsichord and knew how to dance, although not well. She was more inclined to trip over her own feet than move about gracefully. She also knew how to shoot and could ride as well as her brother. Her father had taught her because he wanted to spend as much time as possible with both his children.

Thank the heavens the dance was over. It was time for the honors. And as she dipped into yet another curtsey before her uncle, she could already see the letter to her father forming in his mind.

Dear James, I am happy to report that I have found a wonderful match for Carrie . . . .

"Thank you," Sir Geoffrey said as he led her from the floor.

Carrie smiled sweetly and gently fanned her cheeks with her handkerchief.

"Would you like some punch?" Sir Geoffrey asked.

"Oh, yes," Carrie said. "That would be lovely."

As soon as his pink silk coat and powdered wig disappeared in the crowd, Carrie casually slipped through the set of doors that were opened wide to catch the spring breeze. Outside was a wide porch that overlooked the gardens behind the mansion.

It was nearly as bright outside as it was indoors. The moon was full, and she knew the pale blue of her dress would make her easy to spot from the ballroom. And trying to hide in the gardens might lead to disaster if Sir Geoffrey found her there. Especially if John or her uncle heard about it. She'd be married off before she had time to turn around.

Huge ferns placed on columns decorated the area, and Carrie made for one in the shadows. She heard Sir Geoffrey's voice calling her name from the ballroom, so she picked up her pace and dashed around the column.

Suddenly she was falling forward, barely catching herself with her outstretched arms before she landed on her face.

Carrie felt her hoops flatten as she landed on them and realized that her skirts and petticoats had flown up into the air. But of more concern to her was why anyone would stack wood on a balcony. Then she realized it was not wood, but possibly a set of very strong limbs she had tripped over; a pair of hands found her shoulders and pulled her to her feet.

"Are you hurt?" a deep voice asked quietly from somewhere above her head.

She looked up, almost afraid to see who it would be. Whoever it was had just gotten a good look at her backside—she was sure of it.

"It's you," she said when she recognized the copper hair. It had to be he. Who else had hair that color?

"Aye," he said. "'Tis me." His lips curved in a quirky smile and he dropped his hands to his sides as he backed up a step, which put him against the outside wall of the palace.

In her fall she had lost a few pins, and bits of her hair fell around her ears. Then Carrie realized she'd lost her cap too, so she looked around her feet for it.

She bent to retrieve it and the wind caught her skirts, which threatened to send her sailing off the balcony. She straightened suddenly and was rewarded with a burst of stars as her head crashed into something solid.

"Heavens," she said, and placed her hand on her forehead as she wondered whether she might faint.

"I humbly beg your . . ."

"Miss Murray?" a voice called out, and her head cleared immediately. An image of Sir Geoffrey bending over her prostrate body filled her mind.

"Shhh," Carrie said and reached up to place her hand over the stranger's mouth. She tried to move out of sight against the wall and heard him groan.

"Please," she whispered. "I don't want him to find me."

"Then gerroff me foot," he whispered back. "The heel of your shoe is smashing my toes."

"Sorry," she mouthed.

An arm snaked around her waist and lifted her up so that she rested against a solid hip. The wind ruffled the ferns and covered the faint sounds of footsteps. He cocked his head as if listening, and Carrie held her breath so as not to make a sound.

Her cheek was at the same height as his. She was so close that she felt their ears touch; the intimacy of it was strangely exciting. She felt her shoes slipping off and instinctively curled her toes to keep them on.

He smelled nice. Fresh, clean, like the outdoors. Unlike many of her recent companions, he wasn't covering up body odor with perfume.

"Miss Murray?"

The voice was distant now, but Carrie dared not move, even though the bone of his hip gouged through her skirts into her thigh. The wind died down and the air quieted until all she heard was the sound of a heartbeat.

Was it hers or his? He was so close, it was nigh impossible to tell. It suddenly occurred to her that if they were discovered, everyone would think her the worst kind of wanton: the governor's niece hiding in the ferns with a colonial while a titled gentleman was searching for her. But she didn't care. She'd heard enough gossip about her failed engagements to last a lifetime. And she'd endured enough of Sir Geoffrey to last several.

Slowly the stranger lowered her to the ground, making sure he put her a safe distance away. Carrie looked down and saw long, silk-clad feet poking beneath the hem of her skirts.

"Where are your shoes?" she asked, looking around once more for her cap.

"Over there," he whispered, pointing toward the railing on the side of the balcony. "They pinch. But I believe being pinched is better than being smashed."

"As opposed to tripping over logs?" she said. She spied the piece of lace when she looked where he was pointing.

It was lying on one of his shoes. The wind must have blown it there.

"Logs?"

Carrie pointed at his calves and noticed the muscles standing out beneath the silk.

"Aye, I was sitting with them stretched out," he admitted. "But I wasnae expecting company. I was merely trying to give the poor things a bit of rest from their torture."

"Try wearing them every day," Carrie said. "And dancing in them." She peered under the frothy leaves of the fern to see if anyone else was on the balcony.

"I'd prefer to go without," he said.

Carrie made a dash for the rail just as the wind picked up again, but to her horror, her cap floated between the rails to the garden below, quickly followed by one of his shoes, which she accidentally kicked in her haste.

"Heaven forbid," she said as she watched her cap flutter across the lawn.

"It's just a wee scrap of lace," he said.

"I can't go in without it," Carrie said. "They'll think I've been up to something."

"Ye have been."

"But not what they'll think. And if they see you come in too, my brother will have to defend my honor."

"Lord help us," he said. "And what of yon ponce that was looking for ye? Will I have to fight him too?"

Carrie took her eyes off her cap and looked up at her companion. He did not seem to understand the seriousness of the situation. As a matter of fact, he seemed to think it was quite amusing. As if he'd have no trouble beating her brother, or the ponce, er, Sir Geoffrey.

"Are you patronizing me?" she asked.

"Is that a dueling offense?"

"You are," she said. "You know, your shoe is down there too."

He joined her at the rail and looked over the side. "Ye can fetch it when you get your cap."

"Me? I can't go down there. Sir Geoffrey might see me."

"And?" His lips twitched as if he were trying not to laugh.

"What if he follows me? What if my brother catches me with Sir Geoffrey in the garden?"

"Cannae he kill the ponce while he defends your honor and solve your problem?"

"He could make me marry Sir Geoffrey."

"So if he catches you with me, he has to defend your honor, but if he catches you with yon ponce, then he forces you to marry?"

"Yes." Carrie stamped her foot. "No." She shook her head. He was serious now. As if he'd been offended. His lips were compressed into a thin line, and she saw a tick in the hollow of his cheek. His eyes, once a bright, beautiful blue, had become dark and stormy. "Who are you?"

"Connor Duncan, milady." He swept into a bow. "Thank ye for doing me the great honor of letting me compromise you."

"If I just had my cap," Carrie said, "there would be no problem. Can't you get it? Please?" She looked up at him. He had to help her. She had a chance to start over again in this new country. A chance to put the gossip behind her.

She saw his eyes change. The anger left them, taking the stormy darkness with it. He shook his head, but swung a leg up on the rail, to Carrie's delight.

"Ye pure mad daftie," he mumbled. "And here I am, a gormless eejit, listening to you." He swung his other leg over. "I'll hand it up to ye," he said. "Then I'll be on my way."

He lowered himself by his arms until he dangled from the rail and then dropped to the ground. Carrie was too shocked to speak. For some reason, she'd thought he'd take the stairs on the opposite side of the balcony. The drop was over twice his height, but it didn't seem to bother him.

"Wait," she said. "Your shoe."

She dropped it over the rail, then immediately realized that he hadn't heard her. It landed on his head, and he jumped and turned to look up at her.

"Sorry." Carrie leaned over the rail.

"Where's the frippery?" he asked as he rubbed the top of his head.

"I see it." Carrie leaned out. The wind was blowing it again. "Over . . ."

The wind picked up her hoops again and blew them straight up. She was off balance, leaning out too far, and they carried her over. She went flying over the side.

"Oop!" she exclaimed as her arms flailed about, trying to find something to grab on to.

Somehow she landed in his arms, which was a blessing except for the fact that her hoops were over his head. She felt him gasp as he landed flat on his back with Carrie on top of him.

Carrie yanked down her skirts, and he groaned as her knee went into his stomach.

"I'm sorry," she said. "Are you hurt?"

He lay with his eyes closed and a pained expression on his face, his arms flung out at his sides.

"Mr. Duncan?" she said.

He opened one very blue eye and looked up at her.

"I think I would ha' rather fought the duel," he said.

Chapter Six

"I say. Miss Murray? Are you hurt?"

"Heavens," she said and scrambled away from Connor, her knee this time hitting his throat.

Connor gasped and looked up to see the ponce in the pink silk looking down from the balcony.

"Take your hands off her, you . . . you . . . heathen!" the ponce yelled out.

Connor looked to the right and to the left. As near as he could tell, his hands were still spread out beside him on the ground and nowhere near the daftie lass.

"Psst!" The daftie was scrunched up between the wall and the shrubbery, pointing at the ground. "My shoes," she mouthed.

Connor heard voices approaching on the balcony and saw a lantern bobbing through the garden.

"Please . . ."

She needed an entire regiment just to look after her wardrobe. Connor kicked her shoes toward her as he slowly stood up. His shins throbbed from her kick, his ribs ached from her knees and his Adam's apple throbbed from her last assault. It was all he could do not to grab his stones, fall to his knees, and cry.

"Take my hands off whom?" Connor roared as he looked up at the group assembling above.

"Off Miss Murray, of course," the ponce said.

Miss Murray was at the moment slinking through the shrubbery, and he supposed it was his mission to keep them from noticing her. At least that was what her panicked eyes told him as she looked his way.

Connor raised his hands and shrugged his shoulders. "There's no one else here." Why did he feel the need to help her? He should probably be urging her uncle and brother to lock her up in her room before she hurt another innocent bystander.

Aye, you're as daft as she is. The English would never believe a Scotsman to be innocent. More likely, they'd have you flogged for assaulting her.

"But I saw her," the ponce protested.

"Are ye pished, man? Ye saw the wind blowing, nothing more." He looked upward, almost wishing the ponce would say something so he could throttle the man. It would feel good to throttle him, since he was the reason he had just been kicked, kneed and fallen upon.

"But . . ." The ponce looked over the side of the balcony and saw nothing. From the corner of his eye, Connor caught the sight of blue silk flitting around the side of the palace and allowed himself a small smile. She'd escaped. And just in time, since the regulars had arrived.

Three redcoats came into the garden, one carrying a lantern and the other two with muskets ready.

"Is this how you treat all of Lord Dunmore's invited guests?" Connor said as he raised his hands in surrender.

"More likely you were trying to sneak in," one of the redcoats said.

"Nay, ye eejit, I was trying to sneak out," Connor said. In one quick motion, he grabbed the barrel of a musket, buried the stock in the belly of the redcoat holding the other and placed the end against the head of the man with the lantern.

"Mr. Duncan!" Connor glanced up to see Lord Dunmore and Andrew both looking down at him. Beside Lord Dunmore stood an officer in full regalia. His hair was the same golden blond as that of the daft lass.

Which meant he was the brother, the officer he was to guide to Fort Savannah. It was bound to be an interesting trip. But he'd much rather make the journey than bide his time in gaol.

"Is there a problem, Connor?" Andrew asked.

"Nay, Andrew," Connor said and handed the musket back to its owner. "I was just leaving."

"Why is everyone outside when there is such lovely music inside?"

Connor was sure his jaw dropped to the ground. The daftie stood on the balcony, just as pretty as you please, with her pins back in place. But she was still missing her cap.

"We had a bit of an altercation below," the brother said. "And someone seemed to think you were a part of it. Where have you been?"

"I had to go to my room for a moment," she said. "For personal reasons."

"What personal reasons?" her brother asked.

She seemed nervous, and Connor watched as she stood on tiptoe and whispered rather loudly in her brother's ear.

He caught the end of it. Something about relieving herself. Connor grinned as he saw the three men on the balcony try to compose themselves. She had relieved herself of an especially annoying suitor. Went to great lengths to do it. Perhaps she wasn't as gormless as he'd first thought.

"Good night, Mr. Duncan," Lord Dunmore said. "We shall see you day after tomorrow."

Still grinning, he gave the redcoats a cheeky salute and turned to go.

"Connor?" Andrew called after him.

Connor turned back.

"Your shoes," he said. "Or maybe I should say, my shoes?"

Connor waved up at Andrew and picked up his shoes. The redcoats gave him a wide berth as he strode away, whistling a jaunty tune.

A flash of white caught his eye. The cap, caught up under a shrub. He turned back to see if anyone was watching. The redcoats seemed to be in conference; about him, no doubt. He'd better watch his back until he left town. With luck, they wouldn't be in the contingent going to Fort Savannah.

He looked up and saw the balcony was empty except for one figure moving toward the rail.

'Twas the lass. Carrie. He'd heard Lord Dunmore call her Carrie, even though he remembered her given name was Caroline. He saw the moonlight shining upon her hair, giving it a silvery glow, along with the pale blue of her dress. She looked like a fairy sprite standing there. A very dangerous fairy sprite. He was lucky she hadn't killed him, what with her throwing shoes at his head and falling on him. Although his quick glimpse of her long, slender legs might be worth the price of the bruises he'd been given.

No wonder all her fiancés had died.

Connor snatched up the lace from the ground and stuffed it in his breeks. He saw her hand cover her mouth, as if she were laughing.

Then the ponce came up beside her.

"She's no' for the likes of you," Connor muttered. "She said so herself."

But she was a pretty thing, even if she was daft.

He walked in his stocking-clad feet, not minding the dampness of the dew, or the fact that the silk would be ruined, to where his mare was tied among the buggies and horses. He stuffed Andrew's shoes in his saddlebag. He replaced them with his moccasins, drew off his stock and stuffed it in with the shoes.

A bit of rum was what he needed. In a smoke-filled tavern. Anything to drive the scent of lavender from his head.

Aye, the lassie smelled good. When he'd drawn her up to save his toes, he could not help noticing. And picking her up had been effortless, like holding a babe. He'd held her against his hip with one arm, as if she were nothing more than a feather.

There was no doubt in his mind that her brother would have called him out if he'd known that a Scottish bondsman had laid hands on his sister.

He wasn't good enough to marry her. She'd said so herself.

But she sure was bonnie, with her golden hair and sky-blue eyes.

Which had to be the reason his gut was all twisted up inside. It wasn't the first time he'd heard those words from the English.

Connor didn't see the broad boulevard as he turned his mare toward the pub. Instead his mind went back to a rutted track in Scotland eighteen years earlier.

The tenth anniversary of Culloden. His tenth birthday.

He'd made the trek with his mother. They'd set out a few weeks before the anniversary and walked from the ruins of Castle MacLachlan and the small hovel in which they lived. What little food they carried with them ran out several days before they arrived, forcing them to accept shelter and scraps of food from those they met along the way.

Cumberland had decimated the country, but not the spirit of the people. Ten years after the battle, the memories were still as fresh as if it had happened yesterday.

People warned his mother about showing the plaid. But she would not be swayed. She wore it around her shoulders as if it were armor, tattered as it was.

"Honor your father, Connor, for he was a brave man," Anice said as they stood before the cairn that marked the graves of the MacLachlans.

"Why is he here?" Connor asked. "Why is he not with the Duncans?"

"Your father chose to stand with my clansmen, and so he died with them and is buried beside them."

"How did he die?" Connor asked.

"Some coward took him from behind," she said. "He died with his claymore in his hand and his brains bashed out."

"Are all English cowards?"

"Nay." She placed a hand on her son's thin shoulder. "There are good and bad in every clan, in every country. A man should be judged by his merit, not by his clan. Be strong, be true, and you will grow to be a man your father would be proud of. Fortis et Fidus."

"Fortis et Fidus," Connor repeated after her.

"Someday, when ye are older, I will tell you of a good English soldier that I ken. But not today. Today is a day for remembering the men who died here, not the ones who walked away. Now say a prayer for your father's soul."

Being a good Catholic lad, he did as he was told and wondered, as he always did, about what his life would be like if his father were still alive, and not dead at the hands of an English coward. Then they turned to go. . . .

Connor stopped in front of the tavern. The smart thing to do would be to go back to his room and enjoy the comfort of a bed once more. Who knew how long he'd be on the trail as a scout for the English. Who knew how long it would be before he could go home.

Connor dismounted and tied his horse to the rail.

He'd never see home again. He'd never see the stormy sea off the coast of Scotland or the dark blue of the lochs or the shaggy sheep browsing on the moors. He'd never see the highlands rising up from the earth as if they would tear it asunder.

He'd built a small cabin up on the Blue Ride, on land left to him by Sir Richard. But it was a cold, lonely place. And he had no one who cared if he lived or died, save Andrew.

The tavern was bustling. Those not good enough to be on the invitation list for the governor's ball were making do in their own way, thumbing their noses at the gentry with bawdy songs and boisterous laughter.

The raucous gathering didn't suit his mood, but a drink might make it better, so he found a table in the corner and gave a coin to the maid when she slapped down a tankard of rum in front of him. She was smart enough to know when a man needed company and when he didn't.

Unfortunately, there were those who wouldn't take no for an answer. No matter how much you screamed and cried and begged.

It was easy enough to understand why the Indians wouldn't. They were trying to protect their way of life. It was the only way they knew. But the English . . . they were supposed to be civilized.

Connor tossed back the rum, felt it burn its way down his throat, and was grateful. The maid hastily set another one in front of him, and then another.

If only the rum could burn out the memories of the things he had seen. Or the things he had heard.

They were on the road to Inverness when the patrol found them. Four English soldiers and an officer on horseback, and his mother walking down the middle of the road as proud as you please with the plaid thrown over her shoulders.

They tried to escape across the fields, but the English ran them down. They tied him by his neck and his hands to the trunk of a tree. Then they told his mother they'd hang him if she did not oblige them. So she did, silently, while they grunted and groaned above her with Connor watching, the rope so tight around his neck that he could not make a sound.

They all had their way with her. All but the officer, who said he wouldn't soil himself on a Scottish whore who spread her legs for anyone. She wasn't good enough for him to waste his seed on.

Then they burned the plaid and put the rope around her neck.

Before they pulled her up, she said her last words to him: "Fortis et fidus."

Her hands scrabbled at the rope and she kicked the air as her feet sought the ground.

He tried to fight them. He kicked the one who held him in the stones and ran to his mother and tried to hold her up, but one of them hit him from behind.

When he woke he was in chains in the back of a cart on his way to London, along with some prisoners from Inverness. He didn't even have the benefit of a trial. They just put him on the ship with the others and sent him to the colonies to be sold.

"Thank God for Sir Richard," Connor said, and toasted the air.

"Wallowing, are we?" Andrew said, joining Connor at his table.

"Well, the ball was such a pleasure," Connor said.

"I hope you get this out of your system before you take to the trail tomorrow."

"What?" Connor asked. "The rum?"

"No, you big eejit," Andrew exclaimed. "The hatred."

"Tomorrow," Connor said, ignoring Andrew's observation. "Ye said take to the trail tomorrow."

"I did," Andrew replied. "The governor got a missive from Fort Savannah. There have been several attacks, and people have been taken. So he's moved the departure up a day. You're leaving first thing in the morning."

"Why aren't ye going?"

"I am going. I'm going north," Andrew said.

"But ye should go with me," Connor protested. "Aren't ye the man who found the place?" Connor's tongue felt thick, and he seemed to have lost control of his eyebrows. "They should call it Fort Lewis."

"I only found the spring," Andrew said as he hauled

Connor to his feet. "The English found the fort. They can call it whatever they want."

"Aye, the pigs," Connor said. "They'll call it whatever they want. They do whatever they want. They hang whoever they want. And they tell us who we can't want."

"What are you going on about?" Andrew asked.

Connor reached back for his tankard. "I'm talking about the daftie lass, of course," Connor said as he drained it.

"Come on, lad, you've had enough." Andrew took the tankard and put it back on the table. "You reek too." He waved a hand in front of his nose. "Why couldn't you get drunk on some good Irish whiskey?"

"Because I'm not gooenufferherrrrr." Connor stretched out his tongue. It didn't seem to be working correctly.

"Well then, it's a good thing you're getting away from her, whoever she is," Andrew said as they stumbled out the tavern door. "Perhaps absence will make the heart grow fonder."

"Yesh," Connor said. "Probably shafer for me too. Out on the frontier with the shavages instead of ducking from all the things shesh thrown at my head."

"I'm sure you deserved every bit of it," Andrew said as they reached the horses. He placed Connor's arms over his saddle.

"I think I'll jush lie down a bit," Connor mumbled as he laid his head on the saddle. "I'm a bit pished."

"Yes, you are," Andrew said as he heaved him up onto his mare. "Just a bit."

Chapter Seven

His head hurt. As if someone had split it with an ax. Connor ran his hand over his scalp just to make sure there was no blood. His fingers snagged on something, and he could not for the life of him figure out what it was. He rolled over on his back with a groan and held his hand before his face, hoping to be able to identify the object in the dim light of predawn.

It was a piece of lace. A lace cap, to be exact.

"Ye are a fool," he mumbled as he stumbled from his bed. A piece of paper fluttered to the floor along with the cap, and he picked it up and moved to the window to see if it could be read by the light from the street.

Leaving today. A.

"Yes, I know," Connor said. He wadded the paper and flung it away, then did the same with his shirt.

"I hope it was Andrew who removed my breeks," he said when he realized that he wore none.

His face flamed as red as his hair when he realized that if Andrew had removed his breeches, he must have found the cap.

"You're well rid of Williamsburg," he told himself as he pulled on a pair of well-worn leather pants and his moccasins. "With luck, she'll be married and back across the water before you return."

He looked around his room and stuffed his shirt and breeches into his pack. He looked at his stockings. They were stained from the grass, but he stuffed them in also. Finally he picked up the lace cap from among his rumpled sheets.

The scent of lavender assailed his senses, and he sucked it in as if it would cure the pounding in his head.

It didn't. He stuffed the lace in his pack, picked up his belt and hide shirt and went out into the crisp morning air. He dunked his head in the trough to clear it and splashed water across his chest to rid himself of the smell of rum.

He pulled an ivory toothbrush from his pack, another habit that Sir Richard had pounded into his head, cleaned his teeth, then picked a sprig of mint from some herbs drying on a rack behind the inn and chewed on it as he pulled on his shirt.

He put on his belt, slid his knife out and back in to make sure the dew would not lock it in its sheath. He added another belt that held two dragoon pistols, one on either side, and stuck his tomahawk in also.

He had plenty of shot in his box, plenty of tinder for his long rifle. He had stocked up on everything the previous afternoon, but if the governor was providing supplies, he might as well take more.

He slung his horn across one shoulder and his ammunition bag across the other. The only thing left to do was saddle his horse and pick up his boots.

Connor was sure the cobbler would be thrilled to see him this early in the morning.

The city was just coming awake after he roused the cobbler from his bed. Slaves swept stoops and pumped water as he rode by the houses, munching on biscuits and ham bought from a street vendor.

The peaceful sounds of dawn faded as he came closer to the governor's mansion. Connor turned down the drive and was greeted with chaos.

Wagons, horses, packs, soldiers and slaves were everywhere. And in the middle of it all was the blond officer on a snow-white stallion, shouting orders and pointing with his sword.

"God help us," Connor said. He easily found Andrew towering over the madness near the steps and guided his mare through the maze to where his friend waited.

"This fool will be lucky to find his own arse," Andrew said, nodding at the officer.

"The Shawnee shouldn't have any trouble locating them," Connor said. "I feel as if I'm back with Amhurst."

Connor turned to see Captain John Murray coming his way. It seemed as if his horse was bringing him, whether he wanted to come or not. Connor's mare stretched out her neck and bared her teeth.

"You are the scout?" Captain Murray said by way of greeting.

"Aye," Connor said. He let his eyes run over Murray's stallion. He was a showy beast, built for speed. It occurred to Connor that with his mare's endurance, they would make a fine colt.

"Connor Duncan," Andrew said. "Captain John Murray."

"You know the area we're going to?" The stallion danced around, trying to get his muzzle to the mare's arse. Murray jerked his head back and turned him, keeping his eyes on Connor all the while.

"Aye," Connor said. He was not inclined to be helpful.

"Connor knows all the land north to the lakes and west to the Ohio, and some beyond," Andrew put in.

"Yes, I heard you were a captive of the savages," Murray said as his stallion went through the turn again. "And you speak their language?"

"Aye."

"Connor speaks several languages," Andrew said. "Most of the Indian dialects, French and some German."

"Really?" Murray said, as if he found that hard to believe.

Connor felt the urge to wring Andrew's neck. The captain was talking down to him, and he did not need Andrew to sing his praises.

"I speak Gaelic also," Connor said. He looked Murray in the eye. "If ye feel ye hav' a need for it."

"I'm sure I won't," Murray said with a distinct curl to his lip. His stallion made the circle again.

Connor nodded. He knew where he stood with the man.

"Do you think you can get your men into some kind of order?" Connor asked, jerking his head toward the men and wagons. "So we can be about the king's business."

Murray's horse circled again, and this time Connor's mare nipped at his neck. The stud lashed out with his hooves, nearly unseating Murray.

"Your mare is in season?" Murray asked.

"Aye."

"Then keep her away from my mount," he said. "His blood line is impeccable. I won't have him servicing any nag."

"Then I suggest ye ride at the end of the line," Connor said brusquely. "Since I have to be at the front to guide you."

Murray dug his spurs into his horse and moved off without another word.

Andrew shook his head and rolled his eyes. "I should go with you," he said.

"Why?" Connor asked innocently. "Are ye afraid ye will miss something?"

"Only a hanging."

"He'd look good at the end of a rope," Connor said. "If he's no' scalped first."

The two men watched in silence for a moment as the regulars fell into line. They even had a drummer, which caused Connor to roll his eyes.

"Do you think the fool kens that the wagons and such won't make it up the trails?"

"I told him," Andrew said. "But this is the way the king's army travels. Far be it from me, a lowly Irishman, to tell the captain how to command his company."

"At least I've the sense to save my breath."

Andrew nodded, as if pondering the situation. "Give this to Charlie." Andrew handed Connor a letter for his brother. "Tell him I plan to be there soon."

"I will."

"And try to keep your temper."

Connor lifted his hand and looked directly at Andrew. "I promise no' to kill any redcoats."

A big grin spread across his friend's face, and it only took a glance for Connor to realize that it was not directed at him.

He looked over his shoulder and felt his jaw drop.

"This should be interesting," Andrew said.

Riding up the line toward Captain Murray was the daftie lass. And she was riding astride, no less. Behind her, another horse was loaded down with baggage and a tiny slave woman who seemed to be in fear of her life.

Connor moved his mare closer to Captain Murray, whose face had turned as red as his coat.

"Caroline," Murray said. "What do you think you're doing?"

"I'm coming with you," she said, as pretty as you please.

Connor could not help grinning at the thought. Luckily there was a wagon between him and the pair, and they paid him no mind. Her company would make for an interesting trip. That is, if she didn't ride off the side of a mountain and take him with her.

His eyes swept over her. At least she was dressed appropriately, not wearing one of those silly habits that genteel women liked to ride in. She wore a striped skirt over her petticoats, a linen bodice and a straw hat. Her golden hair was safely tucked into a cap beneath the hat and her blue eyes danced with excitement. Best of all, her shoes seemed to be safely tied to her feet and in no danger of coming off and landing on his head.

"No, you are not," Murray protested.

"I'm not one of your soldiers, John. You cannot order me around."

"You are my sister and in my care," he said. "And the best thing I can do for you is to leave you here."

"I want to see Father," she said. "And after the circumstances of last night, I think it best if I leave Williamsburg for a while."

Connor felt his gut clench. The circumstances of last night? Had there been repercussions after he'd left the ball? Would Murray call him out once they hit the trail, where he would have no one to second him?

Nay, ye fool, he would have already done so.

Something else must have happened.

"Really, Carrie," Murray said. "You must stop injuring every man who shows an interest in you."

"Can I help it if Sir Geoffrey is so weak that a table falling on him sends him straight to the infirmary?"

Connor sucked in his cheeks in an effort not to laugh out loud.

"You cannot go," Murray said.

"Stop me," she replied.

"I shall have you removed."

"And I will scream my head off if you do. Then I will follow you."

She's as stubborn as she is daft.

"Where we are going is extremely dangerous. You could be hurt, or even killed."

Murray had a point there. Connor wasn't sure that the man realized how dangerous it was. And he'd hate to see any harm come to the lass. But then again . . .

"I will be surrounded by the finest troops His Majesty has," she said. "If I am not safe with them, then where am I safe?"

Connor lifted an eyebrow. She was quick; she had her answers ready. And apparently Murray didn't. If he left her behind, he would be admitting that his troops were not qualified to protect her.

The captain's jaw was clenched tighter than a whore's fist over a coin. He knew he was bested, and by his sister no less. Plainly, he did not like it. Not one little bit.

"Very well, Caroline," Murray finally said. "But the first time you become a hindrance, I shall send you back."

"I promise, John, I will not be an inconvenience to you or your men."

"See that you aren't," he said and dug his spurs into his stallion. The beast jumped forward with a flick of his tail, and Connor narrowed his eyes in disapproval at the rough treatment of the animal.

"It's not easy being the son of a bastard," she said.

Connor looked back and saw her blue eyes resting upon him.

"Is it any easier being the daughter of one?" he asked.

She considered his question for a moment. "I think probably it is," she said finally. "I don't feel the need to prove anything, as my brother does."

Connor shook his head. As far as he was concerned, Murray had nothing to prove. He was English. They ruled the world. What more did the man need?

"Tell him to try being the son of a Scottish outlaw," Connor said. "It might make him appreciate his circumstances more."

He turned his mare, but she stopped him. "Your father fought at Culloden?" she asked.

He felt the familiar wave of pain. Culloden was so much a part of him. It defined who he was, at least in the eyes of those who saw him. "Aye."

"As did mine," she said. "You couldn't have been more than a baby then."

"I was born on the field," he said. "The very day of the battle."

"Your mother was there? She saw it?"

"Aye." Why did he answer her? What compelled him to go on? "She saw it."

He didn't want to talk about the past. But the way she was looking at him unsettled him.

"She must have been very brave," she said. She turned to her maid. "Come on, Patsy, we'd best stay out of my brother's way for a while."

"Yes, ma'am," the little slave woman said. Connor watched Carrie position her horse close to one of the wagons as the drummer began his count and the soldiers began to march.

"Eejits," he said.

Patsy was struggling to control her horse, so Connor went to help her. He guided her to a wagon and looped the reins over a rail.

"Are ye scared to go?" he asked her.

"No, sir," the little maid said. "Just never been on a horse afore."

"If it troubles ye too much, ride in the wagon," he said.

He noticed one of the lesser officers talking to Carrie with a sheepish look of longing on his face.

"Exactly what are the circumstances that send your mistress to the wilderness?" he asked Patsy.

Patsy's mouth opened in a wide grin. "Miss Carrie done knocked a table over on Mr. Sir Geoffrey at the ball last night because he wouldn't leave her alone. Mr. Sir Geoffrey done said it broke his foot and had a case of the vapors, which was just fine with Miss Carrie," she said. "They was people talking all over the place about it last night. How Miss Carrie had done cursed another one of her suitors, and Mr. Sir Geoffrey was lucky that he didn't die on the spot."

Connor laughed and Carrie looked his way.

"So let that serve as a warning to all who yearn after her," he said, his eyes boring into the soldier who rode alongside Carrie's horse.

"Yes, sir. Best watch out where Miss Carrie is concerned. She'll either break your heart or break your leg."

Apparently her brother had the same notion, for he barked at the soldier talking to his sister, and the man immediately rode on as Carrie settled into her place close to the wagons.

"I will watch out," Connor said.

Chapter Eight

They followed the James River for several days. The road was dry and the countryside rolling and fairly easy to travel. They made good time.

Carrie just wished the drummer would stop. He did not play constantly, but every time they drew near to a settlement, he would start up. Always, the people would come out of their houses or look up from their work to watch the soldiers go by.

John insisted upon the drumming even though she overheard Mr. Duncan suggest that it might not be such a wise thing to do where they were going. John acted as if the men couldn't march without the drummer's cadence.

Her brother mostly ignored her, except for the evenings, when they ate dinner together in his tent. His lack of interest in her did not bother Carrie. She was used to his ways. His career had been the focus of his life since he'd returned from his last posting in the highlands of Scotland.

As the days on the trail turned into weeks, the thing that did bother her was the fact that Mr. Duncan ignored her, even though he seemed to be quite fond of Patsy. He fetched water for her maid every evening and helped her set up the tent and then break it down in the morning. Patsy was quite taken with him and was always going on about Mr. Connor.

All he ever said to Carrie was "Good morning" or "Good evening," and occasionally he'd add a "Miss Murray" into the mix.

She loved the way *Murray* sounded on his tongue. The way the *R*s rolled off.

What would it be like to hear him say "Carrie"? And why was he so determined to ignore her, in spite of the almost intimate moment they'd shared the night of the ball?

Perhaps because you acted like a crazy wanton that night.

Then why had he protected her that night? Even when she'd insulted him by saying he wasn't good enough to marry her. At least not in her brother's opinion.

Carrie looked at the broad, buckskin-clad back at the head of the column. Mr. Duncan's hair, bright as new copper, was unbound across his shoulders, and his seat was easy in the saddle, as if he were a part of the horse.

He fit here. He belonged. Not in a ballroom. Not in the city, but here, out in the wild.

And they were in the wild now. What before had been rolling farmland and wide roads was now a narrow track with dense woods on either side. Occasionally they would pass a small farm with a rustic cabin and a family and a few slaves or bondservants working the fields. The inhabitants would always pause in their work to look up and watch the troop go by.

They were climbing. It was hard to see the mountains for all the trees, but the land was definitely rising.

They were entering dangerous territory. John and his troop marched on as always, but Connor . . .

His body was covered with weapons. A large knife, what looked like a two-sided ax, two pistols, and his ammunition pouch were all stuck, tied or looped within easy reach around his waist. In his left hand he carried his rifle, and his right hand rested easily on the reins. He seemed to be ready for anything. But surely he did not expect an imminent attack. It wasn't as if they were on the frontier.

At the moment they were riding across a rolling meadow that allowed a scenic vista of the mountains rising up in every direction. She began to understand where the term "Blue Ridge" has come from. The sides of the tree-covered ridges held a bluish cast in the bright, clear sunlight of the warm spring day. The bright red of the men's coats was a harsh contrast to the soft greens of the long spring grass and the deeper hue of the evergreens. The sight of their weapons properly held against their shoulders with bayonets attached formed a sharp contrast with the lacy white of the blooming dogwoods scattered around the edge of the wood. It was a peaceful setting, yet Connor looked ready to fight.

Carrie realized this was just the excuse she was looking for. She guided her mare to the side of the column and increased her pace to catch up to their guide.

"Mr. Duncan?" she said, as she moved in beside him.

He didn't seem surprised to see her. Perhaps he'd known she was coming.

"Is there a problem, Miss Murray?" he asked without turning to look at her. "Did ye perchance lose a shoe?"

Carrie looked to see whether he was laughing at her but could not be sure.

"No," she said. "They remain right where they belong—upon my feet," she said.

"For which the top of my head is eternally grateful," he replied.

"I feel that I owe you an apology, Mr. Duncan," Carrie said, after tossing a quick look over her shoulder to see where her brother was. She saw him in conversation with one of his officers. His eyes were upon her, though, so she knew she'd better hurry.

"For trying to kill me?" Connor said. "Apology accepted. Ye are not the first to attempt it, and even though ye tried very hard, ye were not successful."

Carrie couldn't help laughing. "That's not what I meant," she said.

"Ye are not sorry ye tried to kill me?" This time he looked straight at her, his face showing an obvious look of mock surprise.

"Yes. I mean no," she said. Carrie could not help herself. She placed her hand on his forearm and felt the hard flex of muscle beneath the buttery soft hide. "I apologize for insulting you. What I said about my brother calling you out."

He shrugged his shoulders, tossing off her hand with the movement as easily as if she were nothing more than a pesky insect. "Donnae fash yourself. 'Twas nothing that I have not heard before."

His words were casual enough, as if the insult did not bother him, but she noticed an underlying strain in his voice.

"Have you been in the colonies long, Mr. Duncan?"

"Long enough," he said. "Does it matter?"

"No, I just wondered because your accent is so strong."

" 'Tis a part of me. I spoke more Gaelic than English when I came here. My mother spoke both, and she made sure I knew both too."

"Is your mother still in Scotland?"

His eyes turned to her, so very, very blue. "My mother is dead," he said. The tick in his jaw returned.

"I'm sorry," Carrie said. "I lost mine also. At Christmas time."

He had no reply for her beyond a slight nod of his head.

"Do you feel that we are in danger here?" she asked after a quiet moment. She wondered if she were annoying him. She should leave him alone and go back to her place in the column, but for some reason she couldn't. Perhaps it was because this was the most interesting conversation she'd had since they'd begun the trek.

"Do ye?" he asked.

Carrie looked around. She saw the meadow and the forests and the mountains rising up in the distance. She heard the chatter of the squirrels in the trees and the call of the birds, along with the steady tromp of the troop, the creak of leather, the jangle of bits and spurs and the rumble of the wagons.

"No," she said. "I don't. But you must."

"Why do ye think so?" His face was genuinely curious.

"Because you put on your weapons today," she said. "Before you had them in your pack or looped across your saddle. But today, you have them close."

He lifted his brow and offered a slight smile at her observations.

"In the past there have been attacks in this area," he said. "I thought perhaps I should be ready."

"Do you really think we will be attacked?" Carrie looked around again, as if she could spy Indians hiding among the trees.

"Nay," Connor said. "Not today. But I want your brother to think about the possibility, so that when I do express some concern he will listen."

"What makes you think he would not listen?"

"Have you heard of Amhurst?"

Carrie shook her head. "Should I have?" she asked.

"He was an officer of your king," he said. "And not a verra bright one."

"Are you saying my brother is not intelligent enough to lead his command?"

"I am saying that the English think they are the only ones who know what they are doing. Your brother is new to the colonies. And he has not seen the way the Indians fight."

"How do they fight, Mr. Duncan?"

"They fight to stay alive, Miss Murray. They do not stand in the middle of a field and shoot at each other. They stay behind trees and rocks and use them for cover as they shoot their enemies down. They use surprise as their ally and terror to their advantage."

"They sound like cowards to me," Carrie said indignantly. Mr. Duncan was not only insulting her brother but her father as well. "Have they not the honor to face their enemies face to face?"

"Aye," Connor said. "But the Indians have their own way of fighting."

"God is on our side, Mr. Duncan," Carrie said. "He will protect us."

He laughed. "I've known him to be on several sides all at once," Connor said. "Do you not think the French said the same thing when they fought against us?"

"Yet we won," Carrie said.

"Aye, we did," he agreed. "And it took a miracle."

"Are you Catholic?"

" 'Tis a strange question. Why do ye ask?"

"I find most Highlanders are. I was just wondering."

"I was raised to be one. But there is a lack of priests in the area." He grinned unrepentantly. "I like the Moravians."

"The Moravians?" Carrie asked.

"Down in Salem," he said. "They are a peaceful lot. And they make good food."

Carrie wondered again if he was serious. "Is that your only qualification for worship?"

"I find it much easier to give God my full attention if my stomach isnae complaining."

She laughed. Talking to him was interesting, pleasant, almost fun, when the hollow of his jaw was not ticking.

"So what do you do when you are not leading English troops into the wilderness?" Carrie asked.

"I have a place." His eyes softened, as if they were seeing something inside. " 'Tis south of here."

"Tell me about it."

"There's not much to tell. A cabin, a stream and a glorious meadow with lush grass within the shelter of a mountain."

"It sounds wonderful," Carrie said. She could see it. The cabin, snug and warm in the winter, with smoke pouring from the chimney. Or cool in the summer, with the door open to catch a breeze. Tall grass waving in the meadow along with brightly colored wildflowers and a stream bubbling merrily along.

He looked at her, his eyes slightly crinkled on the corners, as if he were trying to look inside her head.

"And what are your plans for this place?" she asked, relieved to see his jaw relaxed.

" 'Tis my dream to fill that meadow full of fine horses with the name Duncan attached to them."

"This mare," Carrie said, as she let her eyes roam over the fine lines of his chestnut. "Is she part of your dream?"

Connor rubbed the mare's finely arched neck. "My Heather is the start," he said. "It took several winters of work to find just the right one. But I did. She has stamina, but more important, she has heart. She will make a fine mother. The task is to find the right stud."

Carrie looked back at her brother, who was moving toward them. "I think I can recommend one," she said with a smile.

His jaw tightened. "Nay," he said. " 'Twould ruin the impeccable blood line."

"Is there something amiss?" John asked.

"We were just talking, John," Carrie said. She noticed the tick once more in Connor's jaw. "I am most interested in the countryside."

"Ride on ahead," John said to Connor, ignoring her. "Find us a place to make camp for the night."

"I have a place in mind," Connor replied. "We should be there well before nightfall."

"Then go prepare it." John's voice was crisp, demanding. The tick in Connor's jaw became more evident.

Carrie bit her tongue. Her brother was behaving like an ass.

"It's not likely to have moved or changed," Connor replied.

"I've given you an order," John said. He grabbed the rein of Connor's mare and both horses came to a stop off to the side of the trail.

"I am not one of your soldiers," Connor flung back. He pulled his rein away, and his mare kicked out toward John's stallion as the stud put his nose against her tail.

"I could have you whipped for insubordination." John jerked his stallion away, but the horse only circled, returning to the same place.

"I would like to see you try it." Connor sat calmly on his mare and arched an eyebrow in invitation.

"John!" Carrie finally said. "This is ridiculous."

"Stay out of this, Caroline," John ground out. "I suggest you go to your place in line, unless you wish to be escorted all the way back to Williamsburg."

"I must apologize for my brother, Mr. Duncan. He is both proud and stubborn, traits he inherited from our mother," Carrie said.

"Thank you for your concern, Miss Murray," Connor said. He clearly enunciated each word, and in doing so lost some of the musicality of his accent. His face was rigid, without emotion, except for the tick in his jaw.

Carrie moved her horse away from the two men and fell back into line, but she kept checking over her shoulder. It wasn't long before she saw Connor fly by on his mare, and then John rode up beside her.

"I must insist that you stay away from that man," he said.

"And I must insist that you have no say over whom I may or may not talk to." She was livid. Her palm itched with the desire to slap him.

"That man is hardly more than a common criminal. He was brought here as a bondservant."

"He has obviously fulfilled his bond," Carrie said. "The

colonies are full of former bondservants who now contribute to society."

"Both of his parents were outlaws," John continued. "Or so I was told by our uncle."

"Only because the Scots lost the battle of Culloden," Carrie replied.

"How dare you speak that way?" John said.

"And how dare you speak the way you just did to Mr. Duncan?" Carrie's temper rose. "Father would never treat a man in his service that way."

"And have you spent time with Father in the field to know how he treats his men?"

"You know I haven't, John," Carrie said. "But you do know that Father taught us you will gain more loyalty by treating your men with respect and kindness than you will by browbeating them and insulting their intelligence."

"How I treat my men, including Mr. Duncan, is none of your concern," John said. Carrie noticed that her brother's jaw could give Connor's some serious competition in the angry tick department.

"You are right. But I wonder, John, what it is about Mr. Duncan that makes you so angry. He seems more than capable of safely leading us to Fort Savannah."

John looked at her, and Carrie saw his face change from that of rigid commander to loving brother. Her anger at his actions slipped away as his eyes searched her face. "I do not like the way he looks at you, Carrie," he said.

"He looks at me?" Carrie asked. "I haven't noticed him looking at me. He's barely even spoken to me until today."

"He looks at you. He watches you." They rode in silence for a moment. "Did anything happen with him the night of the ball?"

"Don't be ridiculous, John." Carrie couldn't believe how easily the lie came out. "Sir Geoffrey barely left my side the entire evening. How could anything have happened with Mr. Duncan?"

If he knew what had really happened the night of the

ball, John would call Connor out, even though it was all her fault. Connor had been nothing more than an innocent bystander. But explaining that to John, especially when he was already biased against Connor, would be next to impossible.

"He's not good enough for you," John said. "And don't let him talk you into thinking otherwise."

"John, we were just discussing the scenery. And religion."

"I'm sure he's a Catholic. All the Highlanders are."

"He said he was Moravian."

"Another foreign sect," John said in disgust.

"John, being English doesn't make you God," Carrie said.

"No. But it does make me the law in this land. Don't go near him again," he said and galloped off.

Chapter Nine

It seemed as if the eejits had found the place he'd marked for camp. Connor hailed the sentry as he rode through the gathering dusk.

Murray had done his best to make Connor's life miserable after their confrontation on the trail. After the lass had gone by the two men took a moment to stare each other down. Seeing he would gain nothing by arguing with the man, Connor had taken off to find a place to camp for the night.

The area he had in mind, a slight rise over a twisty creek, was still there, as he'd known it would be. Connor hung a scrap of red cloth on a stick in the middle of the field, where the troop would be sure to find it, and had just decided to scout ahead for any sign of Indians when one of the lesser officers rode up and said that Captain Murray needed him back with the troop and to make haste.

Murray then sent him back along the trail they had just traveled, to take care of one of the wagons that had lost a wheel. It was the one Patsy rode in, and he found her cowering inside it as if Indians were about to attack while three soldiers struggled to replace the wheel.

"It would ha' been much easier to do it if you'd unloaded it first," he pointed out to them as two struggled to lift the wagon while the other held the repaired wheel.

Connor found a fallen tree lying in the wood that was stout enough to serve his purpose. He stripped off his shirt and set to work chopping the tree into three thick pieces that they were able to use as a lever to raise the wagon and reattach the wheel.

By the time they caught up with the troop, dusk was upon them, and Connor's temper had reached its limit. He wanted nothing more than a bath, a meal and a nice, long sleep, but most likely Murray would find some other nonsense for him to attend to.

The sight of the horses tied to their line set a grin on his face. He unsaddled his mare, gave her a quick run over with a soft rag and led her into place right beside Murray's white stallion. He loosened the tie on the stud, and with a good-luck slap on both their rumps, went whistling off to find his dinner.

If he was lucky enough, he would be long gone before Murray ever realized that the blood line of his precious stud had been tainted. The noise behind him gave him assurance that the stallion was making the best of the situation, and Connor's grin widened.

Then he saw the lass struggling with her tent. His temper flared again. Could the brother not see fit to send someone to help her? Murray deserved a sound thrashing.

Connor stalked by the mess wagon, where he saw Patsy fixing two plates. At least the lass treated the maid decently. She was not above sharing her food, and the maid slept inside the tent, even if it was on the ground instead of on a cot.

"Is it giving you a bit of a stramash?" he asked as he

dropped his shirt on her baggage and picked up a corner of the canvas.

She blessed him with a genuine smile. "I thought I had it figured out by now," she said as she tried to poke a pole through a loop.

"It helps if you're a bit bigger than your opponent in a fight," he said.

"Do I seem that hopeless?" Carrie asked.

"Only from a distance," he replied.

She laughed. "Please," she said. "I would hate to cause my brother any further embarrassment."

"Aye," he agreed. "I ken he can embarrass himself well enough on his own."

She laughed, then quickly covered her mouth and looked toward the soldiers gathered around the campfire, as if she were afraid she would be heard.

"He has told me to stay away from you," she said as Connor went about the business of setting up her tent.

Connor shrugged. " 'Tis not unexpected," he said. "He is your brother."

"Yes, he is," she said. "And I would like to thank you for not thrashing him earlier today."

Connor looked over his shoulder at her. "So ye think I could if I wanted to?"

"I think he deserved it," she said. "Whether or not you could is something I'd rather not find out."

"I'll bear that in mind next time he makes an ass of himself."

She laughed again, and Connor stopped working to look at her. She stood in the gathering dusk with merriment dancing in her eyes and the fire lighting her hair. Her striped skirt had a streak of dirt across it, and a piece of petticoat hung across the tip of her shoes, where she had undoubtedly torn it.

She looked up at him, and his gut clenched so tight that he felt his breath catch.

"Ye pure mad daftie," he mumbled.

She looked confused. "I beg your pardon?" she said.

"Here is Patsy," he said. "With your dinner. Sit down and eat whilst I finish the job."

The two women arranged themselves on a fallen log while he went about the business of putting up the tent.

Donnae look her way . . . .

He reminded himself over and over again. He should not have let her come. He should have told her brother it was too dangerous.

If only he had realized the biggest danger was for him.

"Would you like me to fix you a plate, Mr. Connor?" Patsy asked.

Connor finished erecting the tent and picked up his shirt. "That would be nice," he said. "I'll just wash up."

He headed down the slope through the trees toward the creek.

The water was icy cold and did much to clear his head and soothe the heat in his body as he splashed it over his face, scrubbed it into the stubble of his beard and allowed it to trickle down his bare chest. He added a few more splashes across his chest and grimaced when he got a quick whiff from under his arm. A bath would be nice, even if it was freezing cold. But right now his stomach needed food more urgently.

Connor stood to go and ran his fingers through his damp hair to comb it into some sort of order.

He stopped, however, when something across the creek caught his eye, and he cursed himself for a fool as his hand went for his knife, the only weapon on him. He'd taken everything else off when he was helping with the wagon. If he was lucky, he'd die in one quick stroke.

He relaxed again when he heard the *pretty, pretty, pretty* trill of a red bird and answered with the same call.

"I saw you earlier today from the ridge." A tall, slender Cherokee stepped out from behind the thick growth of mountain laurel on the opposite side of the creek. "You are not hard to miss with that blazing head of hair."

"Ye could not find me in the autumn," Connor replied. "I missed you this past winter, Efrem." His friend hopped across the creek and came toward him with a big grin on his face.

"But you did not miss having the women all to yourself," Efrem retorted.

"And here I thought you were a man of God." Connor laughed as he clasped hands with the man.

"I aim to share my blessings with everyone," Efrem replied with a laugh of his own. "After all, the meaning of my name is . . ."

"Very fruitful," Connor finished for him. "They didnae expect you to repopulate the earth when they baptized ye, ye fool."

"Shhh," Efrem said, and placed his finger to his mouth. "It works."

"So the women at the mission in Pennsylvania have not caught on to your wicked ways?"

"They are grateful to me for keeping them warm on a long winter's night."

"How did you convince the Moravians that your intentions were honorable?"

"They see me as their greatest success."

Connor smacked his friend on the back of the head. "One day they will catch you and string you up by your stones, ye gormless half-wit."

"And I will ask for my heavenly father's forgiveness," he said and kissed the small carved wooden cross that hung from a thong about his neck. "I've come to give you news," he said, suddenly serious.

"Of the treaty?" Connor asked.

"Of the war," Efrem said. "They declared it at Fort Dunmore."

"There is war on the Ohio?" Connor asked. Without

thought he turned and looked upward toward the camp, where fires glowed between the trees. He felt the familiar fear once more as it grabbed his throat and squeezed tight.

"Already there have been deaths on both sides."

"Ye must tell Murray," Connor said.

"I have heard of a General Murray."

"Nay, his son, the captain."

"Where are you bound with this crew?"

"Fort Savannah."

"I see Andrew's hand in this."

"It is," Connor said. "Where 'bouts have ye been?"

"I traveled down the Shenandoah," Efrem said. "I have no news of fighting from Fort Savannah, which is good, I suppose."

"The Shawnee will come that far east," Connor said. "They have recently. Thus our mission. Come, tell Murray what you know."

They had started up the incline when Connor remembered his shirt, which he'd hung on a branch before his quick bath. He went back for it, then followed Efrem up the rise. Above his friend's head he caught a flash of white and heard a screech. He caught up with Efrem and they entered the clearing just in time to see Carrie fall over backward into the tent. Patsy must have been inside because a muffled scream was heard as the entire thing collapsed around the lass.

Some of the soldiers came running toward the tent, while a few had the presence of mind to pick up their guns and aim them toward the woods.

Efrem dropped his rifle and put up his hands as Connor jumped in front of him.

"Perhaps you should have told them I was coming," he said.

"He's a friend," Connor shouted. "With news."

The men looked doubtful and kept their rifles aimed at Efrem's bare chest. Connor could not blame them. It was probably the first time they had seen an Indian.

His friend's black hair hung down his back to his waist, with an eagle feather wrapped in a side lock. He wore leather breeches similar to Connor's, moccasins and a striped vest over his bare chest. Around his neck he wore the cross, along with several other thongs with feathers and stones attached to them. Connor was fairly certain there were a couple of decent shirts in Efrem's pack—he would have worn them during his stay with the northern Moravians. But apparently he'd chosen not to wear any today.

The lass managed to disentangle herself from the tent with no help from anyone just as Murray arrived on the scene.

"He's a friend," Connor repeated to Murray. "He has news."

"You were not attacked?" Murray asked Carrie as she watched the canvas undulate when Patsy moved about beneath it.

Connor felt his temper flare once more at Murray's obvious disdain for him and his word.

"No," Carrie said. "I fell, nothing more." She looked at Connor, her eyes wide and begging for forgiveness. "Could you help me find Patsy?" she said.

"I'm right here!" The maid's voice sounded muffled but spirited as she squirmed about, no doubt searching for an opening.

"Help me, Efrem," Connor said.

Efrem gave the soldiers his most charming smile and followed Connor to the tent as all eyes remained upon them. Connor found the front flap and the two men held it up as Carrie stuck her head inside and pulled the maid out.

"Oh, Lordy," she said when she saw Efrem. "Is he a real live Indian?"

"Nay," Connor said with a straight face. "He's a Moravian."

"I apologize for my actions," Carrie said, extending her hand to Efrem. "I'm afraid I was startled. My name is Caroline Murray. But you may call me Carrie."

Murray cleared his throat.

Connor noticed that Efrem kept his eyes on the captain even as he bent over Carrie's hand in a bow. "I am pleased to meet you, Miss Murray," he said.

"Efrem was orphaned by the pox and raised by the Moravian in Bethabara," Connor explained. "This is Murray," he added.

"Captain Murray," Murray added in an annoyed tone. "Duncan said you have news."

So he had been listening . . . Yet the regulars still stood around them with their rifles ready.

"He does," Connor said as he stared Murray down.

"Come with me," Murray ordered.

Efrem looked at him, and Connor knew he would get an earful later on. But for now his news must be told. It might result in Murray's sending the lass back.

If Murray possessed the sense to do it.

"Where did this news come from?" Murray asked as the three men settled in Murray's tent with some of the lesser officers in attendance.

"Fort Dunmore," Efrem said. "Settlers are fleeing to the east. The tribes across the Ohio did not appreciate all the surveying parties that showed up this spring. They captured three men and sent them back with the warning that any others who crossed the river would be killed. The whites responded by attacking and killing several Shawnee. Now there is full-scale war to the north and west of here."

"So we can expect an imminent attack on Fort Savannah?"

"That would be my guess," Connor said. "The Shawnee consider everything from the mountains west to the Ohio as their hunting ground."

"How do I know that you're not part of them?" Murray asked.

"Because he's a Cherokee," Connor said. "There is a difference between tribes." He tried to keep his voice calm. "And a Christian."

"He looks like a savage to me."

"Yet he sounds just as English as ye do," Connor said. "More so than I."

"The Shawnee and Cherokee are not friends," Efrem said. "The tribes in the alliance feel that there is not enough land for us all."

"The land you speak of belongs to England," Murray said. "And the savages shall soon learn to be happy that we allow them a place to live."

"If only ye would," Connor said. "The tribes granted us everything east of the Ohio, but that was not enough."

"They granted us?" Murray said.

Connor wondered if throttling the man would make him see the reality of the situation. He did not have any concept of what the Shawnee were capable of. He did not know the savagery that would result if they were pushed to protect what they felt was rightfully theirs.

He looked at the faces of the officers gathered around. A few were grizzled, old, had seen their share of battle, some possibly in the war with the French. But most were young, untried, away from their homes for the first times. They possibly had heard stories of Indian torture. But until you saw it, until you heard the screams and knew that your turn would come . . .

"Ye should send the lass back," Connor said. "Your sister. It isnae safe for her."

"She's well protected," Murray said. "She's surrounded by His Majesty's finest."

Connor looked at him in disbelief. Then he realized that the only reason Murray disagreed was because he had said it. If he had kept his mouth shut . . .

Connor stood, his head pushed against the top of the tent. He towered over Murray, who sat at his traveling desk as if he were in the middle of the English countryside.

"We must travel hard and we must travel fast to get to the fort. The wagons will not make it. The country is rough and even the horses will have a hard time. From tomorrow on the trail climbs and dips and the passage is narrow. The country is wild. There are plenty of places for ambush."

"I am sure that is why Lord Dunmore hired you to guide us," Murray said. He looked up at Connor as if considering him.

"Tell the men to add what they can to their packs," Murray said to one of the younger soldiers behind him. "We will leave the wagons behind." The man snapped a salute and started out of the tent. "And tell my sister that she may only take what she can carry on her horse. She will have to make do without her luxuries."

Connor shook his head. "I only hope she can keep the luxury of her scalp," he said.

Later, when the two men settled around a small fire with their dinner plates, Efrem asked, "Do you think they teach them how to be pompous?"

"Where did a Cherokee learn such a word as that?" Connor asked.

"You had your teachers," Efrem said, "I had mine. Did I tell you that there are some in Bethlehem who want to take me back to the old country to show me off?"

"Do they expect ye to put on your war paint and show them how to scalp?"

"Something like that," Efrem said. He looked over at the soldiers. "Until those who hold the power stop trying to force others to their ways, there will be trouble."

"Do ye think we could ever all live in peace?" Connor asked. "With all our different ways?" He poked at the fire with a stick and a log fell, sending sparks up into the sky.

"You and I do, my brother," Efrem said. "But I can count more nations as my enemies than I can men my friends."

"As can I," Connor mused. "Just because of where I was born." His eyes darted toward the guards, and he noticed there were more on patrol than usual. At least Murray had taken some of his words to heart.

"I know my people would be better off if yours had stayed across the sea."

"It's not as if I wanted to come here," Connor said.

"Would you go back? If you could?" Efrem asked.

Go back. To Scotland. How many nights of his boyhood had he yearned for just that. To be back in the hovel where he and his mother had lived after the castle had been burned. To hear his mother call him in to eat or fuss because he had not done his chores. To work with the war horses that had somehow survived the horrible years after Culloden because his older cousin had the foresight to keep them hidden. To hear stories of his father and his grandfather and his uncles, who had all died on the battlefield, leaving the family desolate, but proud and strong and still willing to fight.

Connor looked toward a tent that was set slightly askew close to the mess wagon. "Nay," he said finally. "There is nothing left for me there."

The only thing he wanted was here.

Chapter Ten

Mist rose from the ground like a shroud as Connor and Efrem picked their way down to the creek in the faint light of dawn. The camp above was coming to life as the regulars sought to condense the supplies for the long trek into the mountains. The lass's tent was silent when they passed, and Connor cursed her brother once again for being a fool.

Murray should send her back to Williamsburg, where she'd be safe.

Though it was early summer, the water was icy cold; their bath would be hasty. Both men stripped down to their short linen breeks and shared a bar of soap. The heavy fog lent the air an eerie silence that neither one of them wanted to break. Not a word passed between them except for a grunt from Efrem when Connor punched him in the arm after he snagged the lace cap from among Connor's things.

They dressed in silent camaraderie, and Efrem shook his head in mock disgust as Connor stuffed the cap down inside the waist of his breeks. The two men gathered their weapons and packs and were on their way back up the hill when they heard sounds that gave them both pause.

Someone was in the creek. A heavy splash upstream from where they had bathed froze both men in their tracks.

Connor raised his rifle, ready to shoot if and when the fog parted. Efrem checked the prime on his.

"Patsy?" Carrie's voice sounded through the fog as if she were a part of the ethereal mist. Efrem elbowed Connor in the ribs and gave a slight toss of his head toward the creek.

Connor raised his eyebrows as if considering the possibility of returning to the stream.

Then they heard shots up above, followed by a horrific yell.

A chill ran down Connor's spine. Surely not. But the sounds of several battle cries convinced him otherwise. Then more shots, yells and screams, all coming together in a terrifying moment that made his skin break out in a sweat, even though he felt chilled to the bone.

"Shawnee," he said and took off at a run.

Carrie froze where she was, terrified to move as the sounds seemed to come at her from all sides.

The camp was under attack. And she stood shivering in her shift in the middle of a creek.

What should I do?

Clothes. *Put on your clothes.* Carrie scrambled from the creek and grabbed her clothes. Her hands shook as she searched for her stockings. She heard the horrendous yells. She heard the terrifying screams. She heard the repeated sound of weapons firing.

And she could not find her stockings.

"God help us," she said.

Surely she was going to die.

She turned in the mist. She knew someone was there. Should she call out? What if it was Patsy? Or John?

The mist swirled and mysteriously parted. And without saying a word, Connor scooped her up in his arms and jumped across the creek. Over his shoulder she saw Efrem gather her clothes and then he too came across, only slower, more cautiously, as if he were covering their trail.

"We must hide," Connor said. He ran through the woods effortlessly with her in his arms. She saw that he carried a pack on his back, and his rifle was slung over one shoulder.

"What about John? And Patsy?"

"We cannae help them. We'd all be killed."

"We can't leave them."

"We must," he said without breaking stride.

"You've abandoned them," she said.

He stopped and put her down. She noticed she was standing on a rock that placed her chin level with his. "Put on your clothes," he said.

"You ran." She wanted to slap him. Or claw out his very blue eyes. Eyes that looked at her with pain and fear. He was a coward. Her brother was back there fighting, and would most likely die. And the man hired to lead them all through the wilderness had run away from the fight. "Give me your gun," she said. "I'll go back for him."

His jaw clenched tight and she saw a tick in the hollow of his cheek.

Connor moved past her and Efrem held out her clothes.

"We were in the creek just like you when it happened," he said. "There was nothing we could do."

"What were you doing in the creek?" Carrie asked, as if she did not believe him. They were cowards. Both of them.

"Taking a bath, same as you," Efrem said.

Carrie's eyes widened as she took in his damp hair. She turned and saw that Connor's was the same, hanging in wet tendrils around his shoulders, dampening his shirt.

"Get dressed," he said.

"I'll see if we were followed." Efrem turned back the way they'd come.

"The fog is lifting," Connor said. "They'll be able to see us soon."

Carrie yanked on her stockings and petticoat. She picked up her corset.

"You'll have to help me," she said. She was shivering un-controllably. She wondered if it was caused by a chill from the water or fear.

Connor looked at her corset as if it were some strange, foreign thing. "Ye don't need it," he said. He took it from her, rolled it up tight and stuffed it in his pack. She quickly finished dressing with her teeth chattering so hard, she thought they would fall from her mouth. Her hands were shaking so much she could not lace her shoes, so Connor bent and tied them for her.

"I'm sorry," she said. She touched her fingers to the back of his head and felt the dampness there.

He looked up at her, and she once more saw the pain in his eyes. "The lucky ones will die back there," he said. "I hope your brother is one of them."

"I don't understand," she said.

"Ye donnae ken what they do to prisoners?"

"No."

"Someone is coming," Efrem said. Carrie looked up in surprise. She had not heard a sound.

"I will have to carry ye," Connor said. "Ye donnae ken how to hide your tracks."

He scooped her up again and they took off at a run, this time straight uphill. Carrie looked at the ground be-hind her. There was nothing. Their passage was silent. Not so much as a twig was broken, or a frond from a fern. Not a petal on a wildflower was disturbed. And Efrem's eyes scanned the ground as he ran, to make sure. How did they do it? Was some sort of Indian magic?

She kept her arms tight around Connor's neck. He

smelled fresh and clean, and she realized he had shaved when her cheek moved against his.

He was just as surprised at the attack as she was. As they all were. She could tell he'd had no idea it was coming. If he'd been in the camp, he would most likely be dead.

And she would be dead also.

"Ye donnae ken what they do to their prisoners."

It was better to be dead than a prisoner? Did the Indians not ransom their captives? Had she not heard her uncle say that Connor had been a prisoner of the Shawnee?

So he would know . . . .

Her arms tightened around his neck.

"We must hide," Connor said. "We cannae outrun them."

Because of me. They cannot outrun the Indians because he's carrying me. And if he puts me down, they will be able to trail us.

I don't want to die . . . .

"This way," Efrem said. "I saw a place when I came in." He veered left abruptly, leading the way.

They were now going downhill, and Carrie hung on for dear life. She was afraid Connor would fall.

"There," Efrem said, pointing toward a huge hemlock tree that had fallen over recently; its branches were still green. "I'll cover our tracks,"

"Get beneath," Connor said. "And don't make a sound."

Carrie moved as carefully as she could, ducking under the branches and hoping desperately that she hadn't left a sign. Water droplets rained down on her back and she realized that Connor was throwing broken branches on top of the tree.

She looked down at her clothes and realized that the color would give them away. If only she had not changed out of the brown striped gown and into the pink.

For some reason she'd wanted to look pretty today.

Pretty in her pink striped skirt, covered in blood and her scalp gone.

Connor crawled in beside her, and Efrem came in on

the low side. Both eased their rifles and ammo pouches
out beside them. Would it be enough? The shots still
sounded on the opposite ridge. The screams and yells
were just as terrifying as the first ones she'd heard.

Connor handed her a pistol.

"Do ye . . ." His mouth was right next to her ear. His
breath caressed her, warming her.

Carrie nodded and checked the prime.

"Save it for yourself," he said into her ear once more.
Her breath caught in her throat. He expected her to use
the weapon on herself?

A twig snapped, the sound just as terrifying as the gunfire, which was slowing down.

Fear tightened her throat and she dared not breathe.
She felt Connor move and realized that he was covering
her body with his, trying desperately to hide the pink.

She felt Connor's nod. It was if he and Efrem shared the
same mind. They communicated without speaking. She
tried to turn to look at their faces, but she couldn't. Connor's weight was too great, as if he wished to smash her into
the earth. She felt the length of his legs over hers, felt the
hollow of his stomach as it curved over her backside. She
felt the strength of his arms as they flowed around her. She
felt the whisper of his breath on her neck. He was everywhere, but there wasn't enough of him to hide her from
the coming terror.

They were going to die and it was her fault.

Efrem pointed. A rabbit went by with its ears flattened,
running like mad, as if the hounds of hell were on its heels.
It was frightened of something. Something behind it.

Then they heard something bigger crashing through
the woods. Something sobbing in terror as it careened
back and forth with no direction.

Patsy.

Carrie gasped, but before she could call out, Connor's
hand went over her mouth, clamping it shut so that she

could not make a sound as she watched Patsy run down the trail.

And just as silently Efrem rolled out of the shelter and bounded away on silent feet.

They waited. Carrie felt her heart pounding against the cold, hard ground, but also felt the slower, even thump of Connor's against her back.

She willed hers to stop its racing. She concentrated on slowing it down until she felt her heartbeat fall into unison with Connor's.

Thump. Thump. Thump.

The sounds of gunfire were gone. There were no more screams, no more yells, no more sounds of death. Nothing but the call of a bird, which sounded strangely out of place.

Then, to her amazement, she heard another bird call, and Connor moved off her.

"They're gone," he said as he crawled from their hiding place.

"How . . . how do you know?"

"I know," he said. He looked back beneath the fallen tree and smiled reassuringly as he reached for the gun that she held clenched tightly in her hand. She was afraid to let go of it. She was afraid she would need it. But when she saw his smile, she released her hold and let him pull her from the shelter.

She was grateful for the strength of his grip as he helped her to her feet. She was shaking so hard she couldn't stand.

" 'Tis safe, lass," he said as he caught her. His arms tightened around her, and she felt the touch of his mouth on the crown of her head. "They've gone."

"Pa . . . Pa . . . Patsy?"

"Look," he said, and turned her toward the ridge.

Efrem and Patsy were coming down the trail, and the maid burst into tears when she saw Carrie.

"Lordy, Miss Carrie, I thought they done killed everyone."

"How did you escape?" Carrie asked as the maid fell weeping into her arms.

"I was going back toward camp from the stream when I heard the shots, and I hid. They couldn't see me in the fog. Then one of the soldiers fell down dead in front of me and I ran off." It was hard to understand her, she was crying so hard, but they got the important bits of her story. "Miss Carrie, I know he was dead, coz his head was split in two."

"Heaven forbid," Carrie said as she patted Patsy's bony shoulders. "You're safe now. Mr. Connor said so."

She looked up at Connor and almost faltered on her words. Even though the attackers were gone, she could see the worry evident in his eyes.

"I want to go home," Patsy cried.

"We will," she said. But Connor frowned and shook his head, and then he and Efrem stepped away, their heads together as they talked quietly.

"What about John?" Carrie asked. "Did you see him?"

"I didn't see nobody," Patsy said as she wiped her nose on her sleeve.

"We must go," Connor said. Efrem was already moving up the trail.

"What about John?" Carrie asked. "What if he's hurt?" She suddenly realized that the sun was pouring down on them. The fog had dissipated, leaving behind a beautiful morning. The woods around her seemed obscenely beautiful when she knew that death was just across the creek.

"We should move on," Efrem said.

"Back to Williamsburg?" Carrie asked. It seemed so far away. As if in another lifetime. Was it just a few weeks since she'd danced at the ball?

"Nay," Connor said. "They are moving the way we came. We dare not meet them on the road. Fort Savannah is closer. We'll keep going that way."

"I can't leave without knowing if my brother is dead or alive," Carrie said. "What if John's been taken prisoner?"

"I pray to God that he hasn't," Connor said.

"Please," she begged. "I have to know."

The two men looked at each other, and then both nodded. "We must move quickly," Connor said. "And ye must do what I say, when I say it."

"I don't want to see," Patsy said.

"You don't have to," Carrie assured her.

The two women fell behind Connor while Efrem brought up the rear. Patsy held on to Carrie's arm as if she would never let go as they made their way down the trail.

And as they crossed the creek and started the climb to the remnants of the camp, Carrie realized that she really didn't want to see either.

But she had to know.

Chapter Eleven

It was as he expected. Bodies lay everywhere, most missing their scalps. The ones with their scalps were Shawnee. They'd left their dead behind, which meant they were traveling fast and light.

It also meant they would not take prisoners. At least the lass would have the comfort of knowing her brother was dead.

Connor watched her carefully. This carnage was not a sight for a lady to see. But beyond covering her mouth with her hand, she bore it well. She looked about at the bodies with her innocent eyes open and sympathetic to the tragedy as she searched for her brother.

The supplies were scattered as if they'd been tossed aside. The attackers had been looking for weapons and ammunition, nothing more. The wagons burned where they stood, and Connor noticed the cook hanging from the back of the mess wagon, his foot caught on something inside and his arms dragging against the ground. He would like to bury all the bodies but knew there was no time. They needed to reach the fort, where they could find some semblance of safety behind its walls.

And with the sun now burning down on their heads, he knew the stink of death would soon fill the camp.

Was there anything he could have done to stop this massacre?

I should have scouted ahead. I should have seen the signs.

He had been planning to do so. But then Murray had sent him back to fix the wagon.

Would Murray have listened even if he'd seen the signs and warned him? The man measured everything Connor said as if weighing the importance of the words against his knowledge as an officer of the king. The captain had listened when he'd told him about the need to travel light and fast driving the rest of the march. Perhaps he would have heeded Connor's warning.

"I can't find him," Carrie said. "I've looked at all the bodies and he's not here."

She stood in the middle of the carnage with her arms wrapped about her body as if trying to hold in her emotions. Her hair dangled about her ears and across her eyes. She'd probably lost her pins when they'd taken shelter.

"Did they take him prisoner?" Carrie asked. She seemed hopeful. "He's an officer. They could ransom him. They know he could be ransomed, don't they?"

"They took no prisoners this time, lass," Connor said as gently as he could.

"They only took the weapons," Efrem confirmed. "And the horses."

Connor didn't want to consider that. He'd realized his mare was gone at the first shot he'd heard.

But he'd known the risks when he'd taken the job.

A movement beneath one of the wagons caught his eye, and with a quick signal to Efrem the two men cautiously moved that way.

It was one of the young officers. Connor and Efrem dragged him out from beneath the burning wagon, and Connor wished right away they had left him.

"Thank the Lord, Miss Murray," he said, even though he was terrified. "You are safe."

He was shot through the gut. A slow, agonizing death for this one. And Connor could tell by the look in the lass's eyes that she would not leave him behind; nor would she tolerate shooting the man to give him a quick, merciful death.

"Mr. Duncan and his friend saved me," she said as she dropped down beside the young man. "And he will get you help."

She thought he could be saved. And she also thought Connor was some sort of miracle worker.

"Patsy, find something for bandages," she said. The maid jumped as if shot from a cannon. Connor realized she'd been standing where they'd left her with her eyes screwed shut against the horrible sights.

"He willnae make it," Connor said. Efrem shook his head. His friend was anxious to be gone.

"We cannot leave him," Carrie said.

"We cannot stay here," Efrem said.

"You can carry him," Carrie suggested. She seemed hopeful. Convinced. "We'll make a litter." She looked up at him, and Connor felt a strange ache in his gut. What was it about her that made him so weak?

She pulled his strings as if he were a puppet. It had to stop.

"We cannae," he said. "Would you trade your life and Patsy's for his? He will slow us down and still he will die."

He hated saying the words, especially in front of the young soldier, who looked up at them in terror. But it was better for him to know the truth.

A screech from Patsy made them all jump.

"It's Captain Murray," she yelled. She was down the side

of the ridge with just the top of her head showing. "And he's alive."

"I hope he's in better shape than this one," Efrem said.

"I'll be right back," Carrie said to the young officer, and she darted off to Patsy.

"I'll see about Murray," Connor said to Efrem. He looked at his friend, a silent communication passing between them. He knew that the officer would be dead upon his return. He knew the young man would not suffer. At least not as much as he would if they allowed him to die on his own.

"Be at peace," he said to his friend, and to the soldier, who now seemed to accept his fate.

Connor nodded his head to Efrem and went after Carrie.

He found Carrie with her brother propped in her lap as she dabbed at the blood on his face with a piece of cloth torn from her petticoat.

"He's alive," she said. Murray's forehead had been creased by a bullet. Connor looked up and saw the scene in his mind. The bullet had just missed him and sent him toppling over the crest. The fog that had covered the attack had saved Murray's life.

The attackers had simply missed him. His sword still lay beside him, along with his pistol.

"Your brother is a lucky man," he said.

Patsy scrambled up the hill with a cup of water from the creek, and Carrie used it to bathe Murray's face.

"Wake up, John," she said. "It's over and we're safe."

His blue eyes opened and he sat up suddenly, alert and searching.

"You're alive?" he said. "How?" He looked at Connor and his face turned cold. "And you," he said. "Where were you when this happened?"

"Connor saved me," Carrie said. "And Efrem. They found Patsy too."

Connor felt Murray's eyes upon him. They were taking his measure. And he felt as if the captain found him lacking. But maybe now he understood the danger of this land.

"How bad are the casualties?" Murray asked.

Connor shook his head.

"No," Carrie said. "One is alive. Corporal Peters."

"He willnae live out this day," Connor said.

"All dead?" Murray asked. "Are you sure? We must make sure."

"We have searched them all," Connor said. "And we must leave this place soon."

"Connor says we must make for Fort Savannah," Carrie said.

"That is our goal," Murray said. "I have my orders."

Connor almost sighed in relief. At least he would not have to fight the man on that count. "We must go."

Murray found his feet. Carrie tried to help, but he pushed her aside. He rested with his hands on his knees for a moment and then picked up his sword before he straightened.

"Gather what food you can into packs," Connor said to Patsy. "Take nothing more than what ye can carry on your back."

"I must see to my men," Murray said.

"There's nothing you can do for them," Connor said.

"I must make sure."

The man was as single-minded as his sister. There was no sense arguing with him. He followed the Murrays up the hill. The smoke from the wagon fires rose straight up into a sky that was as blue as the lass's eyes. It would be a sign to anyone looking toward the mountains that the Shawnee were on the move. Connor hoped that those that saw it had sense enough to seek cover.

Efrem knelt next to the corporal with his fingers on his cross and his head bent in prayer.

"How is he?" Carrie asked.

"He's gone," Efrem said. Connor looked down at the still face of the young corporal. There was no doubt in his mind that Efrem had suffocated him.

It was better this way.

Murray looked around the clearing. "I thought you said this was a safe place and easily defended."

Connor did not answer. He could take the time to explain to the captain that the British had announced their coming over and over again with the drumming and the marching and the wagons. He could tell him that instead of scouting ahead for signs of trouble he'd been ordered to fix a broken wheel on a wagon behind them. He could say that there was no defense against silent men creeping up in a thick fog.

Instead he just looked at the broken drum that lay at his feet.

"I got all I could," Patsy interrupted. She held two packs in her arms.

"Are there any munitions left?" Murray asked.

"No," Efrem said. "They took it all."

Murray walked around the clearing, looking at the bodies. He kicked away the remnants of his tent and found his pack and his coat.

He straightened his shirt, put on his coat and strapped on his belt. He slid his sword into its sheath and leveled his gaze on Connor.

It would not have surprised him to see Murray put on a wig. Even though he had no troop, he was still a captain in His Majesty's army.

And he blamed Connor for the disaster. Connor saw accusation plainly written on his face.

There will come a time when I will have to fight him. . . .

And not for the lass's honor as she'd casually mentioned on the night of the ball. It would be for his own.

"Lead on, Mr. Duncan," Murray said. He took one of the bags of food from Patsy and slung it over his shoulder.

Connor moved out, leading them down the ridge toward the river. As he walked on, he prayed with all his might that Murray would not see fit to thrust that sword into his back.

Chapter Twelve

They followed a narrow trail along the river, which raged and tumbled as it had for innumerable years through the deep valley cut by its passage. They moved quickly and silently over a path that was barely wide enough for a horse to pass along.

Carrie seriously wondered when she would be able to take a breath without panting. They had not stopped since they'd left the scene of death behind. At least she was not hampered by her corset.

The morning, which had started out so cool and damp, had given way to a steamy late afternoon. The sun, now hanging just over the top of the mountain ridges, bounced off the wild rapids that tortured her with their inviting coolness. Was it just a few hours ago that she had stood shivering in her shift? Was it just this morning that she'd thought riding a horse through the rolling farmland of Virginia was an adventure?

She knew Connor and Efrem were worried. The looks on their faces were more effective than any words they could have spoken. Connor led them along the river and set a quick pace. Carrie followed behind him, then John, with Patsy and Efrem bringing up the rear. Connor had not said a word since they'd begun their trek. When there was a steep section of trail or a fallen tree, he would help her over, taking her arm in a firm grip that burned into her flesh through her sleeve, then dropping it again as he moved ahead.

She was worried about John. His mouth was set in a grim line and his eyes were drawn down. He had to be in pain. The crease on his forehead from the bullet looked red and angry. She knew his pride. He would never confess he was in pain. And he would drop before he admitted defeat.

How much longer could they continue at this pace? The time for the noon meal was long past and they had not given a thought to breakfast. Connor allowed time for nothing beyond a few handfuls of water hastily scooped up from the river.

Thunder rumbled in the distance. There would be a downpour before evening came, and Carrie wondered where they would possibly find shelter from the storm. All she saw were trees, dense undergrowth and huge boulders strewn through the river.

Still, she could not help marveling at the beauty around her. Dogwood trees scattered lace among the branches, ferns brushed her skirts and mountain laurels heavy with blooms decorated the sides of the mountains.

Rabbits and chipmunks darted away at their passage, and in the branches above, squirrels and jays kept up a steady chatter, as if warning the forest creatures that there were invaders afoot. She was amazed to see bright red birds everywhere and realized that their song was the one that Connor and Efrem imitated when they wanted to communicate. She could now pick out the sound from the songs of the sparrows, chickadees and wrens that frolicked in the branches above.

She had learned to recognize those birds during the first

few days on the trail. Patsy had taught her the names of local trees, and the plants. She'd told Carrie about the crops grown by the settlers, and the richness of the soil. The untapped resources. The potential for wealth to be gained by any and all who dared to beat back the wilderness.

But it was not until this day that she'd really learned what the wilderness was all about. She could not imagine that they were on their way to a settlement when her surroundings were so completely wild and untamed. Was it worth risking one's life to build a home in this savage place?

Carried looked across the river and saw trees so thick that a man the size of Connor could not pass easily between them. They were so dense that she blinked, unable to see anything in the deep brown and green haze. How did Connor even know where they were going? Were they lost? He seemed to be sure of the trail, but to her eyes they were in the middle of nowhere. Yet somewhere, to the north and west of where they now stood, there was a fort. There were homes. There were people clearing fields, planting crops and raising children.

How did they survive? How did they step outside every morning, knowing that they could be killed at any moment? How did they sleep at night, not knowing if their home might be burned down around them while they slept? What drove them to this place?

The green haze gave way to gray as she looked at the light glancing off the river. She felt blinded. She could not see, she could not feel and could do nothing beyond putting one weary foot in front of the other until she walked into Connor's back. He had stopped on the trail.

He turned and caught her arm as if she were falling. Thunder rumbled once again in the distance, the sound of it bringing her back to awareness.

"Are ye hurt?" he asked gently.

Carrie blinked and realized there was water before him. Another river joined the one they traveled along.

"We must cross here," he said. " 'Tis deep and the current is fast, but we cannae take the time to move upstream to the shallows."

John stood behind her with his hands on his knees as if to rest, and Patsy stood behind him, her eyes still as wide as they'd been after the attack. Beside her, Efrem seemed grim.

"We must rest," Carrie said. Her brother's face was pale and covered with a sheen of sweat. His eyes seemed weak and there were dark circles beneath them. "He's hurt."

"There is nothing wrong with me," John said.

"You were shot," Carrie said. "You are lucky to be alive."

"There's a cave," Connor said. "We must try to make it before the storm breaks."

"Move on," John said, and motioned them all forward with his hand.

"Can ye swim?"

"I can," Carrie said. "John too."

Patsy shook her head.

"Jump on," Efrem said. He knelt, and Patsy climbed onto his back, wrapping her skinny arms around his neck.

"The bottom is rocky," Connor said. " 'Tis easy to misstep." He took Carrie's hand in his and stepped into the water.

Carrie turned to look at John. She was worried that he was too weak to fight the current.

The look on his face was blazing, angry and full of hatred. It shocked her so much, she nearly fell when she stepped into the stream. Was he angry because Connor was holding her hand? It was only the strength of his grip that kept her from falling.

Connor gave her a moment to find her footing and then took another step. John splashed in behind her and then moved past them.

The water instantly cooled her. But she knew she'd be miserable once they left it because her shoes and stockings would take forever to dry. Her skirts and petticoats felt like weights around her ankles, and each step seemed harder and harder to take.

John was up to his thighs in the river. Carrie grabbed her skirts and pulled them up. She knew she was moving too slowly when Efrem splashed by with Patsy high and dry on his back.

"Take your time, lass," Connor said. " 'Twill be easier if ye don't go under." He smiled encouragingly at her.

"I cannot believe the settlers came this way with their wagons," she said.

"They didnae. There is another trail, wide enough for wagons, but longer."

Carrie struggled as her foot slipped beneath a rock.

His grip tightened on her arm. "This trail is faster," he said.

"Do you think the Shawnee could be following us?"

"I think they will come this way on their way home."

The water was deeper now. More forceful. The current threatened to sweep her feet out from under her. Carrie held her skirts bunched up to her waist. Efrem and Patsy were on the opposite shore and John was just past the middle of the stream. The set of his shoulders told her he was exhausted. How much longer could he go on?

"I think it will be easier if I carry you," Connor said, and swooped his arms around her. "Although I am sure your brother willnae like it." The next instant she was in his arms. Because her skirts were bunched up, his arm came into contact with the bare skin of her thighs. The heat of his body burned into the cold chill of her skin.

"You will be wet soon enough anyway," he said as the thunder, now closer, punctuated his words.

"Will we make the cave before the storm breaks?" She placed her arms around his neck as he slipped a bit.

"Storms come up fast in the mountains," he said.

Carrie looked off toward the west and noticed the sun had disappeared behind a cloud and a breeze had sprung up, whipping the new green leaves.

Before Connor took another step, the world exploded around them. The boom was so terrifying that Carrie screamed, and she heard Patsy's voice joining hers. Connor bent over her, turning and slamming her face against his shoulder with his hand as chunks of wood flew around them. She felt rather than heard him grunt as thunder rolled across the top of their heads.

"What happened?" she gasped.

"Lightning," he said. Carrie looked toward the bank and saw the remnants of a tree, its trunk splintered. Patsy was crouched on the bank with her arms over her head.

"John? Where's John?"

Connor ran toward the bank with Carrie as she twisted and turned in his arms, trying to find her brother. She saw Efrem drop his weapons and pack before diving into the river.

As soon as her feet hit the bank, she ran toward the place where Efrem had gone in. She caught a glimpse of her brother's head in the water.

"John!" she screamed. Connor's things landed beside her, and he took a moment to wrench something from his forearm before he dove in.

Carrie looked down at her feet and saw a piece of wood, sharp as a knife and covered with blood. She picked it up and looked at the blood on the end of it.

What was happening?

She watched as the two men took strong strokes toward the middle of the river. The force of the current was carrying John rapidly downstream.

The next instant the entire sky opened up. Before she could draw her next breath, she was soaked. The drops pelted against her skin.

"Oh Lordy, Miss Carrie," Patsy cried as she came up beside her. "What we going to do?"

The rain turned to hail the size of the marbles that John had played with as a boy. Patsy screamed again and threw her arms over her head, dashing toward the trunk of a tree. Then, just as quickly, she ran away from it, as if afraid lightning would strike again. The hail pelted Carrie's face, bruising it with the force of the impact, but she refused to take her eyes from the river.

The three heads visible above the water came together. They had him. Carrie had not realized she was holding her breath until she saw Efrem and Connor strike out toward the shore with John between them.

"Get their things," she said to Patsy. The maid immediately stopped her hysterics and went for Efrem's pack. Carrie threw the bloody stick aside and picked up Connor's pack and weapons and ran up the bank where the men were coming in.

"John!"

They stumbled out of the water. Connor and Efrem dragged John up between them and then both men pitched forward and collapsed on the bank.

Carrie pushed her brother over on his back and her hands searched his face for signs of life as she used her body to shelter him from the hail.

John coughed, choked and sputtered up some water, then turned over. Carrie pounded on his back as he gagged and took a long, shuddering breath.

"What happened?" he finally asked. "Were we attacked?"

"Lightning hit a tree," Carrie said. "The blast must have knocked you off your feet."

The hail stopped, turning once more into a sheet of rain. Carrie brushed back John's hair from his forehead to make sure he wasn't injured.

"I'm fine," he said and pushed her hand away.

"They saved you," she said. "Connor and Efrem saved you." She looked at Connor, who was sitting up and examining his arm. "You're hurt."

His forearm was bleeding from both sides. "I seem to have a few splinters," he said.

Efrem took his knife and sliced the sleeve of Connor's shirt up to the elbow. A wound showed in the meaty part of his forearm, worse on the back side than the front. As Connor looked at it with a frown on his face, Carrie realized it was the arm that had protected her head when the lightning struck. Where would the piece of wood have landed if he had not sheltered her? In her face? In her heart? Surely it would have killed her.

"It passed all the way through," Efrem said.

"Not through enough," Connor said. "I had to pull it out."

Efrem stuck the tip of his blade into the wound, and more blood poured out. Beyond a frown and a wrinkling of his forehead, Connor bore it well.

"Chances are there are still pieces inside," Efrem said. "It will likely fester."

"Put some of your stuff on it and it will heal," Connor said. "I'll worry about the rest later."

Carrie ripped off a piece of her petticoat as Efrem dug into his pack. "We can use this to bandage it," she said.

"I fear that at this rate you will run out of fabric before we get to the fort," Connor said as he looked at the ragged hem of her skirts.

Efrem brought forth a small pot and slathered something that looked like grease on Connor's arm. Carrie stepped in when he was done and wrapped the wound. "You saved my life twice today," she said as she tied a knot in the bandage. "And my brother's." She looked up from her handiwork and saw eyes as blue as sapphires looking down at her. Droplets of water hung on to the tips of his eyelashes. His hair, soaked to a rich chestnut from the rain, hung down across his forehead, and he shoved it back with his right hand as she spoke.

"I cannot thank you enough," she said. The intensity of his gaze frightened her so much that she had to look away. She noticed John was on his feet, watching both of them.

Connor said nothing. Instead he touched her hair and pulled out a leaf. He twirled it between his fingers with a crooked smile.

"We are all a bit bedraggled," he said as she took the leaf from his hand. "But at least this rain will wash away our tracks."

Suddenly Carrie felt herself jerked away as John forcefully grabbed her arm and shoved her behind him. "Take your hands off her, you Scottish son of a bitch," he spat out.

"John!" She looked past her brother's shoulder and saw Connor's face turn rigid and the tick appear once more in his cheek. Then he punched John squarely in the jaw. John hit the ground groaning.

"Are you both insane?" Carrie jumped in between her brother and Connor, who towered over him with fists clenched. Patsy sobbed behind Connor, and Efrem held his rifle in his hands with a dangerous look in his eyes.

"Is it insane for me to defend my sister's honor?" John asked as he scrambled to his feet and snatched something white from the front of Connor's breeches.

Her cap. The one she'd lost the night of the ball.

He'd kept it. Her face flushed a bright red as the implications of his keeping the cap and where he'd placed it flooded through her mind.

No wonder John was livid. Her reputation was once again besmirched, and therefore his honor as well.

On the other hand, this was not England, or even Williamsburg. They were in the wilderness, fleeing for their lives. And it was only a scrap of lace. It could belong to anyone.

"John, you are being ridiculous," she said. "Mr. Duncan saved your life and you're carrying on about a lace cap."

"Your lace cap," John said tightly as he waved the cap under her nose. "The one you were wearing the night of the ball."

"Since when do you pay such attention to my wardrobe?" Carrie asked indignantly. "This could belong to anyone." She took it from him. "They are all pretty much the same." She glanced imploringly at Connor, who still looked as if he wanted to kill John. "I am sure a man such as Mr. Duncan has plenty of young women seeking his favor." She placed a gentling hand on her brother's arm. "Please, John. We're in grave danger. This man just saved your life. Don't you think you should be thanking him? And Efrem also?" Carrie tightened her grip on John's arm.

"The women need shelter," Efrem said calmly, even though his eyes were threatening. The rain washed in sheets down his long, dark hair, and Carrie felt a chill as she watched it pour off the cords in his neck and sluice down the hard planes of his bare chest.

She looked at Connor and realized that he stood a full head taller than her brother, whom she had always thought taller than most. He was broader too, across the shoulders, through the waist, arms and his legs. He carried more weight.

Connor had not moved since he'd struck John. Indeed, if not for the tick in the smooth line of his jaw, she would have thought him a statue. His clothes, soaked from the river and the rain, were molded to his long, well-muscled body as if chiseled from stone.

She begged him with her eyes to let it go. To let her lie pass. But his eyes remained upon her brother.

Carrie watched in fear as John stared back at the two men. Surely John would not challenge Connor to a duel. Not here. Not now. He still had his sword, but Connor surely had greater strength. And there was no doubt in her mind that Efrem would side with Connor, and then her brother would be lost.

They would all be lost.

"There is a cave a bit ahead," Connor said. His eyes were upon her. They pierced through her as if he'd just bared himself before her. Then they changed again as he looked at John.

"I'll lead," Efrem said, and turned toward the trail.

Patsy jumped right on his heels as he took off through the trees along the river.

"Let us go," John said. He took her arm in his hand and nudged her toward the trail, in a not-so-gentle manner. Carrie gathered up her skirts and looked at her brother.

It was as if she were looking at a stranger.

"What is wrong with you?" she demanded. "These men saved your life and this is how you act?"

John stopped and turned to Connor, who was gathering his things.

"My sister has reminded me that I have been remiss in expressing my gratitude to you and your friend for your assistance today."

Carrie resisted the urge to give him a swift kick in the shins. He was acting like a fool and was fully aware of it.

But then again, he had almost lost his life twice in one day.

He's hated Connor since the first day he met him. . . .

Then she realized it wasn't just Connor. It was Connor's blood. Something had happened to John to make him feel this way. He had not been raised to be so intolerant. But he had come back from his most recent posting in Aberdeen a changed man. He never spoke of it, but something had happened to him there. Something that had filled him with hatred.

"The sooner we leave, the sooner we'll be out of the rain," Connor said as he slung his pack on his back and checked the prime on his rifle. The words were meant to be light, but his face was serious. The tick was still evident in his jaw.

"You heard our guide," John said to Carrie. "Move."

Carrie took off up the trail after Patsy and Efrem. And even though the rain was supposed to have washed away their tracks, she did not feel any safer. If anything, she felt as if there was a war right on her heels.

Chapter Thirteen

It wasn't much of a cave. More like a shelf in the side of the mountain, with a hollow carved out beneath. But it would provide shelter, which was some comfort since the pounding rain had settled into a drizzle that promised to continue throughout the night.

Connor felt bone-weary. The night before had been a sleepless torment haunted with dreams of things he could not have. The dawn attack had seemed to last a day in itself, and the forced march had been exhausting. Add to that the swim against the raging current of the river and the fight with Murray, and he wanted nothing more than to seek a warm, dry bed, which was nigh impossible considering the weather. But they had covered a lot of miles. More than he'd thought possible with the lass and her maid.

Connor looked at the group huddled beneath the ledge. Murray would drop before he admitted he was tired, but he had to be done in. It was a miracle he was still on his feet. Yet he was and presently staring a hole through Connor that promised a painful death. And Connor was more than willing to oblige him.

Why does he hate me?

Murray was not the first to look at him in that manner. Probably would not be the last.

He knew he ought to stay away from the lass, but it might be easier for him to stop breathing. Even now he wanted nothing more than to comfort her. His eyes fell upon her standing beneath the ledge with her golden hair plastered to her head and her clothing clinging to her body in a damp mess.

Comfort her? Nay. He wanted to kiss her until she couldnae stand and then lie against her, bare skin upon bare skin, until her body warmed to his own.

Best stay away from her.

"I'll find some tinder," Efrem said. He dropped his pack and moved out into the rain once more with his rifle in his hand.

"Won't they see the smoke?" Carrie asked. "If they're out there?"

"The rain will keep the smoke down," Connor said. "And they willnae be bothering us tonight."

"What makes you so sure?" Murray asked. He stood with his hand on the hilt of his sword, as if ready to fight. Did he even possess the strength to draw it?

"We're not worth getting wet," Connor explained. "If they're following us, they know where we're going and how long it will take us to get there. They will bide their time until the weather breaks. We have no place else to go."

"You seem to know a lot about their ways," Murray said.

"I ken the way they think," Connor replied. "Or hae ye forgotten that I spent some time with them?"

"As a captive?" Murray asked, as if he doubted the truth of it.

The man knew the answer. Yet still he questioned.

The lass watched them carefully with more fear in her eyes than he'd seen there earlier in the day. And no wonder, the way they spoke to each other. As if each could barely tolerate the other.

"They saw no need to keep secrets from me," Connor said. "They did not plan on my leaving them. At least not on my own two feet."

"John," Carrie said, "you must rest. We are safe for now. Get some sleep."

"We must all try to sleep," Connor said. "But first we must eat."

"I lost the food," John said. "In the river."

It took a lot for him to admit that. And it took just as much for the rest of them not to show their disappointment.

"I've got some," Patsy said. "I carried some." The maid knelt on the ground and dumped out the contents of her bag. A wheel of cheese, a small sack of dried apples, a side of bacon. It seemed a feast.

It was only then that Murray leaned against the back of the cave and let his body slide to the ground.

The lass went to him and fussed about like a mother with a child. "Take off your coat so it will dry," she said. "And your boots."

It warmed Connor's heart to watch. The scene reminded him of his mother, scolding him when he'd been caught in a downpour while coming home from his uncle's stable. Carrie had no thought of her own damp misery, only concern for her brother.

Efrem appeared beneath the ledge as silently as he'd left, giving Patsy a start.

"No signs," he said as he dropped an armload of firewood on the ground. "If they are behind us, they are taking their time."

Connor nodded. At least for now they could rest.

A full stomach did much to improve his mood. As did the fire. It was wonderful to dry out a bit. Connor stretched his legs toward the flames in the hope that his breeks would dry on the inside as well as the out.

Patsy lay curled on her side as close to the fire as she could get without being burned. Efrem rummaged through his pack and unrolled a blanket, which he placed over her. She grabbed it in her sleep and curled up tighter beneath it.

"She has no meat to keep her warm," Efrem said with a flash of white teeth.

The Murrays sat against the back wall, their eyes closed. There could be no doubt that they were brother and sister. Their features were similar: the shape of the nose, the curve of the cheek. Their hair was the same golden blond, their eyes the same shade of blue, and both had generous smiles when they chose to give them. He'd seen the lass's much more than the captain's. Murray's jaw seemed haughty, while his sister's was more relaxed. She'd mentioned that her brother was like their mother in spirit. Did that mean the lass was like her father, the man they were going to meet?

Would he ever grow tired of looking at her? It was his favorite pastime of late, watching her as she made her way through the camp in the evening, or as she blinked sleepily in the morning, or while she looked in wonderment at the scenery around her. And especially now, lit as she was by the fire with her sky-blue eyes staring at him across the flames.

She must have knocked him daft when she'd dropped the shoes on his head because he'd been acting like a fool ever since.

She checked on her brother and then silently gathered her skirts as she moved around the fire to sit next to Connor.

"Does he sleep?" Connor asked.

"He does," she said. "He didn't want to, but I threatened that I would stay awake as long as he did. Since I've been known to be disagreeable when I get tired, he decided that we would all be better off if I got some rest."

"I will keep that in mind," Connor said. Why was it that

in spite of their dire circumstances, she managed to lighten his mood? "Beware of falling shoes and lack of sleep." He counted off pitfalls on his fingers, and her smile burned brighter than the fire.

"Do ye plan on sleeping then?" he asked.

She stretched her toes toward the fire. "I think I could sleep forever," she said. "But only after I'm dry."

"That is quite a bit of fabric you've got to deal with." Connor lifted the side of her pink-striped skirt where it touched his leg.

"You seem to be making a habit of picking up the articles of clothing I can't hold on to," she said.

Connor felt his face heat up and knew his cheeks were as red as his hair.

"Er, I . . ."

"At least I don't have to worry about the corset," she said, mercifully putting a stop to his sudden loss of speech. She pulled up her skirt into her lap without embarrassment, exposing her ragged petticoats to the heat of the fire.

"Corset?"

"It's in your pack," she said. "Unless you've moved it."

His cheeks flamed once again at his indiscretion. He was lucky Murray hadn't run him through with his sword. He was even luckier that the lass had covered for him. Connor reached for his pack but managed to steal a sideways look at Carrie. Her eyes twinkled merrily in the firelight. He handed her the corset, and with a wide grin she pitched it in the fire.

Efrem lifted an eyebrow from the opposite side of the cave and Connor shook his head at her spirit.

"This is one part of civilization I will cheerfully leave behind," she said. "But on the other hand, I definitely miss my brush." She pushed her hair back from her face.

"Vanity is one of Efrem's greatest sins," Connor said. "I'm sure he has something you can use."

Efrem grinned ruefully from across the fire and once

more dug into his pack. "Don't let Connor trick you into thinking he doesn't worry about his looks," he said as he pulled out a carved comb and tossed it into Connor's hands.

Carrie snatched it from him as if it were a great treasure and immediately went to work on her golden locks. Connor couldn't stop himself from watching as she gathered a bunch in her hand and worked the comb through the tangles, starting at the bottom and working her way up to the top. It wasn't until she got to the back of her hair that she ran into trouble.

"Please?" she asked. "Do you mind helping me with the tangles? I'd rather not wake Patsy."

Connor looked across the fire at Efrem, who was now stretched out on his back behind Patsy. He saw the flash of white teeth in the dim light and knew his friend was enjoying the moment. On the back wall Murray breathed deeply, although he was still sitting up.

Please let him sleep, Connor prayed as he took the comb from her hand.

He gathered up a handful of her hair and carefully pulled the pins free, searching the strands until he was sure none remained. He placed them on the ground between them and then gently pulled the comb through her hair, taking care not to jerk at the tangles.

"Does your arm pain you?" she asked.

"A bit," he said. "But it's not bad, considering the way it could have been."

"Is it wrong to feel guilty that we weren't killed?" she asked. "It could just as easily have been us if fate had not stepped in."

He did not want to consider it. Once again he'd been spared. He should have died long ago instead of Tom. This was a question he'd rather not think about, but she seemed to be waiting for an answer. She seemed to need one, as if she needed to know that it was right to be grateful that she'd survived and her brother with her.

"Was it fate that I decided to bathe in the stream because I could not stand the smell of myself any longer?" Connor asked flippantly, then immediately regretted the remark. He didn't want to insinuate that she must have bathed for the same reason. "Not that you . . ." He let out a heavy sigh. "Sir Richard reminded me countless times to think before I spoke. 'Tis a shame he's not here to smack the back of my head."

She let out a soft laugh. "When we were hiding, I was immensely grateful that both of us had bathed. When one is in fear for one's very life, it helps not to have to deal with unpleasant odors."

Connor shook his head at her silliness. Here she sat in the middle of the wilderness, soaking wet and without any comforts, and she found a way to make light of her situation. She had nearly died today, she'd seen the realities of death, yet she still kept her good humor.

He continued to work the comb through her hair.

"Who is Sir Richard?" she asked as the fire popped and waved before them.

"The man who raised me."

"I thought you were a bondservant," she said.

"I was." Connor felt a familiar warmth at the thought of Sir Richard. "I was bought straight off the ship by a crusty old bastard who felt it was his duty to civilize the Catholic heathen I was. Of course, his idea of civilizing was marching me off into the middle of a war with the French and the Indians."

She turned to look at him, and he gave her a reassuring smile. "He didn't plan on caring for me, but he did, in spite of all the trouble I gave him."

"What kind of trouble?"

"I wanted to kill every man I saw in a red coat."

She laughed out loud, then immediately covered her mouth as Murray stirred in his sleep. He grunted and then opened his eyes blearily. Connor froze in place, checking to make sure his rifle was close at hand.

Don't be daft. Ye can't kill her brother. Even if he tries to kill you.

Murray moved a bit and then lay down with his back toward the fire. In moments they heard steady breathing coming from the back of the cave.

Carrie's shoulders relaxed, and Connor realized that she too was worried about her brother's reaction should he wake and see the man he despised performing such an intimate service for his sister.

He was done anyway. Carrie's hair felt dry in his hands and lay upon them like a golden sheet.

He didn't want to stop. He loved touching her. Without considering what he was doing, he began braiding her hair.

"How old were you?" she asked, her voice quiet now, just above a whisper. "When you came here."

"Ten."

"Just a boy."

"Aye."

"Why did they send you here?"

His hands froze. He could tell her. Tell her about his mother's rape, her death, the words she'd called out to him before she choked to death. He could tell her how the plaid she'd worn burned on the ground between them while the soldiers kicked him and beat him when he ran to help her. He could tell her. But he didn't.

"If you can spare a bit more fabric, I could tie this up," he said instead.

Her hands moved to the back of her head and felt the braid. She looked around in surprise.

"I used to practice on the horses," he said. It was easier than telling the truth. About how as a small boy he'd sit with his mother by the fire at night and comb out her long reddish blond hair after she washed it, then braid it for her while she told him stories of his father. Until he grew older and thought himself too much of a man to do it.

Yet not man enough to help her when she needed it most.

"In Scotland?" Carrie asked as she tore at her petticoats again and handed him a strip.

"Aye." He tied off the end and placed it over her shoulder.

Her hand stroked the length of it and he resisted the urge to do the same. Chances were her brother would cut off his hand if he knew how he'd just touched her. How he wanted to touch her.

Best to leave her alone. To stop thinking about her. As soon as they reached the safety of the fort, he'd leave and never think of her again.

She rubbed her arms as if chilled.

"Cold?" he asked.

"Yes," she said.

"I have a blanket," he suggested and pulled his pack close to find it. He placed the blanket over her shoulders and she settled beside him with her back against the wall, her legs stretched out in tandem with his. "Get some sleep," he said. "Lest we all suffer the consequences ye mentioned earlier."

She smiled at him, yawned widely, and then blushed when she realized she had not covered her mouth.

"Sleep," he said with his own smile. "I'll keep watch."

He settled back against the wall with his arms crossed and quietly watched the fire, hoping she would soon nod off.

He should have made her move next to her brother. But he liked having her near.

And he would be away from her soon enough. There was no harm in enjoying the moment, was there? One small moment to pull out and remember on a cold winter's night.

She moved about a bit restlessly, trying to get comfortable. She should lie down, like Patsy, who was sleeping like the dead.

He turned to tell her and just as he turned, her head hit his shoulder and she settled against him with a small sigh of contentment.

Connor held himself stiffly for a moment, his eyes upon her brother, who still lay with his back toward the fire. Her head nestled against him, seeking comfort, so he moved his arm up and around her and she settled against his chest.

There was no harm in it, was there? It was just for the moment. Just for the night. So that she might rest. His fingers found her temple and stroked the hair there as her breathing evened out.

He closed his eyes and listened to the sound.

Chapter Fourteen

It was John's stirring that woke her. Carrie opened her eyes and saw her brother sit up and rub his hands across his face before she pulled the blanket tighter under her chin and went back to the dream that had been interrupted by John's movement.

Hadn't she been next to Connor when she'd fallen asleep instead of beside John? Her hand went to her hair and felt the neat braid, evidence that she had not merely dreamed the peaceful scene from the night before.

But had she imagined the touch of his hand on her temple as he smoothed the skin there? Was the security of his chest as a pillow part of her dreams or reality also?

"I knew he was a coward," John exclaimed as he jumped to his feet.

Carrie heard the scrape of his sword coming out of its sheath and sat up.

"Who's a coward, John?" she asked.

"That bloody Scot," he said. "They've deserted us."

Carrie came fully awake and looked around the cave. Patsy sat up with her eyes still closed, her mouth moving

up and down as if she were eating a meal. The fire was
cold and the ashes scattered.

John moved from beneath the shelter and looked
around. "They've left us here," he said. "They're probably
hoping we'll die so no one can testify to their cowardice
during the attack."

"They saved our lives!" Carrie rubbed her eyes, trying
to make sense of this latest occurrence as she moved out
in the bright light of morning and looked around.

The wood was deserted. Indeed, it was as if the three of
them were the only people on earth. Birds flitted from
tree to tree and water dripped from the leaves, creating
minuscule puddles on the soaked earth.

She heard the call of a cardinal and another answering.

"They're still here," she said. "I just heard their call."

John pulled her back into the shelter of the cave. "It
could be anyone," he said and pushed her behind him as
he took up a defensive posture beneath the ledge.

"Why are you so quick to condemn him?" Carrie
pointed to the north, where Connor had just appeared.

"Because he's a Scot," John said with a grimace as they
watched Efrem come up from the south. It was almost as
if he were disappointed that the two men had reappeared. "They can't be trusted."

"Yet Connor's saved our lives several times over."

"Connor?" John said. "Since when have you become so
familiar with the man that you call him by his given
name?"

"What is wrong with you?" Carrie asked, annoyed with
herself for the slip. She was tired, she was hungry and
she desperately wanted a bath. And John's acting like an
ass was not helping her mood. "You never were this way
before."

"Before what?"

"Before you went off to your last posting," Carrie
snapped. "Before Aberdeen."

"I've spent some time in the real world, dear sister,"

John said. "Not sheltered in the cottage with Mother mourning the unfortunate deaths of your fiancés. I know what the Scottish are really like. I know they can't be trusted."

"That is just ridiculous," Carrie said. "How can you make such generalizations about a man just because of where he was born?"

"As I said, I've spent some time in the real world."

"Be careful what you say, brother," Carrie said. "Lest all colonials think that English officers are insufferable prigs."

"Be careful who you consort with." John took her arm in a firm grip. "Or I will make your choices for you."

Carrie jerked away from him and rubbed her arm as her eyes found Connor and Efrem talking in the distance. She was certain her skin was bruised. If only she knew why he reacted to Connor this way. Could it really be just because of his Scottish blood?

Something had changed John.

Connor and Efrem, finished with their conference, moved on silent feet toward them. The thought that they would abandon her and John and Patsy was ridiculous.

Wasn't it?

"Good morning," Connor said. His eyes were fixed upon her, and Carrie smiled in greeting.

"Good morning," she replied.

"Where were you?" John didn't ask. He demanded a response, and Connor's jaw went rigid. How quickly she'd learned to read his moods.

"We were looking for signs of the Shawnee," Efrem said patiently.

"And?" John said.

"The trail behind is clean," Efrem said.

"I saw signs ahead," Connor said stiffly. "Not the main party that attacked us, but a smaller group. Ten, possibly, all on foot."

"Can we avoid them?" Carrie asked. "Will we be able to get to Fort Savannah?"

"We should," Connor said. " 'Tis a good two days' march from here. Quicker if we leave the trail and go over the mountain. But the going is hard. It willnae be easy on ye."

"Difficulty is not the issue," Carrie said. "It's not as if we have a choice."

"Nay," Connor replied. " 'Tis not." His eyes bored into her.

He wants me . . . .

He wasn't talking of the passage. There was no mistaking that look. She'd seen it before, but never this intensely. Connor's gaze jolted her insides and made her feel weak, yet powerful. His look was desperate, yearning. It warmed her, burned her, frightened her. Her knees felt weak, as if she would fall to the ground.

And he would catch her. There was no doubt in her mind that he would.

But Connor's desire for her could only lead to catastrophe. John would never stand for it. And she knew her father had higher expectations for her.

You want him too . . . .

Carrie had to admit to herself that she'd been curious about Connor since the moment she'd seen him on the street. Since she'd seen him in the Governor's Palace. Since she'd tripped over him at the ball.

If she were entirely honest with herself, she would admit he was the reason she'd come on this expedition. The night of the ball, after her near disaster on the balcony, she'd heard her uncle tell John that Connor was to be their guide. Without considering the dangers, she'd made the decision then and there to go along . . . because she was anxious to see her father. That was the reason she'd given herself. But deep down inside she knew it was because she wanted to know more about Connor Duncan.

Was he the boy from the docks she'd prayed for all these years?

Did it matter?

"So we're to hide from the savages?" John asked.

"Would you prefer to fight them with the women?" Connor snapped as he turned to face him.

John crossed his arms and looked at Connor, who returned the gaze with the same intensity. And with that look, Carrie realized the two men hated each other.

And she was trapped in between.

Chapter Fifteen

He should have left Murray behind.

Ye could not do that . . . not to the lass . . .

Without Murray, his path would be clear. As they pushed their way to the top of the mountain through the dense thickets of mountain laurel, he considered how easy it would be. Take the lass and disappear into the wilderness and make her his. No one would know. They would think her killed in the attack, or worse, a captive. She would simply be gone, along with her brother. No one would know.

I would know . . . .

Even stronger than his yearning for her was his wish that she want him too. Surely she did. She sought him out at times. She had to have some feelings for him.

He fought the urge to turn and look at her as he crested the ridge they'd spent the afternoon climbing. He knew he was setting a grueling pace. There'd been no rest, no food, nothing but a few quick gulps of water as they made their way over the mountains toward Fort Savannah.

There'd also been no chance to speak with her, or

touch her. Murray was taking great care to make sure he remained between the two of them.

Even now the captain had her arm, helping Carrie up and over the rocky outcropping as she held her skirts and petticoats bunched in one arm so she would not trip. Patsy seemed to be having an easier time of it. She didn't weigh much and was not hampered by her clothing.

Efrem came behind, picking up pieces of fabric that tore away from the lass's skirt. Making sure that their passage would appear to be nothing more than that of a bear lumbering over the mountain.

Or so they hoped.

He had not been entirely honest with his small party about the signs he saw. He'd confided in Efrem, of course, but decided not to tell anyone else. It would only make the passage worse. 'Tis hard to concentrate on where you are placing your feet when you are also looking over your shoulder.

He only wished he'd had time to bury the small family that he'd found dead along the main trail, their scalps gone and their possessions scattered on the forest floor. Had they been traveling west, hoping for a better life?

His small group joined him on the ridge. They were all breathing hard. They were all covered with a fine sheen of sweat. He didn't like the looks of Murray. His face was pale and he had great, dark circles under his eyes. His hair was soaked with sweat. Perhaps he was feverish?

Carrie placed her hands in the small of her back and arched as if sore muscles caused her pain.

If only he could place his hands upon the bare skin of her back and rub the pain away. If only he could take her to a safe place where there was no threat and take the fear away.

For him it was a constant companion. The fear.

Not the fear of death.

The fear of dying at the hands of the Shawnee.

The man he'd found in the early morning hours was

still alive, his life trickling away with the blood from his wounds. He could see his family lying dead around him and he could do nothing but slowly die and weep out his regret for bringing them all to this fate.

Connor ended the torment mercifully with his knife. Just before the blow came, the man looked up at him with gratitude in his blue eyes. Eyes that were nearly the same color as Carrie's.

He would spare the lass that much if he could. He would spare her the fires if they were captured.

"How much farther?" Carrie asked as they looked at the endless mountains before them. Murray stood thin-lipped beside her, his eyes scanning the horizon.

Connor resisted the urge to take her hand as he motioned to the north. "Not today," he said. "Tomorrow, I hope."

"Will we have shelter tonight?" she asked.

"We'll be hard pressed," Connor said. "But we should make it."

He didn't ask her how she felt. If she were tired. If she trusted him to get them there safely. If she feared for her life.

Carrie nodded in agreement. She did not complain, and Connor moved forward and downward. Another mountain behind them. More before them. But at least taking this route they were not vulnerable. And they were making good time. Taking nearly a day off the trek.

His eyes kept moving. His feet kept moving. His ears listened for the slightest foreign sound. And his mind went back to his dilemma

Admitting he wanted her was the easy part. He knew better than to fight against his nature. He'd wanted her since the first time he saw her. Seeking her out was now as natural to him as breathing. But having her was something else entirely. He could think of no way it could work. Especially not with her brother around, wishing he were dead.

Which led to another problem nagging at his brain:
Why did Murray hate him so? Did he think him a coward
because he hadn't joined in defending the camp? It would
have been suicide.

Did Murray blame him for not predicting the attack?
Perhaps he could have if he had not been attending to
broken wagon wheels.

Murray matched him stride for stride as they descended.
His eyes stayed as busy as Connor's. Searching for the
right place to step as they navigated the rocks that pro-
truded from the ground, the fallen trees and the thick
tree roots that scrabbled for support against the side of
the mountain.

Murray's hatred went back to the first day. The first
meeting. He'd looked down his nose at Connor from the
first time he'd met him.

Why?

Ye have no love for him yourself.

It was no secret that Connor hated the redcoats. Yet he
tolerated them and was civil because he had to be to survive. And given a choice, he'd rather be with the English
than with the Shawnee. Both treated him harshly, but at
least with the English, he had a chance of survival.

He had a very good reason for hating the English. The
mystery was why Murray hated him.

There was a stream down below. He'd let them have
some rest. Have a drink. There were a good three or four
hours of daylight left. He knew of another cave up ahead.

He'd give Carrie shelter. He could do that much for her.

Chapter Sixteen

Their pace slowed considerably. It was because of Murray. He was sick but would not admit it. It was a miracle the man was still on his feet. As darkness approached, Connor knew they would not make the cave, so he settled for a dead fall, a once mighty hemlock that spread its branches over the forest floor. He chose the place because it was near the summit of another mountain with a good view of the stream below. If someone came upon them in the night, they would know in plenty of time to make an escape.

Connor and Efrem spread their blankets on the ground and put Murray and the two women beneath the branches with an unspoken caution for quiet. Then they moved out into the near darkness to clear any evidence of their passage and to look for signs of the Indians Connor had seen evidence of earlier in the day.

"Do you think they will make it?" Efrem asked when they were satisfied that they were alone in the forest.

"They are strong," Connor said. "And not given to complaint."

"The little one has surprised me," Efrem said. "And your woman."

"My woman?" Connor said with an eyebrow raised.

Efrem's teeth flashed white in the darkness. "If not now, then soon," he said. "Can you deny it?"

"Nay," Connor said. "I don't deny wanting her. But I doubt I will ever have her."

"The brother," Efrem said. "He is as stubborn as you are."

"Aye."

"You could take her."

"She would not have me then. She must choose me. 'Tis the only way it would work."

Efrem nodded in agreement. "The moon will appear soon," he said. "I'll take the first watch."

They made their way to the fallen hemlock on silent feet. Murray sat outside the shelter with his sword in one hand, his pistol in the other.

"Nothing," Connor said to him as he placed his pack against a tree and leaned against it. "Get some sleep." He closed his eyes. He was so weary. Yet he felt Murray's eyes upon him.

If the man wanted to lose sleep by hating him, then so be it. He would not lose any himself. Efrem would keep watch.

Carrie could not sleep. Her body craved rest, so much so that she felt near to tears, yet sleep would not come. She dozed and chased half dreams and woke with a start due to cramped muscles and bruised bones. When the moon shone directly overhead, its light teasing her through the thick branches of the hemlock as the wind tossed them to and fro, she decided she'd had enough. She checked to see if John was asleep and realized part of her problem was the heat coming from his body. He was burning up with fever.

She should tell Connor and Efrem. Perhaps Efrem had something in his pack that could help her brother. She crawled from the shelter.

As her head came out, a hand covered her mouth and she froze in place.

Connor's face was inches from her own and his eyes gave her the unspoken warning to be quiet. Efrem motioned with his head toward the gully below their shelter. The sound of the wind rustling through the branches overhead covered the noise as Connor guided her on her stomach to a fallen log.

She lay between the two men and looked over the log to the trail beneath. The moonlight was bright enough that she could clearly see the line of men making their way through the forest.

Carrie drew in her breath and held it for fear of making a sound, even though she knew Connor and Efrem beside her were breathing regularly, as if nothing was wrong.

How could they just lie there so calmly and watch?

There were twelve Indians. At first, she was not sure if she would have been able to tell the difference between them and Efrem in a crowd, but then she realized their clothing was wilder, more primitive.

One of the men stumbled, and Carrie was shocked to see his hands were tied behind him and he was being led by a rope around his neck. The one leading him had no regard for his difficulties. He just tugged on the rope until the prisoner caught up.

Two of the men were captives. And one wore a bedraggled red coat.

Efrem motioned to the prisoner in the red coat.

"One of yours?" he mouthed.

Connor studied the man and shook his head. Carrie studied him also, but she did not recognize him. He could have been one of the troop. She couldn't say. Only John would know.

She looked back toward the shelter. Connor laid his hand on her arm and his mouth touched her ear.

" 'Twould be suicide for all of us," he said. His lips ca-

ressed her ear as he spoke. "Would your brother let him
go if it was his man?"

She knew the answer. John would charge full bore
down the mountain if he thought he could save one of his
men. And he'd expect God to turn the battle his way.
There was nothing they could do for the prisoners. Nothing beyond praying, and she did so, adding their ragged
souls to her pleas for safe passage.

The Indians moved on, and when she realized that her
own group was safe she was overcome with a fit of trembling.

She could not control herself. She was so very tired. So
very hungry. So very frightened. She felt the security of
Connor's arms as they came around her and she burrowed her head into his chest. Her hands clutched at his
shirt as she moved closer, pressing her body against the
length of his. She could not get close enough.

"Shush, *mo cridhe*," he whispered. His lips touched the
top of her head. "They are gone and we should be away
whilst we know where they are."

She felt rather than heard Efrem move off. No doubt
he was scouting the trail. She felt remarkably safe as the
steady beat of Connor's heart sounded in her ears.

"I'm worried about John," she said quietly against his
chest. As if that would explain her fear. "I think he's sick."

"He's strong," Connor said. "He'll keep up."

"He will."

"We must wake them."

She didn't want to move. She wanted to stay where she
was, secure in his arms until this nightmare ended.

She should have remained in Williamsburg, safe with
her uncle.

Safe and not knowing if her brother were alive or dead.
Or if Connor were alive or dead. Would it have mattered
to her then? Would he have turned and joined the battle
if she had not been in the stream, or would he have

slipped off into the woods and never been heard from again?

"Donnae worry. I will not leave him behind."

Could he read her mind? She nodded against his chest and he rose, pulling her to her feet as if she weighed nothing. She looked up into his eyes, which were lost in the shadows created by the moonlight. His hand touched her cheek, his thumb moved under her eye and she realized there were tears. Then his hand cupped her chin and tilted her face up.

He was going to kiss her. The fear, the worry, the discomfort, all flew from her mind as her stomach churned with anticipation. The pad of his thumb moved across her lips and they parted, ready . . . waiting . . .

"Wake them," he said and dropped his hand.

She moved to the shelter, her arms wrapped around her waist. Suddenly she felt very cold. So cold that her teeth chattered, yet the weather was mild.

What was happening to her?

"John," she whispered, as she touched his arm. He was burning up.

He did not move except to toss his head, and she shook his shoulders, speaking more firmly this time. "John. We must leave. Now."

Patsy was already awake. She crawled without question from the shelter, dragging a blanket with her. John's eyes fluttered open and he stared up at her wordlessly. The wind moved the hemlock and the moonlight caught his eyes and they seemed to be covered with a glaze.

"John."

He grabbed her arm as if just now coming awake. "Carrie? What? Where are we?"

"In the wilderness. We must be quiet. We must make haste. The Shawnee . . ."

He rubbed his hands over his face.

"Can you stand?"

"I'm fine," he said and shook off her hands.

Efrem had returned when she crawled out of the shelter, leaving John to gather himself. "Do you have something he could take for fever?" she asked.

Efrem shook his head. "Only what could be made into a tea. We can't risk a fire."

"I'm fine," John declared as he came forth. "The Shawnee are about?"

"We saw a raiding party," Connor said. "They passed below us. We need to move away from them. They're on the trail. We'll keep to the ridges above them. I want to get ahead and beat them to the fort."

"Do you think they're going that way?" John asked.

"Aye," Connor replied. "They will scout it out. To see if it's worth attacking."

"Bloody savages," John said.

"Try to keep to the rocks when ye can. We'll leave fewer tracks that way. The moon will set soon, so it will be dark."

"I'm ready," John said.

"We're close," Connor said. Carrie looked at him in disbelief. She could not believe they were still standing, especially John. She knew Connor and Efrem were worried that their pace hadn't been quick enough. Several times during the night Efrem cut away from them, moving toward the west. Several minutes later he would materialize out of the darkness at some predetermined point that only he and Connor recognized. Then they would talk quietly while John wearily leaned against a tree or rock and Patsy looked into the darkness as if someone were watching them.

This time they were waiting for Efrem to appear. They waited on a ridge with a breathtaking view of a long, green valley that curved into the distance. A river cut through the center of it, slicing it in two. The sun was just peeking at them from the east, its rays piercing through the trees, warming their damp skin.

"Ye can rest a bit," Connor said to her. She knew his words were for John. She also knew John would stand till he died rather than let Connor know he was hurting.

Men and their pride. She had none left at this point.

Connor moved off into a thick stand of underbrush. She guessed that he was relieving himself and sought to do the same. Patsy was just now scrambling back from her own private moment and Carrie turned in the same direction.

She moved off to the side a bit, took care of business and sat down on a huge boulder that jutted out of the ground.

If only she could sleep. Just lie on the warm rock and sleep forever. Carrie could barely keep her eyes open as she stared off into the distance.

Connor said we were close.

She thought of shelter. A hot meal. A warm bath. Safety. It nearly brought her to tears. Where was the fort? All she saw was wilderness. There wasn't even a welcoming wisp of smoke to speak of civilization.

"Miss Carrie?" she heard Patsy call out. She really shouldn't be out in the open as she was. She slid from the rock and stepped on something that moved beneath her foot. A sharp pain hit her calf and she jumped sideways with a small cry as it hit again.

She landed on the ground and saw the snake looking at her, its angular head undulating before her with its mouth open in a steady hiss. Copper and tan stripes decorated its skin. It was nearly as thick as her arm and as long as her legs.

"Copperhead." Connor jumped over the rock, grabbed the snake by its tail and cracked it like a whip before she could draw a breath to scream. The snake's head exploded in a rush of blood, and Connor flung the thing into the underbrush.

"Did it bite you?" He grabbed her arms, his face intent.

"Yes," Carrie said. "My leg."

Connor flipped up her skirts just as John and Patsy arrived.

"Take your hands off her!" John ordered.

Connor ignored him. He tore at her stocking, shoving it down her calf to expose two wounds, one above the other, each with four holes that pierced the skin and oozed blood.

Carrie gasped in disbelief. Would she die? Had she survived an Indian attack and three days' trekking through the wilderness just to die now, when they were so close to safety?

Her heart jumped into her throat when she looked up and saw John standing behind Connor with his sword touching the side of Connor's neck.

"I said take your hands off her." John's face was as white as the fluffy clouds overhead. His eyes were watery, pale, and the circles under them were a deep purple. Did he even know what he was saying?

Then John was lying on the ground. It happened so quickly that if she had blinked she would have missed it.

Connor moved his arm, hit John behind the knees and knocked him on his back. His knife was out of its sheath and at John's throat in the same moment.

"She's been snakebit," he said clearly. "Twice. We must get the venom out."

"Will I die?" Carrie asked disbelievingly.

"Ye willane die. Not if I can help it. But ye will be very sick."

"Heaven forbid," she said helplessly.

"Time is important," he said to John. "Do ye understand?"

John nodded. He looked as thunderstruck as she felt.

"I must cut you," Connor said. He turned his back to John as if nothing had happened between them, and knelt between her legs, which were still exposed, still splayed before her. The knife spun in his hand. "I must suck it out."

Carrie nodded, as if having him suck on her calf were perfectly normal.

"Ye cannae scream, no matter how much it hurts."

"I won't."

"Hold on to me, Miss Carrie," Patsy said as she took her hand. "Bite on this."

Connor picked up her foot by the ankle and turned it upward so the bites were exposed. Carried grabbed the small bit of wood Patsy offered and stuck it between her lips.

"I'm sorry," John said. He managed to get up and move behind her. He put one arm around her and leaned her back against his side.

This could not be happening to her. Connor stuck his knife in the wound, and she groaned as a strong wave of pain shot up her leg.

I will not scream. I will not scream. I will not scream. Please God I will not scream.

Tears coursed from her eyes as the blood poured from the wound. She bit down on the stick. Before she had a chance to consider what he was doing, Connor cut the other wound and put her calf to his mouth.

He sucked out a mouthful of blood and turned his head to spit it out. He sucked on the other wound. He sucked and he spit on one, then the other in quick succession until the pain numbed her. She could not feel her foot. She could not feel her calf. She felt a strange pulsing throb shooting up her leg and her head felt large and cloudy, as if she were in a fog.

"We need Efrem," Connor said when he finally stopped.

Carrie leaned back against John and Patsy and took the stick from her mouth.

"Look at that, Miss Carrie," she said. "You nearly bit it in two."

She didn't care. She didn't want to see it. She just wanted to rest against John. She didn't want to move. She wanted to sleep. If only she could sleep.

"He has medicine in his pack. A poultice."

She heard a ripping sound and almost giggled when she saw that Connor was ripping away a piece of her petticoat. She would run out before they reached the fort.

He wrapped it around her calf.

She'd be dead soon, so what difference did it make? No need of petticoats. No need of corsets. No need of lace caps.

The only thing she needed was Connor.

"Connor?" she said.

He looked at her. His hand reached out, but to her it seemed very far off. He was going away. She reached up her hand, but all she touched was darkness.

Chapter Seventeen

Connor picked her up. "We must hurry now," he said. She felt light as a feather in his arms. But he knew that wouldn't last long. How long could he carry her? They still had the valley to traverse. The most dangerous part. The part Efrem was now scouting.

He would carry her until he died if need be.

"What about Mr. Efrem?" Patsy asked.

"He kens where we're going," Connor said. "We've stayed here too long."

"You mean to carry her the entire way?" Murray asked.

"She clearly cannae walk," Connor said. "And ye can barely carry yourself."

Murray opened his mouth to speak and then shut it again.

I just hope we'll make it to the fort in time.

A man could survive one bite. A woman also. But he'd seen a man die from three. The lass was small. She was weak from the trek. Could she survive two bites?

He moved off the ridge. Whether the others followed or not, he did not care. Whether they left signs or not, he did not care; nor did it matter now. The Shawnee would either find them or not. The only thing that mattered now was the lass.

They reached the river. It was wide and shallow, with large boulders scattered through it. The beauty of the scene made one want to linger, but today was not the day to do so. Connor's arm ached from his wound, which was now festering, and his shoulders throbbed from the effort it took to carry the lass. He had to rest. He could go no farther. He knelt by the water, moved Carrie over his knees and scooped up a handful. He let it dribble over her lips.

"Carrie," he said. "Ye must try to drink."

Patsy came with her apron, which she had dipped in the water. She wiped Carrie's face and neck while John observed. The man looked like death, yet his first concern was for his sister.

"Carrie," Connor said as he scooped up another handful.

She opened her eyes as the water touched her lips. She took his hand in both of hers and he tilted it toward her mouth so she could drink. Connor took the apron from Patsy and wiped Carrie's face with it.

John turned away then, as if the sight of her holding onto Connor's hand sickened him. He knelt by the river and splashed water over his face and head.

"You said my name," she said.

Connor looked at her in confusion.

"I've been waiting to hear you say it."

"Carrie?" He said it slowly, letting his tongue caress the sound of her name.

She smiled weakly. "Yes. Carrie."

"Ye are a daftie lass," he said with a grin.

"So you've mentioned." She twisted her head. "John?"

"Here," Murray answered.

"How are you?"

"I'm as well as can be expected."

Connor was surprised. It was the first time Murray had admitted any weakness.

"We should have a look at your leg," Connor said. "Can ye sit for a bit?"

"Yes," she said. Connor placed her on the ground and lifted her skirt.

Her leg was swollen horribly from her knee down to her toes. Angry yellow bruises streaked from beneath the cloth tied about her calf.

She made a face at the sight.

"The cold water should help," Patsy said. "Ease the swelling."

Connor nodded. "Just a bit," he said. "We cannae stay long."

He moved away and with a toss of his head invited Murray to come with him. Patsy helped Carrie remove her shoes and stockings and helped her place her legs in the water. Connor watched the women as Murray finally came to his side.

"Efrem should have caught up to us by now," he said.

"Do you think they have him?"

"Efrem is too smart to get caught. I think he is trying to lead them away from us."

"What makes you so sure he's not their prisoner? Or dead?"

"He would have warned us before . . ."

"Before what?"

"He would kill himself before capture." Connor did not want to think about that. "We would have heard the shot."

Murray's lips tightened into a thin line. "He could have used his knife. They could have captured him before he had a chance."

Connor shook his head. "He would have warned us." Efrem would die to protect them. It was his way.

"What of my sister?"

"I do not ken," Connor said. "Efrem has a poultice that would help, but he's not here. Without it . . ." He looked at the women. Carrie was lying back on the bank with her arm flung over her face. She needed Efrem's help. Or a doctor.

"Do you mean she may die?" Murray asked incredulously.

"She willnae die," Connor said. He refused to think of it. "She will be very sick, but she willnae die."

He would keep her alive by sheer force of will if he had to.

"You say that as if you have some control over it," Murray said.

"You shouldnae have let her come."

He expected Murray to explode in a fit of temper. He expected him to tell him to leave his sister alone, that she was not for him and was none of his concern. He expected all of that and looked forward to the confrontation. He needed an outlet for his anger. For his fear.

Instead, Murray rubbed his hand wearily over his face and looked over at Carrie.

"There are a lot of things I should have done differently on this expedition," he said as he turned back to Connor. "And I will make sure that the mistakes I've made will not happen again. The responsible parties will be punished."

The man is daft from his fever. Does he think he can find the Shawnee that attacked the camp and take them to trial?

"We must be away," Connor said. "The fort is close. Within the hour."

"Then let's not waste any more time."

He heard the call as they approached the women: the cardinal song that meant Efrem was approaching. Carrie heard it too and slowly sat up.

It was the next call that sent a chill down Connor's spine. An angry jay.

Efrem was coming. And he was not alone.

"We need to move now," he said. He scooped Carrie up in his arms and took off at a run, not caring if Murray and Patsy were behind him or not. If they had any sense, they would be. He heard footsteps pounding behind him and took a moment to glance over his shoulder as they moved into the thick woods. Murray had Patsy by the hand. In her other she clutched Carrie's shoes and stockings.

"But Efrem—" Carrie said. She clutched Connor's neck. "I heard his call."

"They are on his trail."

"Put me down. I can run. It will be easier."

"Ye cannae walk." His heart was pounding in his chest. His breath came in gasps. She was not heavy, but he was weak from the trek, weak from lack of food, weak from exhaustion. It would be easier if he had his arms free. As it was, the tree limbs tore at both of them.

"And you cannot go on carrying me. Not like this."

"Can ye hang on to my back?"

"I will."

He stopped by a fallen tree and put her down. She almost fell when she tried to put weight on her foot, and he grabbed her.

"What are you doing?" Murray asked. "What is happening?"

"Efrem is coming and he's being followed," Connor said as he handed Carrie his pack. She slung it over her shoulder while he checked the load on his rifle. Then he bent down and she jumped on his back.

"How do you know that?" Murray demanded.

"He told me," Connor said.

"Oh, lordy," Patsy said.

"Have your weapon ready," Connor said as he adjusted Carrie's weight. She wrapped her arms around his neck and her legs around his waist without concern that her skirts were pushed up to her bare thighs.

"And don't shoot Efrem," he said as he took off again, this time with his rifle in his hand.

He had barely hit his stride when he heard Efrem's signal again.

"Efrem is close," he called over his shoulder. He heard a

crashing sound to his right and caught sight of his friend paralleling them. It was not long before Efrem was running before them, his long hair fanning out behind him.

His appearance told the story. His clothes looked ragged and he was dripping with sweat. He'd been running for a long time.

"How long?" Connor asked.

"Minutes," Efrem called back.

"We'll have to make a stand."

"Can she run?"

"Nay."

"I can," Carrie said. "It's the only way."

"We must get closer," Connor said.

"They are behind us," Murray shouted.

Connor looked back. He saw nothing, but he could hear the sounds of bodies crashing through the forest. There was no need for stealth now.

"Oh, lordy," Patsy cried out.

"Why don't they shoot us?" Carrie asked.

"They wish to capture us," Connor gasped. "To taunt those at the fort."

Connor knew the Shawnee would be able to take them down easily before they made the safety of the walls. And they would not kill them. At least not right away. They would stake them out and cut them so they would die slowly and miserably of pain and thirst while those inside the walls watched. The Indians knew it would be harder on the men inside to watch women die. And the soldiers would have no choice but to watch them die. To come out of the fort would be suicide. And in watching the deaths, the men would become disheartened. They would think about leaving.

Which was what the Shawnee wanted.

Their pursuers were gaining on them. He could not run any faster. He heard Murray and Patsy gasping for breath behind him.

"Efrem," Connor managed to call out.

"Ahead," Efrem gasped.

Connor saw it. A tree, recently felled by lightning. It stretched into the clearing. And in the distance, he saw the fort.

Efrem slid in behind it, his rifle pointed behind them. Connor fell in beside him and Carrie scrambled off his back.

Patsy hurtled over the tree as if she'd been thrown, and Murray dived behind her just as a shot splintered the wood.

"Make for the fort," Connor said to Murray. "Stay low. We'll cover you."

He handed Carrie one of the pistols he carried. "Take this." His hand closed over hers. "Ye know why."

Carrie nodded. "What about you?" she asked.

"If we kill enough of the Shawnee, they will help us," he said looking toward the fort. Another shot rang out, and they all ducked as wood splintered into the air.

"We'll keep them busy until you're safe," he said to Murray.

Efrem fired and immediately flipped over on his back to reload.

"Go before they get around us," Connor cried out as he fired over the tree. He flipped over on his back, just as Efrem had. Powder. Shot. Ram it home. It took seconds.

"*Go!*" he roared over the sound of Efrem's shot.

Patsy took off as if she were shot from the rifle. She ran bent over, her back hunched in the grass so that she barely showed above it.

Connor fired as Efrem reloaded. He flipped over. Carrie was still right next to him.

"Please go," he said.

The lass grabbed his jaw with one hand and quickly kissed him before she staggered away, pulled by her brother. It happened so quickly that he stared after her dumbstruck as she leaned heavily on Murray, both of them bent over and running as best they could.

Efrem fired. Connor had lost his rhythm and nearly dropped his powder as he reloaded.

"She's got spirit," Efrem said as Connor turned to fire.

"Fortis et Fidus," Connor said, and was pleased to see one of the Shawnee drop to the ground as blood spouted from his chest.

When he turned to reload, he saw Patsy sliding through the gate of the fort. Carrie and Murray were still struggling. Between her leg and his fever, they were hard pressed to make it.

Now would be a good time for the regulars to appear.

"What's taking so long?" Efrem asked as he dropped another Shawnee.

The odds were against them. They were two against ten, and even though they had hit some, they were still outnumbered.

Connor turned again and was relieved to see the gate open and redcoats filing out, taking up position to fire and then marching ahead until they reached the two struggling to make their way to the fort.

"Let's go," he said. He fired and reloaded, slung his pack on his back and crept forward as Efrem fired. As soon as Efrem turned to reload Connor fired, and then Efrem moved past him.

Connor was relieved to see the Murrays being carried through the gate.

"They're in," he said as Efrem fired.

He covered Efrem as he reloaded. The Shawnee were at the dead fall where they'd first made their stand. The time to move was now.

He reloaded as he ran and Efrem covered him. By the time they were halfway to the fort, the regulars were covering them with steady gunfire, and both men bolted through the gate with a prayer of thanksgiving.

Connor's eyes swept the fort for Carrie. She was nowhere to be seen, nor was Patsy.

They've taken her to the doctor then . . . .

The realization that they were all finally safe swept over him. It must have hit Efrem too, because both men collapsed against a wagon and grinned at each other in celebration. The nightmare was over. They laid down their rifles and clasped each other's hands, their long friendship making words unnecessary.

Murray came up with regulars on either side of him. The man should be in the infirmary. But he was still standing. There was more to the captain than a red coat.

Connor stood, ready to be gracious. Ready to forgive. Ready to accept the man's gratitude, because he knew what it would cost him to voice it.

"Mr. Duncan, you are under arrest for desertion and dereliction of duty," Murray said.

Connor looked at him, dumbstruck, and the redcoats grabbed his arms before he had time even to think about moving.

Efrem slid his knife from its sheath.

"I wouldn't if I were you," Murray said. "I still have not decided if you were part of this or not."

"Donnae sacrifice yourself on my account," Connor said to Efrem while his eyes remained on Murray.

"Clap him in irons," Murray said as the men took him away.

GET UP TO 4 FREE BOOKS!

You can have the best romance delivered to your door for less than what you'd pay in a bookstore or online. Sign up for one of our book clubs today, and we'll send you **FREE* BOOKS** just for trying it out...with no obligation to buy, ever!

HISTORICAL ROMANCE BOOK CLUB

Travel from the Scottish Highlands to the American West, the decadent ballrooms of Regency England to Viking ships. Your shipments will include authors such as CONNIE MASON, CASSIE EDWARDS, LYNSAY SANDS, LEIGH GREENWOOD, and many, many more.

LOVE SPELL BOOK CLUB

Bring a little magic into your life with the romances of Love Spell—fun contemporaries, paranormals, time-travels, futuristics, and more. Your shipments will include authors such as KATIE MACALISTER, SUSAN GRANT, NINA BANGS, SANDRA HILL, and more.

As a book club member you also receive the following special benefits:

- **30% OFF all orders through our website & telecenter!**
  (Plus, you still get 1 book FREE for every 5 books you buy!)
- **Exclusive access to special discounts!**
- **Convenient home delivery and 10 days to return any books you don't want to keep.**

There is no minimum number of books to buy, and you may cancel membership at any time. See back to sign up!

*Please include $2.00 for shipping and handling.

YES! ☐

Sign me up for the **Historical Romance Book Club** and send my TWO FREE BOOKS! If I choose to stay in the club, I will pay only $8.50* each month, a savings of $5.48!

YES! ☐

Sign me up for the **Love Spell Book Club** and send my TWO FREE BOOKS! If I choose to stay in the club, I will pay only $8.50* each month, a savings of $5.48!

NAME: _____

ADDRESS: _____

_____

TELEPHONE: _____

E-MAIL: _____

☐ **I WANT TO PAY BY CREDIT CARD.**

☐ VISA   ☐ MasterCard.   ☐ DISCOVER

ACCOUNT #: _____

EXPIRATION DATE: _____

SIGNATURE: _____

Send this card along with $2.00 shipping & handling for each club you wish to join, to:

Romance Book Clubs
1 Mechanic Street
Norwalk, CT 06850-3431

Or fax (must include credit card information!) to: 610.995.9274.
You can also sign up online at www.dorchesterpub.com.

*Plus $2.00 for shipping. Offer open to residents of the U.S. and Canada only. Canadian residents please call 1.800.481.9191 for pricing information.
If under 18, a parent or guardian must sign. Terms, prices and conditions subject to change. Subscription subject to acceptance. Dorchester Publishing reserves the right to reject any order or cancel any subscription.

JOIN NOW!

Chapter Eighteen

"How is she?" Connor's hands gripped the bars over the small, ground-level window of the cell he'd occupied for the past six days. He could not help noticing how filthy he was when he saw the dirt ground into his skin, but he did not care. He had more pressing things on his mind at the moment.

Efrem, crouched on the ground outside, said the same thing he'd told him every other time he'd asked. "No change. Anne Trotter is still with her."

"She used the poultice ye gave her?"

Efrem nodded patiently.

"She gave her the tea ye brewed?"

Once again Efrem nodded.

"And she still has the fever?"

"She's still calling out for you, Mr. Connor," Patsy said hopefully. She leaned over Efrem with her hands on her knees so she could see into the cell.

"I don't think that makes him feel any better," Efrem remarked dryly as Connor flung his empty plate against the wall.

The sounds of heavy boot treads pounded against the ground. The regulars were drilling. Their marching shook dirt through the cracks in the boards that served as the ceiling of his cell. A cell that was hardly more than a root cellar set into the ground. It was barely high enough for him to stand in and just long enough to lie in if he stuck his feet through the bars of the door. A bucket served his other needs. A horrendous stench rose from it through the small barred window. It was a miracle that Efrem and Patsy didn't retch from the smell.

"I have good news," Efrem said. "Murray said you could have a bath."

"How generous of him," Connor said. "Considering we saved his life and all."

"His father is expected some time today," Efrem continued as he ignored his friend's sarcasm.

"Which means he'll finally get to hang me."

"Oh no, Mr. Connor," Patsy said. "They ain't going to hang you. They just want to give you some lashes."

Efrem and Connor both bestowed a look on her that would have most men seeking cover.

"I heard Mr. Murray talking to the post commander," Patsy said by way of explanation. "He wants to give you fifty lashes in front of the whole troop. They's gonna muster the militia and they want to make sure that none of them run off, so they's gonna make you an example."

"He's calling me a coward," Connor said. His hands gripped the bars as if it was Murray's neck beneath his fingers. "Yet he doesn't have the courage to call me one to my face."

"Guilt can make a man do strange things," Efrem observed.

"Aye," Connor agreed. "So can fear."

Something was dreadfully wrong. She couldn't quite put her finger on it. If only she wasn't so hot. If only she did not feel as if her leg were five times bigger than the rest of her body. If only someone would answer the questions that were constantly on her dry, parched lips when the fever let her drift to the surface.

"Where am I?"

"Fort Savannah," a woman named Anne told her over and over again. "Safe."

"John?"

"He's better. His fever is gone."

"My father?"

"On his way."

"Connor?"

"Hush, child," Anne would say. "You must rest now."

"Where is Connor?" she said. "I want to see him."

"Go to sleep now," Anne said again.

And her fevered brain came to only one conclusion.

Connor was dead. He had not made it to the safety of the fort. He'd died saving them. Efrem too, because she could not recall seeing him since she'd entered the fort. She hoped Connor was dead. He seemed to have an aversion for capture. As if it were more horrible than dying. She knew enough about him to know that he would kill himself before he allowed himself to be captured. After all, he'd told her to do the same. He'd given her a gun for that very purpose.

She could not even recall coming into the fort. She must have fainted from the pain, the fever and the fear before she even came through its gates. The only familiar face she'd seen was Patsy's, and it seemed as if her maid was never around. As though someone were keeping her away.

He must be dead.

And they didn't want her to know.

And for some strange reason she did not care if she ever rose from her bed again. There was no reason to get up. No reason to get better. No reason to go on. She could not stop mourning for something that was never meant to be. She lay curled on her side and wondered where her life would lead her now.

"How are you this morning?" It was Anne again. Anne with a tray of food that suddenly made her stomach realize exactly how long it had been since she'd had a meal. Carrie kept her eyes closed tight and hoped that her stomach would not give her away.

She heard Anne set down the tray and then felt the woman's hand against her forehead. "Fever's gone," Anne said. Carrie risked a look by opening the eye against her pillow part way and saw a dark-haired woman who could not be more than ten years older than she pulling open the curtain that covered the window. Bright sunshine poured into the room and across the gaily colored quilt that covered her bed.

She felt a shadow between her bed and the sun, and her eyes twitched with the knowledge that Anne was studying her.

"Perhaps we should send you back to the palace," Anne said. "It seems as if you're used to the pampered life of a princess. Or course, we'll have to find men willing to risk their lives to get you there. And since we need the men for the militia . . ."

Carrie opened her eyes in resignation. It seemed as if her period of mourning was over.

"I'm Anne Trotter," her torturer said. "Can you sit up?"

Carrie rolled over on her back and slowly sat up as Anne plumped and propped the pillows behind her, then quickly placed the tray of food on her lap.

"I find that a full stomach makes even the worst of circumstances look better," she said in satisfaction.

"Thank you," Carrie said. "I know you've been taking care of me since I became ill."

"We were afraid we were going to lose you the first night," Anne said. "Luckily for you, Connor knew what to do."

Carrie felt a painful twinge in her heart at the mention of his name.

"He was a good man," she said. "He saved our lives many times over."

"He still is a good man." Anne snorted. "No matter what your brother says."

"*Is* a good man?" Carrie looked hopefully at Anne.

"He always has been as far as I'm concerned."

"Then he's not . . . not dead?"

Anne looked at her as if she were daft. Which, according to Connor, she was. "He wasn't last time I saw him. The smell might kill him and I'm sure your brother's plans for him will make him wish he were dead, but he's alive and madder than a wet hen as far as I know." She put her hands on her hips and looked at Carrie with an arched eyebrow. "What makes you think he's dead?"

Carrie felt her face turn red. She'd been too forward. Too presumptuous. Too . . . daftie. The reason Connor had not come to see her was because he did think she was daftie, crazy or terribly inconvenient. She had assumed too much. She'd thought he had feelings for her.

I kissed him . . . .

The memory came flooding back. The fear. The urgency. The realization that he had carried her for miles and was willing to lay down his life so she could reach the safety of the fort.

Surely he had some feelings for her. But if he did, then why wasn't he here?

Did you expect to find him sleeping on the floor beside your bed? As if John would allow that.

She realized that Anne was still standing before her, watching her, waiting for an answer.

"I must have dreamed it or misunderstood . . ." Carrie realized how absolutely pathetic she sounded. "Er . . . the fever . . ." She took a bite of the eggs on her plate. They were delicious, and she quickly decided that eating was the best plan for the moment.

"Do you live here at the fort?" Carrie asked.

"We have a cabin not far from here," Anne said. "My husband Richard, and our son William. We came here for safety when the trouble started. Richard is out now, rounding up the militia." Anne went about the process of tidying up the room, which already seemed to Carrie as neat as a pin.

"Heaven forbid. Are we at war?"

"Lord Dunmore has ordered an attack. The army is to assemble here and then march west. Apparently he's leading the expedition himself. The courier said he was moving toward Winchester. General Lewis is coming here.

"Is there any news of my father?"

"We expect him to arrive at any time."

That was good news. Wonderful news. Suddenly the day seemed much brighter.

"Would you like a bath?" Anne asked as she picked up a blanket.

"That would be lovely," Carrie said. "My clothes . . ." She was wearing nothing but a shift, and a strange one at that.

"Clean and mended," Anne said. "Although your petticoats were nearly beyond repair. I believe Patsy's been hard at work trying to fix them."

"How is Patsy?"

"She's fine. Worried about you, of course. She's been watching William for me and mooning around after Efrem. I'm afraid she's quite taken with him."

"He's very gallant," Carrie said. "And a gentleman." She had to smile at the thought. In the world she grew up in, Efrem would be the last person society would call a gentleman.

"In spite of what he looks like?"

Anne was observant. And direct.

"You mentioned that my brother had plans for Con . . . Mr. Duncan?"

"He plans on having him whipped." Anne folded the blanket as she spoke, the motion of her arms relaying the force of her anger. "He's called him a coward and said he deserted the troop when you were attacked."

Carrie's fork hit the tray with a clatter. She looked up at Anne in shock.

"But he saved my life. He saved our lives. Surely not." Carrie shook her head. She could not comprehend the words. "Where is Connor?"

"In the cell," Anne said. "Basically a hole in the ground that serves as a jail."

"I think I'll wait for my bath," Carrie said as she flipped off the quilt. "I need to speak to my brother."

"I was hoping you'd say that," Anne replied with a smile. She opened a wardrobe and handed Carrie her clothes, all washed and carefully folded. On top of the stack was her lace cap. Carrie took it in her hand as if she were seeing it for the first time. Wasn't it funny how something so simple, something so innocent, could lead to so much trouble? Would Connor be in this predicament now if not for her impetuousness the night of the ball? Or would he be dead? And John dead with him?

"You weren't wearing a corset," Anne added.

"I hate corsets," Carrie exclaimed as she put the cap aside and reached for her stockings.

Chapter Nineteen

She would have loved to storm into John's room. But her sore calf made it difficult. As did the fact that he wasn't in a room but in the middle of the fort grounds, overseeing the drilling of the troops.

John saw her limping toward him and ran to meet her, concern written all over his handsome face.

"Should you be up?" he asked. "Should I summon the physician?"

"Yes, John, I think that would be a very good idea." Carrie waited until they reached the privacy of a nearby porch to shake off the hand he had placed under her elbow. "Perhaps he can tell us if you have lost your mind."

"My mind?" John seemed totally confused. "Whatever are you talking about?" His hand went to her forehead. "Are you still running a fever?"

Carrie swatted away his hand. If anyone else touched her forehead, she would scream. "Why did you arrest Connor?"

"Regulations state that anyone caught deserting is to be arrested and tried for said crime."

"Don't spout army regulations to me, John. Connor didn't desert. He just wasn't *in* camp when we were attacked."

"Under very suspicious circumstances."

"He was taking a bath," Carrie retorted. "As was I."

"Carrie—" John pushed her back against the wall and quickly looked around to see if anyone was listening. "Do you not care what that sounds like? Do you not realize what people will think if they hear you say something like that?"

"I don't care what people think, John. I haven't done anything wrong. And neither has Connor. As a matter of fact, he did everything right. He saved my life. He went back for you instead of leaving you there to die. He risked his own life over and over again to get us here safely. And all you can do is condemn him?"

John crossed his arms and looked down at her. Carrie could tell by the set of his jaw that he would not relent.

"What happened to change you?" she asked in frustration. "You used to be fair-minded. You used to judge a man on his merits. Not because of his blood."

"I am the same as I have always been, Caroline."

"No . . . you . . . aren't." Carrie ground out the words as her frustration with her brother rose.

"Carrie, I am afraid you are not seeing Mr. Duncan clearly." John's voice was patient. With just a hint of annoyance. As if he was talking to a child.

Carrie resisted the urge to kick him in the shins.

"I'm afraid you've been carried away by the excitement and danger you were exposed to in the wilderness," John continued. Carrie's temper rose. She considered it a miracle that she did not kick him.

"Mr. Duncan has done a very good job of convincing you that he is something I know he's not." John's voice dripped with superiority and satisfaction.

"What is that, John?" Carrie demanded.

"He is not an honorable man. He can't help it. It's in

his blood. And I've heard things about his history. His father was, after all, a rebel, and his mother was hanged for sedition."

"His mother was hanged for sedition?"

"According to our uncle . . ."

"I don't care what his family did in the past," Carrie put in before John repeated more tales. "And I will not let you convict an innocent man."

"Our father will be the judge of that," John said. "I will put the facts before him and let him decide."

Carrie recognized the challenge. John was an officer in His Majesty's army. His word held great weight.

But her father was a fair man. Surely he would recognize the truth.

"As will I, John." Carrie limped past him. "Or should I address you as Captain Murray? My brother John seems to be missing."

She moved out into the packed dirt of the yard, not caring how John would react to her last words. On a day like today, it would be a blessing to be a man. It would definitely make her feel better to hit something. Or someone.

Why be vague? She wanted to hit John. She wanted to punch him in the mouth and then shake some sense into him.

She looked around, seeing the fort for the first time from the inside. Spiked logs, much taller than her head, surrounded a conclave of small cabins that were built up against the palisade. There was a well and a corral and a shelter for horses. A fat sow was penned in one corner and innumerable chickens scratched in the dirt.

About halfway up the walls were walkways where men stood watch with rifles in hand. The soldiers were still drilling, and a small group of children marched off to the side with sticks as pretend rifles on their shoulders.

Smoke rose from a chimney in one long, low building, and she presumed that it was the mess hall. A dog lolled on the porch of the building and a fat orange cat washed its face on top of a rail.

At that moment, Patsy came around the side of a cabin lugging a bucket of water.

"Patsy!" Carrie gathered her skirts and hobbled toward the maid. "Where is Connor?"

"Mr. Connor?" Patsy asked, as if she'd never heard the name before.

"Yes. Mr. Connor. Where is he?"

Patsy chewed on her lip and looked around nervously.

"My brother told you not to say anything, didn't he?"

"Er . . . no . . . er . . . yes, ma'am." Patsy sighed.

"Anne told me," Carrie said. "Now take me to Connor."

"But I can't, Miss Carrie. Not right now."

Carrie looked at the bucket. It contained soapy water and some filthy clothes. She recognized the pants Connor had worn on the trail. Which meant Patsy had just left the man. Carrie took off in the direction from which she'd seen Patsy come.

"Miss Carrie! Wait!" Patsy dropped the bucket, splashing water all over herself, and ran after her mistress. "You can't see him right now."

Carrie gathered her skirts and moved as fast as her injured leg would let her. John didn't want her to know about Connor being in jail? John had told Patsy not to say anything about Connor?

She was tired of John bossing her around and trying to protect her reputation. She was a grown woman. She could manage quite well on her own. And she was more than capable of making her own decisions about whom she would associate with.

Murray's idea of a bath was laughable. Three buckets of water and a sliver of soap carried to his cell by armed guards who acted as if he were Cornstalk come to take their scalps. Perhaps the dirt that covered him gave them the impression that his skin was of a darker hue.

Efrem had yet to return with his pack and a change of clothes. One of the guards begrudgingly slipped a razor through the bars so he might shave. Then both men stood watching him.

"Do ye think I'll slit my throat to save Murray the trouble?" Connor asked with a grin as he examined the razor. It wouldn't surprise him if Murray had sent him a dull blade just to make the process uncomfortable.

One of the men gave him a condescending smirk before they both left. Connor ignored them. They wanted a reaction from him and he was not going to gratify them.

He unwrapped the bandage from his arm, which had healed quite nicely in spite of his wretched conditions. Efrem's poultices often worked miracles.

Shaving was the first order of business. Once he'd completed that task, he quickly soaped up his hair and down his body, praying that lice had not set up residence during his confinement. There were no rats, so perhaps he was safe from that aggravation.

The cell was damp and cool, tolerable during the heat of the day but chilly now; the water in the buckets felt just a few degrees above freezing. If he were free, he'd soak in one of the hot springs that bubbled up through the ground out in the valley.

But he wasn't free.

The thought of the whipping to come did nothing to warm him. He did not deserve the punishment, but considering the alternative . . .

He dumped a bucket of water over his head.

"Connor!"

He dropped the bucket and looked up in shock at Carrie peering through the window.

He was practically naked. And very cold. Very, very cold.

Connor snatched up the bucket and held it in front of his private parts.

"What are you doing?" she asked.

"Are ye daft?" he roared. "I'm taking a bath."

"Heaven forbid," she said. "That's what got you in trouble in the first place."

"Miss Carrie, you can't talk to Mr. Connor now."

"Oh, stop it, Patsy. Mr. Connor and I are past the point where propriety is an issue."

"You are?" Patsy asked in wonder.

"We are?" Connor echoed. He looked around his cell for something, anything, with which to cover himself and settled on the ratty blanket on his cot. He wrapped it around his waist and moved to the window.

"Weren't you doing something?" Carrie said to Patsy, and the maid scampered off.

"How are ye, lass?" Her face was pale and she still had circles beneath her eyes, but the blue was clear and sparkled with life.

"I'm fine, thanks to you," she said. He let his eyes roam freely over her face, memorizing the lines of it.

"I hear Anne Trotter has been taking care of you."

"She has."

"She's a fine woman."

"I'm afraid I left her in a bit of a rush when I heard the news about you."

"Donnae trouble yourself. 'Tis nothing."

"It's all my fault."

"How can ye think that?"

She hesitated, as if she did not want to speak. She looked out toward the grounds for a moment, then turned back to him. The rays of the sun, straight overhead at this hour, shone upon her golden hair.

He would never grow tired of looking at her.

"My brother seems to think there is something between us . . ."

His gut clenched.

"Is there?" She seemed anxious. As if his answer was very important to her. As important as it was to him.

What could he say? Was there? He certainly wanted there to be. He wanted it more than anything he'd ever wanted in his life. But wanting something and having it were two different things.

His fingers curled around the bars at the window. When hers did the same, he could not resist the urge to run his thumb over her hand.

"I have nothing to offer ye, lass." He looked from her hand to her face. "Nothing at all."

"I didn't ask you about your prospects, Connor," she said with a slight smile.

"'Tis simple enough. I have none." He returned her smile with one of his own.

"Answer my question. Is there something between us?"

She was kneeling in the dirt in the middle of the wilderness while he was in a cell about to be lashed. It wasn't exactly the kind of life she was suited for.

Did he want her? Every part of his being screamed out for her. But what kind of life could he offer her? A cabin in the wilderness? Every day a chance that they could be killed or captured by the Shawnee? And aside from Indian attacks, there were the risks of everyday life. Of childbirth. Of illness. Of accidents.

He supposed they could live in Williamsburg, or one of the other towns. But how would he support her? He had no skills beyond those of a woodsman and the natural ability with horses that he'd inherited from his father. Could they live on a stablehand's pay?

No. She was meant for better things than he could offer her. And yet she sat in the dirt waiting for his answer, looking so lovely that it made his heart ache.

"There is nothing between us," he said, and turned away from the window. "You'd be better off with someone else."

"And you call me daft." Her voice held a hint of disgust, and Connor turned back to her in surprise. "You, Mr. Duncan, are an idiot. Probably a bigger idiot than my brother."

"I am?"

"How many times in your life has a woman sat in the dirt and practically handed you her heart on a platter?"

She seemed to be gathering up her anger and Connor wasn't sure what would happen next.

"Is that what ye were doing?" he asked.

"You know I was. And don't pretend that you didn't know what I was doing." She rolled her eyes in disgust. "I can't believe you won't admit it."

"It's not that I won't admit it," Connor explained. He felt a bit befuddled. This wasn't the reaction he'd expected. "It's just that I cannae give ye things. Ye need more than what I can provide for ye." For some reason, he'd thought there would be tears instead of this bubbling anger.

Carrie rose up on her knees and stared down at him. "Are you trying to say you know what's best for me?" Her jaw was tense. As if she was grinding her teeth.

"Aye." Connor almost sighed in relief. "I do."

"Ohhhhhh!" She stood up. "You are just like the rest of them." Connor peered up through the bars and watched her stomp her foot in righteous anger, only to exclaim in pain as she jammed her injured leg. She lifted her skirt and rubbed the calf.

It was quite a nice view as far as he was concerned.

"My mother knew what was best for me. All my fiancés knew what was best for me, even though they did not have enough sense to stay alive. My uncle and aunt knew what was best for me, and my brother certainly knows what is best for me, or so he says. Now I've got you telling me what's best for me. I just wish someone would ask me what I think is best for me."

Connor clamped his mouth shut as she went on with her tirade. At the moment he was sure silence was the wisest course.

He was most definitely relieved to see Efrem appear.

"You are better," he said to Carrie.

"I was," she huffed. "Perhaps you should ask your friend

how I am now since he *knows what's best for me.*" She stalked off with an uneven gait that seemed almost comical when seen from behind.

He was wise enough not to laugh.

"What was that all about?" Efrem asked as he shoved Connor's clothing through the bars.

"She wanted to know how I felt about her."

"Did you tell her?"

"I told her she'd be better off with someone else."

"She wasn't happy about it."

"Nay. She wasn't."

"You should have stolen her away when you had the chance."

Connor grinned up at his friend. He should have. She would be his now.

"Ye see now why I didn't," he said. "She would have bitten my head off."

Efrem nodded in agreement. "But you still want her."

"Aye. I want her."

Chapter Twenty

"Why are all men so . . . so . . ." Words failed her as she made her way across the fort. She didn't even know where she was going. Her leg throbbed, she felt weak and dizzy from her confinement, yet her righteous anger carried her on, even though she limped.

"How dare he not admit it," she raged on. "How dare he!"

"Miss Carrie!" Patsy ran up to her. "Shouldn't you be resting, Miss Carrie?"

Carrie stopped with her jaw clenched. "Because that's what's best for me?"

Patsy blinked. "Er, um, Captain Murray sent me to find you. He said you need your rest."

"Oh, he did, did he?" Carrie placed her hands on her hips and looked over Patsy's shoulder to where she saw her brother in conference with several officers of the king. It would serve him right if she gave him a good dressing down in front of everyone, and she was tempted to do so. But she would only succeed in embarrassing both herself and her brother.

The relief she had felt upon realizing they were all safe

was gone. Instead a sudden dread settled upon her shoulders like a heavy cloak. It weighed her down.

What was it she felt for Conner? She had to admit that the reason she'd sought him out was to get help understanding exactly what she felt. But now she was more confused than ever.

There was something that drew her to him. Something that had happened before the expedition. Was it fate that had guided her out onto the balcony the night of the ball?

The walls of the fort suddenly felt as confining as her forgotten corset. She longed to walk outside, beneath the giant trees, where she would have the solitude to think. However, the sight of the guards reminded her that the threat from the Shawnee was still very real.

Patsy stood beside her, her face twisted with worry.

"Perhaps I *should* rest." Carrie sighed.

At that moment there was a shout from the wall, and the gates of the fort swung open.

A troop rode in, a party of ten men dressed in the same type of rustic clothing that Connor wore. Carrie paid them no mind and continued on her way until a familiar voice called out to her.

"Papa?" The man walking toward her wasn't what she'd expected. But the stride was one she would know anywhere, and the face beneath the dirt and growth of beard broke into a familiar smile as his arms stretched wide to fold her into a rib-crushing embrace.

"What are you doing here, child?"

"I came to see you." Carrie looked at her father. His bright blue eyes seemed sad as he looked down into her face.

"You look more like your mother each passing day." His hand stroked her hair and cupped her chin. "I'm sorry I wasn't there . . ." His voice broke and Carrie felt a catch in her throat. "At the end."

"Oh, Papa." Carrie buried her head beneath his chin

and felt the strange scratch of his beard on her scalp as he held her close for a moment.

Surely everything would be set right. Her father was here. He would take care of everything. She looked up as if to make sure it was really he.

The beard was very unfamiliar. Especially since it was more silver than gold. The hair at his temples showed silver too. He was covered in dirt and dressed in hide and linen. She had never seen him this way, and the look on her face must have showed her confusion.

"I have found that a red coat makes an excellent target," he said. "Especially when one is in the wilderness."

"John learned the same lesson the hard way," Carrie said.

"John?" Her father's face turned from happy smiles to instant concern. "Is he hurt?"

"He's fine," Carrie said. She turned to where she'd seen John moments earlier. He was standing off to the side, along with the other officers, allowing her a private moment with her father. "However, his troop did not fare as well." She knew her brother must be anxious to see their father, but at the moment she did not care. He would have his time with their father soon enough.

"You were attacked?"

"Yes. And if not for the courage of our guide, both John and I would have died."

Carrie could tell her father had a hundred questions all fighting for importance in his mind. She wasn't surprised when the first one he asked concerned her.

"Why are you limping? Were you injured in the attack?"

"No, afterward. A snake, a copperhead, I believe Connor called it . . ."

"Connor?"

"The man who saved us."

"I must meet this man," her father said. "But first I should talk to John."

"I'm afraid John's version of what happened is a bit different from mine," Carrie said quietly as she heard the officers come up behind her. She stepped aside, but stayed close at hand as the officers saluted in turn and welcomed the general to Fort Savannah.

"Your baggage arrived here safely a week ago," the fort commander said.

"Excellent," the general said. "I am ready for a bath, a change of clothes and a hot meal."

"I'll have my quarters prepared for you, General," the commander said with a smart salute and marched off, leaving the family alone.

"I am glad to see you well, John." Her father clasped her brother's hand. "Your trip was difficult?"

"It was," John said. "There are things I need to discuss with you in private."

"Of course." Her father placed his arm around Carrie and pulled her to his side. "Can you give your brother and me time to discuss official business?"

"I will go see to your meal," Carrie said.

"She should be resting," John said. "The trip was most difficult for her."

"I am fine, John," Carrie said. "Just a bit tired. Seeing Papa has greatly revived my spirits." She gave her brother a look that let him know she could be just as stubborn as he when it suited her. "Thank you for your brotherly concern," she added.

Her father dropped a kiss on top of her head before following John.

"I sure hate to see Mr. Connor get whipped," Patsy said as she came up beside her mistress. "I seen a man get whipped one time and it was terrible."

"Mr. Connor isn't going to be whipped," Carrie said. "Not if I have anything to say about it."

"It sure would be nice to hear what Mr. John has to say about things," Patsy said.

"Yes, it would. But John demanded privacy, and I have no right to be present when they discuss military matters."

"Still . . ." Patsy rolled her eyes dramatically. "If someone just happened to be behind that cabin and the little window off to the side of the chimney was open, someone might hear what was going on inside."

"Patsy." Carrie placed her hands on her hips and looked down at the maid. "Have you been spying on my brother?"

"Well . . ." The maid grinned. "Mr. Efrem was worried about Mr. Connor."

"And you'd do anything for Mr. Efrem."

"He did carry me over that awful river. And he let me use his blanket."

"Yes, he did." Carrie looked over at the cabin. "He did indeed."

"We were unprepared for the attack," John said.

Patsy was right, Carrie realized. With the cabin window open, the voices carried right to her. From the other sounds she heard, she could tell her father was shaving, and memories of her childhood and his infrequent visits washed over her. When he was home, she'd wanted to spend every minute with him. She recalled watching the strange contortions of his face as she watched him shave. Carrie settled down in a most unladylike squat behind a barrel and hoped that Patsy would warn her in time if anyone came near.

"Did you post sentries?"

"Yes. But the fog made it impossible to see."

"What did your scout—" Carrie heard the splashing of the water in a bowl. "Mr. Duncan? What did he do? Did he tell you of the risk?"

"He mostly complained about the noise of the drummer and the wagons," John said. Carrie bit down on her knuckle to keep from calling out in protest.

"They would attract attention," her father said, and Carrie felt a swell of pride in him. "I have learned the best way to travel through this wilderness is quietly, without calling attention to oneself."

"Father," John said, "we marched as an army to assure the colonists that we were here to protect them."

"Surely you knew the wagons could not make it over the mountains."

"Mr. Duncan told me so. We were planning to leave them behind that very day."

"So you did take his advice."

"When I felt the situation warranted it."

There was a long silence. What was her father thinking?

"Did he ever warn you of an imminent attack?"

"No. After his friend showed up, he said that we were at war and should expect an attack at the fort." There was a moment of silence, and then John added something that surprised Carrie.

"He did suggest that I send Carrie back to Williamsburg."

I wouldn't have gone . . . .

"Which was just as useless as your telling her not to come in the first place," her father commented.

Carrie grinned. Her father knew her well, even if he had not seen her for over three years.

"I never should have allowed her to accompany us," John said. "If she had not survived . . ."

"She did, John. She's safe."

"I thought she would die when the snake . . ."

There was a moment of silence. Was John overcome? Carrie felt an uncomfortable guilt wash over her. She was so angry at John, she couldn't stand to look at him right now. But her heart would break in two if something happened to him. Did he feel as strongly about her?

She'd always thought he ordered her about to protect his reputation. But now she realized he did care for her. She knew he did. He could have easily died in the attack. It was a miracle he hadn't. Or in the river . . . if not for Connor . . .

"Tell me exactly what Duncan did that led you to believe he deserted."

"He and his friend ran from the camp when we were attacked."

"You saw him run?"

"He was not in camp when the attack occurred."

"Tell me everything that happened that morning."

"I was in my tent when I heard the first shot. When I came out, the savages had my men engaged in hand-to-hand combat. My men were taken totally unaware. Most were in the process of preparing for the march, or so it appeared from their dress. I fired at a savage who was fighting with Corporal Simmons. I saw one of the Indians take aim at me as I was reloading my pistol. The next thing I recall was Carrie dabbing water on my face. I was downhill from the camp. The shot creased my forehead, and apparently the impact knocked me into the woods, where I lay undetected by the savages as they finished off my men."

"None survived?"

"They scalped them. All of them. They ravaged the camp for weapons. I lost Sultan also."

Carrie felt the pain in John's voice. In all the desperation of their escape she had forgotten about John's stallion. The horse was his most beloved possession. During the cross-Atlantic voyage she had often remarked on how much time he spent doting on the horse belowdecks. Of course he would miss the animal and regret his loss. Was that the reason he hated Connor so?

" 'Tis my dream to fill that meadow full of fine horses with the name Duncan attached to them."

Connor had lost his dream in the attack too. If he were deserting he would have taken his mare with him.

"I'm sorry, son. I'm sorry you had to go through that."

It was not the voice of a commanding officer talking to a subordinate. It was the voice of a father talking to his son.

"What of Carrie?" her father asked. "How did she survive the attack?"

"She was not in camp either."

"Where was she?"

Carrie knew the answer. An innocent whim. An early morning bath hidden by the heavy fog. Something so simple had saved her life.

"She was with Duncan."

"What?"

"The story is simple enough. She was bathing in the creek. He was bathing in the creek."

"Together?" her father asked incredulously, and Carrie felt her cheeks flame. How could he think that?

"Duncan has been after her since the first moment he saw her. I think he used the excuse of the attack to steal her away."

"But they came back for you, did they not?"

"He forgot about the maid. She was witness to it all. When the maid followed them, he had to bring her back. Or else kill her."

How could he twist the truth this way?

Carrie had serious doubts about her brother's sanity. Had the bullet that creased his head somehow altered his perception?

"She's totally infatuated with the man," John continued. "She sees him as our savior, when in truth the attack was just a handy excuse for him to have his way with her."

She had heard enough. John needed to be stopped. And as if God himself agreed with her, there was a heavy pounding on the door that caused Carrie to jump and almost fall flat on her face. She peered around the corner to where Patsy was innocently waiting on the porch. The maid shrugged her shoulders as if to say she had no idea what was going on.

Carrie ducked under the window as she made her way toward the front of the cabin.

"Charlie. Come in." Carrie heard her father introduce John to a man named Charles Lewis and then stopped when she heard the man mention Connor's name.

"Why is Connor Duncan being held?" Lewis demanded.

"The charges are desertion," John said.

"That's a lie," Lewis said.

Carrie heard the sound of a crash, and then her father spoke.

"John," he said in a warning tone.

"This man has questioned my word." John's voice was angry, and Carrie could well imagine that his hand was most likely on his sword.

"Connor Duncan would no more run out on a battle than I would," Lewis said. "And since he is not an enlisted man, you have no right to hold him."

"Captain Murray," her father commanded. "Sit."

He's made it worse . . . this Lewis man . . . he's made John hate Connor more because of father's discipline. . . .

"How long have you known Duncan?" her father asked.

"Since he was a lad. Since he came here as a bondservant to Sir Richard Abbington. He was with us when we marched on Fort Duquesne, and he wasn't more than twelve at the time, yet he fought as a man and didn't shed a tear when he saw what the French bastards did to the Scots who fought there."

Carrie knew the story. Even though she was a small girl at the time, she'd heard her father tell her mother of it. The Scots' heads were impaled upon posts with their kilts displayed beneath. She'd had nightmares for weeks after that and promised herself she would never sneak from her bed again in the middle of the night to listen to the grown-ups talk.

Connor had witnessed that battle. What other horrors had he seen? He talked of the Shawnee as if they were horrible. What could they do that was more horrible than that?

"He wouldn't run from a fight unless he knew it was useless to begin with," Lewis continued. "I would have him by my side in any battle and mark my words, if you persist in punishing him, not a man in this militia will march with you upon the Shawnee."

"That is sedition," John said.

"He does not speak sedition, John," her father said. "I have spent time with this man. I trust his word, and he knows the ways of the colonists."

"So you take his word over mine?"

The anger in John's voice was tangible. What drove him to judge Connor in such a way that he would stake his reputation and career upon this issue? Could he not admit the mistakes he'd made? This country was new to him. Could he not learn from the people who knew it instead of judging them for things he did not understand?

"I must weigh all the words I hear." Her father. Always the voice of reason. Always a calm port in any storm that brewed around him.

"My brother Andrew looks upon Connor as a son," Lewis continued. "And he is the general of the militia."

Carrie heard the sounds of heavy footsteps on the floor. John. He was leaving. She dashed from beneath the window and stepped up on the porch just as he came out the door. Her calf screamed from the exertion.

"May I see Father now?" she asked, and hoped that John did not notice her convenient appearance.

He ignored her and stalked away.

"Does that mean good news for Mr. Connor?" Patsy asked.

"Shush," Carrie said, and knocked on the door. "I saw John leave," she said when her father called out for her to enter.

Her father looked much more familiar now. He was in uniform, although his coat hung over the back of a chair. The beard was gone and his hair was neatly combed into place.

"My daughter, Caroline Murray," her father began, and Carrie curtseyed. "Charles Lewis."

"I believe I met your brother in Williamsburg."

"Andrew. He's on his way here as we speak." Lewis looked at her father as he bowed toward Carrie. She knew the message was meant for him. "I will leave you two to your reunion," he said and left.

"Papa, I am greatly concerned for John," Carrie said.

"As am I," he said. "But first I need to hear your version of what happened on the trail."

Carrie thought back to what she'd overheard. What exactly had John said against Connor?

"Connor was a complete gentleman," she began.

Her father smiled at her. "Have you been listening where you should not, daughter?"

She looked at her father in confusion.

"I never asked about Mr. Duncan's actions." He tilted his head toward the window.

Carrie felt her cheeks flame. Her father knew what she'd done.

"Nothing unseemly has happened between Connor and me," Carrie said. "In spite of what John thinks."

"What were you doing the morning of the attack?"

"I woke before dawn. When I went out I saw that it was foggy. So foggy that you couldn't see your hand at the end of your arm. I thought I could have a bath without anyone noticing, so Patsy and I went down to the stream that was below our camp."

"Where was Duncan at this time?"

"I didn't know, but he was also in the stream. Down from where I was. The fog was so thick I couldn't see, and the sounds were distorted. I sent Patsy back up to the tent for my shawl, and that's when the attacked happened. I was standing in my shift in the middle of the stream and I didn't know what to do. The next thing I knew, Connor and Efrem were there, and he picked me up and carried me to safety."

"And then?"

"I called him a coward for leaving the camp. Then I saw he had been doing the same thing as I."

"How could you tell?"

"His hair was wet . . . and he . . . smelled better." Carrie flushed again. "We hid beneath a fallen tree. He lay atop me so my skirt wouldn't show." Carrie folded her hands in the same pink-striped skirt, which showed several mended tears. "Efrem hid our trail so the Indians wouldn't find us."

"What did he say when you called him a coward?"

"He didn't say anything. He just said the lucky ones would die because of what the Shawnee do to their prisoners."

"He was right," her father said. "His life and his friend's life would have been lost, along with yours. He did the right thing."

Carrie nodded. "The Shawnee were headed east, so Conner and Efrem decided we should come here rather than return to Williamsburg. I made them go back to camp because I wanted to know if . . ."

"It was lucky for John you did."

"They were all dead. All scalped. Except for Corporal Peters. He was still alive, but he died while I was with John. We gathered what food we could find and left. We stayed by the river the first day. Then a storm came up. Lightning struck a tree close to where we were, and John was thrown into the water. He almost drowned. Connor and Efrem pulled him out." She recalled the rage on John's face when he'd found her cap stuffed in Connor's breeches. "Papa, I'm worried about John. Something has happened to him. There's no reason why he should hate Connor so. It's almost as if he hates him just because he's a Scot."

"I believe he does," her father said. "A broken heart can do strange things to a man."

Carrie looked at her father in confusion.

"It's John's story and his choice to tell you," her father said. "I don't even know it, except for a letter I got from his commander in Aberdeen, who expressed the same concerns you have. It is the reason he was sent to the colonies."

"The colonies have nearly as many Scots as Scotland."

"Yes, they do." He pointed toward her calf. "Tell me about the snake."

"One night on the trail, we saw the Shawnee pass below us," she began. She could not recall which night it was. They all seemed to run together into one big nightmare. "John was running a fever and I couldn't sleep, so I moved from the shelter. As I came out, Connor covered my mouth to keep me quiet. Then I saw the Shawnee. They were passing below us. They had prisoners. Connor said we should take the trail over the mountains instead of going around them. Efrem went ahead to scout."

She saw her father nod in agreement.

"The next morning we stopped to rest and wait for Efrem, and that's when the snake bit me. I sat down on a rock and it must have been beneath it. It bit me twice. Connor cut my leg and sucked out the poison. Then he carried me. The Shawnee caught up with us close to the fort. Efrem tried to lead them away, but they stayed on our trail. When we got within sight of the fort, he and Connor stayed behind so we could make it across the clearing. I don't even remember coming into the fort. My leg . . ."

"Two bites would have killed you if not for Duncan's quick action."

"He saved our lives many times over, Papa. He doesn't deserve to be punished."

"John seems to think you have feelings for this man."

Carrie looked down at the hands folded in her lap. "Would it be so wrong if I did?"

"What if your emotions are just a result of the dangers you've faced together? What if they're just feelings of gratitude? It's a hard life out here, Carrie. One that I would not choose for you. I would rather see you safe at home in England."

She smiled. "Connor said the same thing."

"He did?"

"Yes, he did."

"I think it's time for me to meet this man." Her father rose from his chair and came to help her to her feet. "And it's time for you to get some rest." He dropped a kiss on her forehead.

"Papa?" She had to know what they were going to do to Connor, but her father waved her on without answering her unvoiced question.

Patsy was waiting for her. "What they going to do?" she asked.

"I don't know," Carrie said. She suddenly felt exhausted. She looked over toward the building that covered Connor's cell. There was nothing else she could do. She might as well get some rest. Who knew what the remainder of the day might bring?

Chapter Twenty-one

He was tired of waiting. He knew something was going to happen before the day was out and he just wanted it over with.

Efrem had come and gone. He'd reported that the gates of the fort were now open, which meant the threat of attack was over. But Efrem being Efrem, he wanted to see for himself. He must have told Charlie what had happened, because then he'd shown up, demanded Connor's release and stomped off when the regulars did not comply. Connor didn't even get a chance to tell Charlie he had a letter in his pack from Andrew.

"Make yourself ready." The guard slammed shut the door as Connor stood and waited for it to open again.

He was tired of waiting, but he was also surprised he was going to be lashed at sundown. Didn't they usually do that type of thing at dawn?

It would have been nice if they fed him first. But then again, they didn't want to see him spew it up again when they lashed him.

Fifty lashes then. Without the benefit of a trial. The

Lord Christ himself only received thirty-nine. Not that he was comparing himself to Christ—Connor quickly crossed himself and asked forgiveness for his blasphemy. But there was a reason for only thirty-nine lashes. The law of that day considered forty a certain death sentence.

"It should be over soon enough," he assured himself.

The English were merciful when you considered the alternative. The Shawnee could make death last for days.

He remembered well the punishment he'd received after his one and only attempt at escape from them.

They left him alone that day. He was skinning a deer, and the woman had gone off. She was always watching him, so he was surprised that she was gone. They never left him alone. He was always in her sight, or else with the men on a hunt. And they only took him to carry back the kill.

Perhaps there was some confusion about whose turn it was to watch him. Or maybe they thought he no longer had any desire to leave. Whatever the reason, Connor found himself alone at midday. Without conscious thought, his feet took him east toward home.

He wondered how far he would get. All he wore were his breeks and a pair of moccasins. The only weapon he had was the small flint blade used for skinning. He was weak from hunger. The old woman made sure he stayed that way. He never got enough food. His size frightened his captors, so he remained gaunt and weak. He knew he wasn't strong enough to survive for the many days it would take to get back to civilization. And he had the Ohio to cross. Yet he kept going.

They caught him at sun up the next morning. They marched him back for as long as he was able to stay on his feet. Half the time they dragged him by a rope around his neck.

The camp was waiting for him. He was sure they would burn him, and he'd die screaming as Tom had. Luckily for him, the old woman wasn't done with him yet.

They stripped him and staked him to the ground. The

women and children switched him until he was raw and then they left him.

He wondered at their mercy. He wondered what was next until the insects came and made a feast of his blood and he lay there helpless, unable to escape the torment. Then came the chills in the wee hours of the morning. He shook until he was sure he would die.

When dawn arrived, the old woman cut him lose. She told him he should be grateful because she'd spared his life. She gave him a salve for his wounds, fed him a bite and told him next time it would be the fires for sure.

"Can we get it over with?" Connor yelled at the guards on the other side of the door. They came for him with their weapons pointed at his chest. One bound his hands, and then they prodded him out with the points of their bayonets.

He'd thought there'd be a post in the middle of the yard but saw nothing. The gate was open, and he wondered briefly if they were going to lash him outside the fort. Instead he was marched to the commander's office, his hands were untied and he was told to go inside.

Connor looked around. No sign of Efrem. Or Murray. Or the lass.

Was there some sort of trial waiting for him on the other side of the door? Connor rapped on the wooden portal.

"Enter."

There was only one man in the room. Even without an introduction, Connor knew exactly who he was: General James Murray. There was no mistaking the set of his eyes or the line of his jaw. Was there anything of the mother in his children?

His mother had always told him he was the image of his father. Now he understood what she'd meant for John Murray was the image of his. And the lass a much softer, more pleasingly feminine version.

"Sit." General Murray indicated a chair before his desk. "You know who I am?"

"Aye, sir." Connor sat in the chair. "I do."

The general leaned back in his seat and put the tips of his fingers together as he took a moment to consider Connor.

"I have a problem, Mr. Duncan," the general said. "And you seem to be the cause of it."

Connor kept his mouth shut and his eyes upon the general.

"Tell me what happened the day of the attack."

"I was bathing in the creek," Connor said. "I heard your daughter call out for her maid when the gunfire began. I took her away from the camp. We found the maid, Patsy, in the woods. Then we went back to look for survivors."

"And you found my son?"

"Patsy did. There was another, but he died of his wounds."

"Why did you not go to the aid of the camp when it was attacked?"

"It wouldnae have made a difference to the outcome of the battle."

"But your actions did make a difference to my daughter."

Connor did not comment. Did the man expect him to brag about saving his daughter's life? Saving her was the only thing that made sense.

"Did you not see any sign of the Shawnee when you were on the trail?"

"I was unable to scout ahead," Connor said. "I was sent back to take care of a broken wheel on a wagon."

"By my son."

"He was the one who gave the order," Connor said.

"Did you agree with the order?"

Connor measured his words. " 'Tis no secret that Captain Murray and I disagreed on many things, including bringing the wagons along in the first place."

The general sat back in his chair. "Charles Lewis speaks highly of you."

"As I would of him if asked," Connor said.

"You were with him in the Indian Wars?"

"Aye. My master was part of the militia."

"You were a bondservant?"

"Aye."

"You couldn't have been more than a child at the time," the general commented.

"I was ten when I came here."

"And how old are you now?"

Connor did not see that his age had anything to do with the subject at hand, but he had nothing to hide. "I just turned twenty-eight."

"So you were born in 'Forty-six?"

"Aye." It seemed to be a strange line of questioning.

"Where were you born, Mr. Duncan?"

"Is it nae obvious?" Connor spouted, then instantly regretted losing his temper. He took a deep breath to calm himself.

"Where in Scotland were you born?" the general asked again with an indulgent smile.

"I was born at Culloden. The day of the battle."

"You were born James Connor Duncan? To a woman named Anice?"

Connor was dumbfounded. He looked at the general. "Aye."

"I fought at Culloden," the general said. "The battle is not one I am proud of. And the aftermath . . ." His voice trailed away. "I came across your mother on the battlefield. She was dragging your father's body off so she could bury him." He looked at Connor. "You have the look of him. He was a big man with long, flaming hair. For the life of me I could not imagine how your mother was able to lift him, much less drag him, especially in her condition."

Connor could picture it. She was stubborn enough to do such a thing.

"When I told her to stop, she asked me what use the king had for dead prisoners. When I told her we were to leave none alive, she asked me to bury her with him."

Connor nodded. He could hear her say it as if she were right there with him.

"When I realized her time was upon her, I took her to a midwife. I was there when you were born. Since my name is also James, she said I could pretend you were named after me. But, in fact, you were named after your father."

Connor bent his head. How was it that he came to be sitting before the very man who had been so instrumental in his birth? He'd never heard this version of the story.

"Your mother was a brave woman. I have often wondered what happened to her and her son."

"She was hanged for sedition after she was raped in front of her son by English soldiers. Then her son was sold into slavery." The words exploded from his mouth.

The general's eyes widened and then closed, as if he felt Connor's pain. "Bastards," he finally said. "Some men cannot see past their hate. And I'm afraid my son has turned into one of them."

Connor gripped the arms of his chair as anger and frustration rolled over him.

"You were just a boy," the general said. "There was nothing you could do against trained soldiers."

"I tried to fight them," he said. His jaw ached, it was clenched so tight, and he had to force the words through. "I wanted to kill them."

"I know," the general said. "There is no worse fear than that which accompanies helplessness."

Connor realized the general was giving him a moment to compose himself. Which meant the questions weren't over.

"What are your intentions toward my daughter?"

Once again Connor was dumbstruck. "Sir?" he asked.

"My daughter."

Suddenly the prospect of a lashing did not seem so bad.

"My son seems to think you have feelings for her."

Connor opened his mouth to speak and then clamped it shut.

"Well, do you?"

"Yes, sir." He could not deny it.

"And what are your intentions toward her?"

His intentions? He longed to marry her. But good intentions would not make a life for her, nor would they keep her safe.

"I have none."

The general's eyes bored into him, and Connor realized just how hard his chair was. He resisted the urge to move about to find a more comfortable position. It was the same look the lass had given him when he'd told her the same thing.

"I cannae provide a decent life for her," Connor said. "And she willnae be safe with me. Ye should send her back to Williamsburg."

I will never forget her . . . .

He knew it in his gut. He knew she was the one woman he could love as his father loved his mother. He knew it just as surely as he knew that there was no future for them. They were of two different worlds. They could not be together.

"I am considering it," the general said. "But she would need an escort, and right now I cannot spare the men." He shuffled some papers on his desk. "You are free to go, Mr. Duncan. However, you are not released from the king's service. As you may have heard, the militia has been called into service. We're marching to Point Pleasant, and I will have need of a man such as you."

Connor stood as Murray rose from behind his desk. "Be careful with my daughter, Duncan," he said. "She is very dear to me."

Connor nodded. There was nothing he could say. She was dear to him also.

Chapter Twenty-two

It was the bird call that made her open her eyes. She was half asleep, aware of everything that went on around her but too comfortable to actually get up.

She looked around the room and noticed it was now dark. How long had she slept?

The answering bird call got her up and moving. She flew out the door and onto the porch as her eyes searched the darkness of the fort.

Most of the windows glowed with the soft light of lamps. Torches burned on either side of the gate, which was wide open. Four people stood there, a woman, a small boy, Patsy and Efrem. There was no mistaking the Cherokee's lean physique and waist-length hair.

Where was Connor? Had he been freed? Who else would have answered Efrem's call? Was he planning on leaving without a word to her? There was no doubt in her mind that Efrem was going. He was carrying his pack, and his rifle rested lightly in his arms.

Carrie gathered her skirts and hopped off the porch. She'd forgotten about her leg, and it buckled beneath her, toppling her into a solid body that had just come around the side of the cabin.

"Oof." She recognized the voice, and her arms wrapped around his neck as he fought to keep them both upright. His hands about her waist steadied her on her feet, and she let her hands slide down until they rested upon his chest.

"Ye will be the death of me, lass," he said. "In more ways than one." His blue eyes twinkled merrily in the light of the torch. His hair was neatly brushed, curling about his shoulders, and his clothes seemed remarkably clean. It was hard to believe he had been a prisoner just a few hours earlier.

"You're leaving?" she asked. He was wearing his pack and his rifle was slung over his shoulder.

"We're taking Anne back to her cabin and staying with her since her husband is gone."

"Without saying good-bye?"

"Why do ye think I was sneaking about your cabin?" he said with a grin.

"You could have just sent Patsy in."

"I would have, but she's a bit distracted." He looked over toward the gate, where Patsy was hanging on Efrem's every word. "Don't worry, he'll let her down easy," Connor assured her.

"Perhaps you should take a lesson from him," Carrie said.

" 'Tis better to hear the truth at once than a lie for all your days."

"Such wisdom," Carrie said. "Perhaps you should make better use of it."

"The right decision isnae always the easiest," he said. His words sounded flippant, but his eyes remained upon her.

She was tired of platitudes. What she wanted to do was knock some sense into him. Make him realize that he really did care about her.

"Since you are out and about, I guess you're not going to be flogged?"

"I told them the one I received today would be sufficient."

"What? They beat you?"

"Nay. I was referring to the tongue-lashing you gave me."

Carrie rolled her eyes. "You deserved it," she said.

"Aye." He picked up a stray curl and placed it behind her shoulder. His hands were tender, caring, yet Carrie well recalled the violence and strength in them when he'd killed the snake. "Your father told me to be careful with you."

"You met my father?"

"We talked. He is the one who let me go."

There was something different about Connor. It could have been because they were safe now and he didn't have the responsibility of their lives pressing down on him. But then again . . .

"What did you talk about?"

"Lots of things." His hand caressed her shoulder.

"About me?"

"That was part of it," he said. "He asked me what happened and I told him."

"And your story matched mine."

"I told the truth, as ye did."

"About everything?"

"Aye."

"What did you say about me?"

Connor looked beyond her shoulder toward the gate, where Efrem waited. "He asked me what my intentions were toward you."

"What did you say?"

His eyes returned to her face and he looked down at her, his gaze lost in the shadows. "I told him I had none." His hand lingered on her cheek.

"Yet here you are."

There was no mistaking the confusion on his face.

"What were your intentions tonight, Connor?" Her anger flared once again. "You came here to tell me good-bye? So say it and leave."

His hand gripped her shoulder. He squeezed it so hard that a pain shot down her arm, but she didn't move. She looked into his eyes, as they suddenly caught the reflection of the torchlight and burned as if they were on fire also. Then his head dipped and his lips caught hers.

Carrie felt as if she were falling. She wrapped her fingers in the loose billows of his shirt and Connor's arms moved around her as she leaned into him. His hand moved down her back, pressing against the layers of skirt and petticoats. He swung her off her feet without taking his mouth from hers and moved her back into the shadows between the cabin and the wall of the fort. He dropped his gun and pack and he pushed her against the wall, his body pressed up against hers.

"I can't," he whispered hoarsely when he finally let go. His mouth trailed down her neck and caressed her skin with his breath. "*Mo cridhe*. I cannae leave you."

Before she could answer, his lips were on hers again, and he pinned her against the wall. She felt the rough wood against her spine and did not care. She couldn't get enough of him.

Her hands moved over his back and into his hair.

"God help me," he said when he once again drew a breath. His forehead touched hers as Carrie gasped for air. "I cannae stop."

"I don't want you to," she said.

"Do ye know what ye say?" His voice was nothing more than a whisper.

"I do." Carrie took his face in her hands so he would look at her. "I love you, Connor. For the first time in my life, this is something I want."

"It cannae happen, Carrie. I cannae . . ."

"I don't care," she said. "I know you love me, too." Then she kissed him.

Connor moaned deep in his throat as she pressed against him, molding her body to the length of his.

Then his head whipped up and he froze, listening. Efrem's call.

"What is it?"

"A warning . . . someone is coming."

"I don't care."

Efrem called out again. This time a different call, one more urgent.

"It is your brother." He stepped away from her.

"How can you know that?"

"We shouldnae take the chance."

"Chance on what?"

"Dishonoring you." She saw the set of his jaw and knew he would brook no argument. "I promised your father." He pushed her toward the back of the cabin. "Go around," he said.

"Take me with you."

"Nay. 'Tis not safe."

"It's safe enough for Anne and her son."

"I willnae risk it." She saw the tick in his jaw in the dim light. "Go."

He picked up his things and disappeared behind the adjoining cabin before she could protest. Her only choice was to call out after him or follow. She gathered her skirts and took off, paralleling his path between the cabins.

John was in the yard. He saw Carrie, realized where she was going and ran to stop her.

"Connor!" she called out. "Wait."

Connor was at the gate. John grabbed her arm just as he turned.

"Are you insane?" he hissed.

"Let go of me." She tried to wrench her arm away, but his grip was like iron.

"You are making a fool of yourself, Caroline." John twisted her around so that they both faced the gate. Connor stood there, facing them. Carrie felt his eyes upon her. "He doesn't even want you." John said into her ear.

"Connor!" she called out.

He turned and walked away.

She couldn't believe it. He was gone. The darkness swallowed him up as if he'd never been there.

John released her arm. "You are going to have to choose, Carrie." He pointed toward the gate, which was being closed by two men. "You can have your family, who only wants what is right for you, or you can have someone who will allow you to humiliate yourself in front of an entire regiment."

"The only one who's humiliated is you, John," she said. She turned away and saw her father standing on the porch of the small cabin that had become hers. Had he witnessed the entire incident?

She didn't mean to embarrass him. Tears came unbidden to her eyes as she went to him.

"I'm sorry, Papa," she said. "I only wanted to talk to Connor."

He opened his arms and she stepped into his embrace.

"Do you love him?" he asked.

"Yes. And I know he loves me, even though he won't admit it."

"He doesn't have to say it," her father said. "He's just showed you that he does."

"I don't understand."

Her father tilted up her chin so she would look at him. "He's doing everything he can to keep you safe. Perhaps we should do the same."

"I won't go back, Papa."

"We will all be leaving soon. Even your young man. We're going to war and I cannot leave you here."

"Then—"

"You will not go with us, nor will you follow us. You are going back to Williamsburg. As soon as Lord Dunmore arrives with his contingent, I will assign someone to take you back. Do you understand?"

"Yes, Papa." She understood his words. But that didn't mean she agreed with them. And her uncle was days away. Which meant that she still had time to convince Connor he was wrong.

Chapter Twenty-three

"You should have taken her."

"I swear, Efrem, if ye say that one more time, I will gladly scalp ye myself."

Efrem laughed. "You just don't want to admit that I'm right."

Connor resisted the urge to punch Efrem in the mouth. Instead he let the branch he was holding snap back as they walked by, knowing it would give his friend a good smack in the gut.

They had spent all morning and half of the afternoon searching for the Trotters' milk cow. Anne always turned it loose at the threat of attack, and the beast had become used to its freedom and escaped every chance it got. Anne was sure the poor thing was in need of a good milking. Connor just thought it needed a stouter rope so it would quit wandering off whenever it chose.

Efrem moved off to the side, leaving plenty of distance between the two of them. A wise move on his part, considering the mood Connor was in. They were on the trail of the cow, but it wandered back and forth without direction. It would be a miracle if they found the creature.

He should not have kissed Carrie. It had been a mistake. He was a fool to think one kiss would be enough.

A week of sleepless nights had done nothing to help the situation. If anything, he was in worse shape than ever. He lay down wanting her and he rose wanting her.

One kiss was not enough. There would never be enough of Carrie.

The sooner her father sent her back to Williamsburg, the better off they'd all be.

Could ye forget her then?

Nay. The memories would linger. Memories of her laughing and talking and looking about the country in wonder. Memories of her lying by his side, trembling with cold and fear and seeking shelter in his arms. Memories of her crashing into him and throwing shoes upon his head that made him smile just to think of them. Memories of the dressing down she'd given him while he stood in a cell wearing nothing but a moth-eaten blanket. Memories of her impetuous kiss when the Shawnee were on top of them, of her warm, willing body in his arms the last night he saw her. Willing for more than just a kiss.

The years stretched ahead, long and lonely, empty and meaningless. What good was his dream of a home and children and the best horses on the Blue Ridge without someone to share it?

I do want her . . . I love her . . .

Connor stopped in his tracks and Efrem gave him a shrug and continued on down the ridge, searching for the cow.

He had to admit it to himself: he loved her. She'd had the courage to say it, and he was naught but a coward.

But he'd always known that about himself. Ever since he was a boy and failed his mother. If only he'd fought harder.

You were just a boy . . . . Carrie's father had been there the day he was born. The fates certainly had had a hand in this episode of his life. The general had said his mother was brave. He'd always known that. And his father's bravery was legend.

Yet when his own trial had come at the hands of the Shawnee, he'd been a coward. He'd been grateful when they chose Tom for the fires instead of him. He'd cried when he saw how his friend suffered and died, and he'd lived in fear that it would soon be his turn.

"Fortis et Fidus."

His father had had a choice. He could have walked away from the battle. But he'd done what he thought was right even though it meant certain death.

"Brave and faithful."

Had his father made the right choice? He'd never know. Was he making the right choice? If he chose to wed Carrie, he had a chance at happiness. But he also had the chance of the biggest regret if harm came to her.

"Ye are a coward, Connor Duncan."

Efrem whistled to him, and Connor saw his friend wave him down. He must have found the cow. They were lucky, then. The meadow was just off the main trail between the fort and Anne's cabin, so they'd have no trouble getting her back.

The cow's freshly butchered body was not what he'd expected to find.

"They just took what they could carry," Efrem said. He had already made a circuit around the meadow, searching for tracks. "It looks as if they were here just a few hours ago."

"Shawnee?" Connor asked, even though he knew the answer. The hair on the back of his neck was on edge and his eyes scanned the tree line, even though Efrem had just made the circuit.

"They must have come from the north." Efrem's eyes followed the same trail as Connor's.

Connor looked off toward the west, where Anne's cabin lay. "We'd better get her and Will back to the fort."

"I wonder if any of the militia ran into them," Efrem said.

"We will ken that when they donnae show up."

They took off at a trot, their rifles in their hands as they paralleled the trail. They had not gone more than fifty paces when they heard a horse on the trail behind them.

"Militia?" Efrem asked Connor, who had turned his head to glance up the trail.

"Nay. 'Tis a redcoat," he said. " 'Tis Murray." He stepped out on the trail with his rifle resting in the crook of his arm.

When he saw Connor before him, Murray dug his spurs deep into the horse's sides. Did the man mean to run him down?

"I think he wants to kill you," Efrem said.

"Aye." Connor handed his rifle to his friend and stepped into the middle of the trail. "He can try if he likes."

Murray did not draw his sword, which was a good thing. Apparently he didn't intend to kill him straight off.

The horse came right at him and Murray leaned out and launched himself from its back. Connor was ready. He sidestepped and grabbed Murray, flinging him face-first in the leaves and pine needles that covered the trail.

Murray came up spitting blood and dirt and swung at Connor. He landed a blow to his jaw and Connor's head snapped with the punch.

"Where is she?" Murray yelled as he swung again.

Connor blocked his punch and returned with a left that spun Murray around. The captain followed up with a punch of his own.

"What have you done with Carrie?" Murray yelled again.

"Are ye daft?" Connor roared back. "I havenae seen her for a week."

"Liar!" This time Murray's hands went for his neck and his knee went for Connor's groin. Connor dropped like a bag of stones with Murray on top of him.

Murray's grip threatened to break his windpipe. Connor

grabbed Murray's wrists and wedged his thumbs between Murray's palms and his neck, loosening his hold. Before he could draw in a breath to relieve his tortured lungs, Murray came back with a punch. Connor blocked it, grabbed Murray's forearms and kicked up, which flipped Murray over his head. Connor twisted around, got on top of his opponent and pinned his arms at his sides.

Connor sucked in air as Murray struggled beneath him. Efrem placed the end of his rifle against Murray's cheek and his struggles stopped.

"What took ye so long?" Connor gasped.

"I thought it a battle of honor," Efrem said with a shrug. "If you wanted my help, you should have said so."

"It's hard to talk when your throat is being crushed," Connor said hoarsely.

"What have you done with her?" Murray demanded. His eyes bored into Connor, showing his hatred.

"I told ye, I have not seen her since I left the fort."

"She went out this morning to find you."

"She left the fort?"

"With Patsy. They fixed a basket to take to Mrs. Trotter to thank her for her care."

"You let her leave the fort by herself?" Connor's throat protested as he yelled at Murray.

"It's not as if she asked my permission," Murray yelled back. "She took off on her own."

"If she stayed on the trail, she would have found Anne's without a problem," Efrem said. "She probably just asked for directions at the gate. They wouldn't think anything of letting her go since they think the Shawnee are gone."

"But they are still here." Connor climbed off Murray and hauled the man to his feet.

Murray quickly jerked away and straightened his coat. "What do you mean, they're still here?"

"We found Anne's cow just a few minutes ago, freshly butchered. Another raiding party is passing through," Connor explained.

"We must find her," Murray said.

"Aye. We must. The first place to look is Anne's."

Murray found his horse and swung into the saddle. "Duncan." His eyes burned as he looked at Connor. "If anything has happened to her, I will kill you." He dug in his spurs and the horse took off down the trail.

"I fear we may be too late," Efrem said. He pointed over the trees. "Smoke."

Connor felt his stomach drop down to his knees. The smoke was coming from the vicinity of Anne's cabin. "It cannae be."

The two men took off at a run.

"If they are still there, Murray will likely be killed," Efrem said as they moved crosscountry, their long legs eating up the distance.

"He's foolish enough to challenge them," Connor said.

They spoke no more. Instead, they concentrated on running, their eyes on the smoke that hovered over the treetops.

"Connor!" Anne stumbled from the woods, dragging Will behind her.

"Carrie!" Connor grabbed the woman and held her up as she gasped for breath. "Where is Carrie?"

"They took her." Tears coursed down her face. "They killed Patsy. I was in the privy when they came. Will saw them sneaking up on the place and came for me. They had surrounded the house before I could do anything."

Anne was a brave woman and had seen a lot, but her voice broke. "They killed Patsy. They tomahawked her."

"Are ye sure they took Carrie?"

Let her be hidden somewhere. Let her be safe. Let it be someone else. Let it all be a bad dream.

Anne nodded. "We hid in the woods. I saw them tie her hands."

That meant something. If they were going to kill her, they would have done it right off. They were taking her back to their camp.

"How long has it been?" His mind whirled.

"A quarter of an hour. Maybe more. We stayed hidden until we were sure they were gone."

"We can catch them," Connor said. "They won't know we're coming."

Efrem nodded, and the two took off at a run again. Connor gripped his gun. His pack was at Anne's. His pouch rested on his hip, along with his horn and his knife and a pistol. How many were there in the raiding party? He and Efrem would have the element of surprise. They could come up beside the Shawnee in the wood. They could pick the raiders off one by one. They could get her back.

Or her captors would slash her throat and leave her bleeding in the dirt.

The house was in flames. The roof had caved in already. Which meant a good amount of time had passed. A half hour or more. How long had Anne hidden before she ran?

He saw Patsy's body lying on the stoop, her head split open and blood running out. He sped by, but Efrem stopped.

Connor saw the trail that led into the woods. There was still time. The raiding party could not travel as fast as he and Efrem could run. The Shawnee had prisoners. They would be slower. He could catch them.

"Duncan!" Murray charged from around the house, his gun in his hand. His face was contorted, wild with grief.

"They took her," Connor yelled. "We can still get her back."

"This is your fault, Duncan," Murray yelled, and raised his pistol.

"We have to go now!" Connor yelled and turned back to the trail. He saw something white up ahead and ran toward it.

He heard the shot, felt its impact in his back and stumbled face forward on the trail. The breath left his body as he hit the ground, and he lay there gasping, feeling the warmth of blood ooze out beneath him.

He reached out toward the white lace that lay alongside the trail. It was her cap. Her white lace cap. He clenched it in his hand.

"Carrie," he said as the darkness came.

Chapter Twenty-four

God help me.

Carrie was too frightened to speak the words aloud. All she could do was concentrate on keeping up as she was led by her bound hands through the dense woods. There were fifteen Shawnee. At least she guessed they were Shawnee, as that was the only tribe she'd heard anyone speak of. There were three other prisoners, a mother with two daughters. The woman seemed hollow, resolved. She just looked straight ahead as they were dragged along. The girls were terrified. All were filthy. They looked as if they'd been on the trail for several days.

Patsy was dead. For as long as she lived, Carrie would never forget the sight of the raised tomahawk above Patsy's head. Or the hollow thunk it made when it struck her skull.

Her skirt bore splatters of blood and brains. She refused to look at it. She was afraid that if the Shawnee saw her be sick they would kill her.

Why had they killed Patsy and spared her? When it had happened, she'd screamed until her throat was raw. She'd cowered on the porch as they threw the branches of fire inside the cabin. They'd dragged her into the yard and she'd been sure she was about to die. Instead, they'd tied her hands, leaving a long piece of thong with which to lead her.

What had happened to Anne? And Will? Anne had excused herself and gone out back to the privy. Carrie had heard a noise and thought it was Connor, returning from his hunt for the cow. Instead she'd found the savages sneaking up on the house. She'd tried to run, with Patsy right behind her.

Patsy was dead.

They'd thought it was safe. The men at the gate had assured them it was. The Shawnee were gone. It had been two weeks since they'd been sighted.

She hadn't even told her father where she was going. She'd prepared a basket of food to take to Anne in gratitude for her care.

It had also been an excuse to see Connor again. An excuse to perhaps pick up where they had left off the week before. A week without seeing him. It had seemed like a lifetime. Patsy needed no encouragement. The girl was so much in love with Efrem, it was amusing to watch. Carrie wondered if her feelings for Connor were as obvious to everyone.

If Connor Duncan had not figured it out by now, then he was more daft than she was.

Daftie lass . . .

She could still taste his kiss after many sleepless nights. Many nights of longing. Many days of loneliness.

And now she would never see him again. She would never see anyone she loved again. She was as good as dead.

Would she be better off dead like Patsy? How many times had Connor told her that being a prisoner of the Shawnee was worse than being dead? Had he not given her a gun to end her own life if she were captured?

What would they do to her?

Had they killed Connor and Efrem before capturing her? Was that why the men were gone so long? She and Patsy had waited most of the day for them to return. She'd been afraid she would have to go back to the fort before she saw him.

She'd been afraid he was staying away because he knew she was there.

Little had she known that there were greater things to fear.

The pace her captors set was so rapid she could hardly draw a breath. Her heart pounded in her ears from fear and exertion. Would it burst?

I don't want to die . . . .

Do ye not ken what they do to prisoners?

What *do* they do?

She had heard rumors, of course. Things talked about in hushed tones in the salons back home. Burning captives and disembowelment and other atrocities. Nothing that she believed. No one could be so cruel. Not even those they called savages.

Carrie looked at her captors. They were lean, hardened, filthy. Their clothing was a hodgepodge of garments they'd picked up along the way and put on over hide leggings. Red coats from soldiers, linen shirts, silk coats; one even wore an apron tied about his waist.

Why had they done this? Why had they come so far and killed so many? Wasn't this country big enough for everyone to live peacefully?

Why did they kill some and take others?

Why did they kill Patsy and spare her?

How long would it take to get where they were going? Where *were* they going?

I am lost . . . .

It was as if the forest had swallowed her whole. Trees swayed overhead, their tops so high and the branches so thick that she could not see the sky. The underbrush was so dense that her skirt ripped and tore with every step. Her arms were stretched out before her so she could not pick her skirt up, which made walking all the harder. The pace was so rapid, it was all she could do to stay on her feet.

The mid-summer sun was hot. And she was thirsty. The river that ran beside them was wide and shallow. She longed to drink from it, to lie down in it and let it carry her away.

It seemed they had followed the river for hours. All she would have to do was follow it back if she were lucky enough to escape. She could find her way.

How far was the fort? It couldn't be far. She could walk it in a day. It had been just past midday when the Shawnee attacked, and the sun was just now going down.

Surely the raiders would stop soon. They couldn't go on like this in the darkness.

But they did. They walked on, their path lit by the occasional glimpse of the moon.

It amazed her that the warriors helped the women over the rough path when they needed it, taking their arms, guiding the way, pulling them up the steep grade or keeping them from falling in the darkness.

Why?

They kept on until one of the girls was in tears. She couldn't stop crying, even when the men threatened her.

"Just kill me, then," the girl cried out.

The warriors talked in their strange language and mercifully they stopped.

The mother did not say a word.

Now then . . . when they sleep . . . Carrie watched them carefully. She would run the first chance she got. She would stay awake and make her way back along the river. She would hide in the underbrush as Connor had showed her. They would stop hunting for her and be on their way.

One of the warriors took her off to the side and motioned for her to squat and take care of her personal needs while he watched. Even though he could not see anything with her skirts billowed out around her, she was appalled. But she needed to go. Her face flamed with heat as the water she made trickled down a gully between her feet.

Then he laid a blanket on the ground and motioned for her to lie down. The fear that she'd kept at bay all day bubbled up in her throat.

Did he mean to rape her?

"No," she said, shaking her head and backing away as far as her leash would allow.

The warrior tugged on it and pulled her in. Carrie kicked and clawed until finally the man picked her up and slammed her on the ground so hard that the breath was knocked out of her body. She lay there and waited until she could breathe again. He wrapped the thong around his arm several times before he settled on the blanket next to her. He rolled her onto her side and placed his arm over her.

She lay there, tense and rigid. She felt every part of his body pressed up against her. She waited for him to do something, anything, but he did nothing, so she lay quietly and prayed that he would not touch her any more than he already had. Her muscles screamed in protest. Her calf, still sore, throbbed horribly. Her stomach felt hollow and her feet were raw. Rocks and twigs gouged into her side, but she dared not move.

There was no fire, but she was able to make out the other women, all imprisoned in the same manner as she. The girls cried quietly and the mother hummed and then sang the words of a hymn.

"Come thou long expected Jesus, born to set thy people free . . ."

She heard the steady breathing of the man who held her captive. Was he asleep? How could he be?

There was no way she could escape. If she dared to move he would feel it. She was exhausted and terrified and wanted nothing more than to close her eyes and pretend that this was all a horrible nightmare.

Eventually the girls stopped crying. The mother stopped

her singing. There was no noise except for the steady
breathing of the sleeping men and the sounds of the night
creatures, who gradually increased their chorus when they
realized there was no threat to them from the outsiders
who slumbered on the forest floor.

It seemed as if all the world was at peace.

God help me . . . .

Chapter Twenty-five

Andrew was sitting beside the bed when he awoke. Connor wearily opened his eyes, blinking in the sunlight that streamed through the window. The log walls of the room told his confused mind he was in a cabin, but the noise from the open window had the sound of a city.

"How long?" his voice rasped.

"Five days," Andrew said. "The shot went clean through, but you had a fever."

"Damn." Connor threw off his blankets and sat up. The room spun and he grabbed his head.

"Where do you think you're going?" Andrew asked.

"After her." Connor looked down at the bandage that was wrapped around his torso. He peeled it back to see the wound. It was healing nicely, thanks to Efrem, no doubt. But still . . .

"Damn," he said again. It was a miracle he was alive. The wound was amazingly close to his heart.

Your heart is in the wilderness with the Shawnee . . . .

"You're lucky to be alive, son," Andrew said. "Would you mind telling me what happened out there?"

Her cap . . . I found her cap . . . where is it?

"How did I get here?"

"Efrem carried you and Murray in on the back of a horse. Anne and Will were with him. He said you were attacked and the general's daughter taken. You were bleeding to death and Murray had a bump on the back of his head as big as my fist."

"Where is Efrem?"

"Eating. He's been out scouting."

Efrem didn't say a word. He's leaving it for me to settle with Murray.

"Where are my clothes?"

Andrew grabbed his arm. "She's gone, Connor. They sent out patrols. The militia is here. They've combed the woods. They found the trail, but then it disappeared . . ."

Connor shook off Andrew's hand. "I ken where they've taken her." He stood up, and once again the room spun, but he fought it, his body swaying as he willed himself to stay on his feet. "I'm going to get her back."

"You know what they'll do to you if they catch you."

"I ken it well."

He knew exactly what would happen. He knew exactly what he had to do. It did not matter. All that mattered was Carrie.

He found his shirt on a peg and pulled it on. It was mended, front and back. Bless Anne.

"Where is Murray?"

"He's been out looking for her."

"Gormless eejit. He's lucky he hasnae been killed several times over."

"He's near mad with grief."

"He should be," Connor roared. "It's his damn fault she's gone." His outburst made his head spin again and he touched his fingers to his forehead. There was no time for weakness or regret.

"What happened out there?" Andrew asked. "Her father has questions."

"Ask Efrem." Connor fought to get his temper under control. If not for Murray, he would have rescued her by now. "I was bleeding to death so I don't recall."

"Efrem hasn't said anything beyond what he told us when he brought you in. And Murray hasn't said anything at all."

"And he called me a coward." Connor jerked on his breeches and his moccasins. He spied his pack in the corner, along with his weapons, and he moved to gather them together.

"At least eat something first," Andrew said. "Since you seem determined to go."

"Aye," Connor said. "I am. And I will." He was weak from the wound and the fever. A meal would help.

The sun was too bright and the compound too crowded. The smell of too many men and animals in a small area was overwhelming. Andrew shouldered his way through the men who were gathered, waiting, for their orders to march.

"What's causing the delay?" Connor asked as he picked his way through the packs and weapons that lay in piles around the yard.

"Lord Dunmore plans to march with us."

Connor let out a laugh. "Out for fame and glory, is he? Does he plan to beat the Shawnee on his own?"

"He plans on putting an end to this," Andrew said.

"Then I wish him well," Connor said. "And tell him to hurry."

They reached the mess and found Efrem and Richard Trotter sitting at a table.

"You have survived," Efrem observed as both he and Richard greeted Connor with wide smiles.

"And I have ye to thank once again."

"And I cannot thank you enough for what you did for Anne and Will," Richard said.

"You would have done the same," Connor replied. He raised a questioning brow toward his friend.

Efrem quickly rose from the table and went outside with Connor. Andrew watched them leave with a frown on his face. He knew there was more to the story than what he had heard.

"What happened?" Connor asked. He felt weak and dizzy, but he had no time to coddle himself. He settled against a barrel while Efrem talked.

"I came from behind the house and saw Murray shoot you," he said. "He was about to put a bullet in your head when I hit him with the butt of my rifle."

"Which gave him a knot the size of Andrew's fist."

"Yes." Efrem grinned. "He was out of it for a day. The only problem I had was getting both of you on his horse. He wasn't so bad, but you were like pushing boulders uphill. It wasn't an easy task."

"So you're complaining about having to bring me back here after you saved my life?" Connor knew his friend was joking. It was their way.

"If I'd known it would be so hard on my back, I would have left you there."

"Ye should have," Connor said grimly.

"You are going after her?"

"Ye know I am. We could have rescued her if her brother wasn't such a fool."

"I found the spot where they spent the first night," Efrem said. "From the tracks, I counted fifteen Shawnee and four prisoners, all women. They met up with more Shawnee the next day. Fifty or sixty, with prisoners and some horses."

"I wonder if they have my Heather," Connor said. " 'Twould be nice to have that mare back again."

"I cannot tell the color of a horse by its tracks," Efrem said. "Nor the temperament of the man. They were pushing hard to get back across the Ohio. They left none behind."

Connor let out a sigh of relief at that news. Sometimes they left a captive behind as a warning—a very gruesome warning.

"What of Murray, then?"

"That is up to you," Efrem said. "It is your battle. He's been searching for her. He leaves every day at sunup and comes back at night. He realizes now the mistake he made."

"He was mad with grief," Connor said. "I would have done the same, I think."

"Blaming someone is always the easy part," Efrem said. "When do you wish to leave?"

"Ye are not going with me."

"That is my choice to make, not yours."

Connor placed his hand on Efrem's shoulder. "I watched one friend die in the fires, and I never thought I would have another as dear to me as Tom was. But I do. And that is something I never want to live through again."

"It is still my choice," Efrem said. "You are weak. I can either go with you or follow you. But if you fall, I will not pick you up or carry you. You're too heavy."

"I will likely knock you out and tie you to a tree," Connor said. He knew there was no arguing with his friend. And he would be glad for the company. But Efrem would not go with him to the village. It would be certain death for his friend, and his own life was all he was prepared to offer.

"You would have to catch me first," Efrem replied with a casual smile. He looked out over the yard and then pulled something from his pouch.

"You had this in your hand when I found you."

It was the lace cap. The sight of it tore at Connor's heart. Loss, anger, anguish and frustration all boiled inside him. He took it from Efrem and stuffed it inside his shirt. "She must have been wearing it."

"I found scraps of her skirt along the way. They weren't trying to hide their passage."

"We could have saved her," Connor said.

"We still can."

Connor appreciated Efrem's confidence. But he also knew the odds were against them. It was a long way to the Ohio, longer still across it and up the Scioto. Then they had to find the village where she'd been taken. And hope she was still there and not sold off as a slave.

Or dead.

His stomach lurched.

"Her father is coming," Efrem said.

Connor saw the general making his way across the yard. "If I must talk to him, then I will do it on a full stomach."

"I'll gather some supplies," Efrem said. "I've done a good job of avoiding him the past few days. I think I'll continue to do so."

He stepped away, and then came back. "I put Patsy in the fire," he said. "I will miss her."

Connor placed his hand once again on Efrem's shoulder and gave him a gentle squeeze. He went inside with the knowledge that the general would soon be in to talk to him. He joined Andrew and Richard at a long table to eat his meal.

The days since their last meeting had not been kind to General James Murray. His grief was evident on his face. But the man also seemed resolved, and Andrew and Richard made themselves scarce when he sat down across from Connor.

"I need to know what happened," he said. There was no preamble. No asking after his health.

"What does your son say?" Connor asked after he swallowed his last bite.

"He doesn't say anything. He just goes out every day and searches for her."

"He willnae find her."

"I know. She is gone. She is lost to us forever." The general covered his face with his hand and took a deep breath. Connor looked away while the man composed himself.

"Tell me what happened," he asked again.

"It does not matter," Connor said. "She was taken and I will get her back."

"How can you?"

"She can be ransomed if we get there in time."

"Whatever the ransom is, I will pay it."

Connor took a deep breath. He did not want to put into words what would happen when he found Carrie. He only knew what he had to do. He just hoped the Shawnee would honor the agreement he intended to make with them. It was the only way. He'd been ransomed before. They would not allow it again.

"I am afraid the price is one that only I can pay," Connor said. The general looked at him, and Connor saw understanding dawn in his eyes. Eyes that were the same color as his daughter's.

"Did my son shoot you?"

"What difference would it make if he had?"

"He would be punished," the general said. "He is a soldier. He knows his duty."

"Ye have lost a daughter, General. I see no need for ye to lose a son too. We all deal with grief in our own way."

"You love her." He said it as a statement, not a question.

"Aye. I do. I loved her from the first. But I was too much of a coward to admit it. She, on the other hand, was not."

The general smiled. "She is agreeable most of the time. But when she makes her mind up about something, there is no stopping her."

" 'Tis my fault she was taken," Connor said. "If I had not

been such a coward, she would not have felt the need to come looking for me."

"You were only doing what you thought was best for her. What was right for her. I, as a father, can appreciate that more than you will ever know."

"I will get her back," Connor said.

"When will you leave?"

"As soon as we're ready."

"Whatever you need . . ."

"I know."

"To think that a chance meeting so long ago would bring us to this place."

"Several things have brought us to this place," Connor said. "And the evil of men is one of them. All we can do is what we think right."

"I believe your mother would be proud of you."

"Aye. I hope so."

Efrem came in. He wore his pack and his weapons, and he was carrying Connor's things. "Whenever you're ready." He looked at the general. "Your son is back."

"He cannae go with us," Connor said. "He does not know the ways."

"He will be difficult to stop."

"I am confident you will find a way," Connor said. He took a final draught of his ale and slammed the cup on the table.

As the men stepped outside, Murray was just coming to the mess. He opened his mouth to speak, but before he could say a word Connor dropped him with a hard left across the jaw.

"Corporal," the general barked out, "place my son in the cell until further notice."

"Yes, sir." Men came and dragged Captain Murray away.

Connor gave the general a wry grin. "Overnight should be enough," he said.

"I'll make it a full day," the general said. "He needs time

to think about things. It will do him good." He shook Connor's hand. "I hope to see you soon . . . son."

Connor nodded. There was nothing he could say. He did not want his last words to the man to be a lie.

Chapter Twenty-six

The captives sat in a circle, their hands all tied before them. Six women, nine men and a boy of about seven who was not related to any of the others. They all tried to comfort him, but he did not seem to want their care. He was curious more than frightened, and Carrie wondered what kind of life he'd known before his capture.

"I have heard that the prisoners they adopt are treated well," Preston said beside her. He was the prisoner they'd seen on the trail the night that John was burning up with fever, the prisoner from John's company. He'd recognized Carrie when her captors joined up with the main group and felt it his duty to protect her. He was older than she by ten years or so, and the army was his life. He had no family beyond his brothers in arms who'd died in the attack.

Carrie did not mention the night they'd seen him pass by on the trail, mostly because to think of it was too painful. The feel of Connor's arms about her. The way his mouth moved against the top of her head. The words he spoke.

Shush, mo cridhe . . .

The girls that had traveled with her told her their brother had been taken by the Shawnee a few years back. Their mother was hoping they would all be reunited. Carrie was worried about the mother. She didn't seem right in her mind. She sang her hymns most of the time, and their captors seemed to enjoy her singing.

She tried to count the days, but they all ran together. She knew a few weeks had passed. Maybe more. They walked from dawn to darkness in sunshine and in rain. They drank water from the river. They ate once a day, but only if there was a kill.

Her clothes hung in tatters. Her shoes were split and barely stayed on her feet. Her hair was a mess of tangles and twigs and leaves. Dirt streaked her skin. There was nothing she could do about it.

Patsy was dead.

Would she ever forget her killing?

She saw it every time she closed her eyes.

Had anyone buried her? Or was she still lying there, her body decomposing or perhaps food for the birds and the animals? Was Patsy as forgotten as she was?

Stop feeling sorry for yourself . . . you are alive.

How long would she stay alive?

"Paul," she said to the boy. "Tell me what they are doing."

He was a pretty young boy with a cherubic face, golden brown hair and great green eyes. They never tied his hands or made him sit with the others. It was almost as if the warriors had taken a liking to him. They let him handle their weapons and taught him words in their language.

"They're getting some boats," he said. Paul stood at the bank overlooking the river, which Carrie had only glimpsed before she was commanded to sit. She knew it was wide. Wider than any she had seen so far. She also knew it was the boundary the war was being fought over. Once she crossed it, all hope was lost.

"I mean canoes," Paul said with a laugh at his mistake. "They had them hidden in the shallows."

"Your father and brother will ransom us," Preston said.

He had said it many times on their trek.

Connor had been ransomed. There was hope. But that was several years ago. Before there was a war. Before all the killings. How would her family even find them? This wasn't a war like the ones her father was used to fighting. This war wasn't civilized.

A civilized war . . .

She almost laughed at the words.

Wars were brutal. People died. Horribly. Tragically. Lives were changed forever. People were lost.

She was lost.

Ye donnae ken what they do to their prisoners . . . .

What did they do that made Connor fear them so? That made him think death was preferable?

The warriors were back. They pulled the captives to their feet and guided them down the bank, helping them so they would not fall because their hands were tied. She was used to it. The one who captured her touched her when he felt she needed help. But he never forced himself on her, and she was grateful for that. None of the women were accosted. Perhaps it was because the men simply didn't have the time or energy now.

They got in the canoes and the warriors paddled across. Carrie watched ripples feather out as the strong strokes of the men cut through the current, taking them across to a wilderness more vast than she'd ever imagined. Did it seem as if the trees on the western bank were taller than the ones on the east? Did the forest seem denser and darker?

And to think that at one time she'd yearned to see the wilderness.

The mother once again raised her voice in one of her hymns. She turned her face skyward, as if she were singing to God himself, and the warriors added their own chant with smiles and laughter.

They were happy to be so close to home.

They pulled the canoes up on a bank and took the prisoners to a clearing that overlooked the river. Then they told them to sit.

It was a strange change from the days past. It was just midday. The prisoners all looked at each other in confusion as the warriors settled into groups to talk. A few of them went about the business of building a fire, and one chopped down a sapling and cut the trunk into a section about three feet long.

"At last we're to enjoy a meal," Preston said hopefully.

Paul hung about, watching everything curiously. One of the warriors set him to dig a hole close to the edge of the bank.

Carrie closed her eyes and let her head drop. She was so tired. So weary. So very, very sad.

They all must be. The prisoners remained quiet. They did not talk much, except to exchange names and where they'd come from in case someone made it back to tell of their fate. There was never a chance to say much more.

The drone of the warriors speaking in a language she failed to understand lulled her into a doze. Her head jerked a few times and then she just let it go.

Her neck hurt. The pain shot down her back, but she was so tired, so weary, she chose to ignore it as she dozed. It was just pain. It would eventually stop, wouldn't it?

She let herself drift as she heard the talk in the background. Just drift. If she listened hard enough, she could hear the sound of the river rushing by below.

Where did it lead? If she were to jump in and let it float her away, where would it take her? West? Did it flow into an ocean? Or did it just run into another river like the rivers she'd walked along to get to this lonely place?

She imagined herself in the river. She lay flat on her back as she had learned as a child in the sea and floated with her hair spread out around her.

She kept her eyes closed and ignored the pain in her neck and concentrated on the river. If she thought about it long enough and hard enough, would it take her away? Take her back.

Back . . . there was no home . . . home was in the past. She'd come to the colonies to start a new life. To build a new home. Home didn't exist, but *back* was real. Back was her father, her brother . . .

Connor.

She saw him then. He ran toward her through the forest, his eyes blazing, his hair fiery copper around his face, his rifle in hand and his belt full of weapons.

He came for her. Her breath caught in her throat. Her heart leapt. Someone kicked her.

"What are you doing?"

Carrie jerked awake.

Where am I?

She was disoriented. Confused. Her eyes focused on a scuffle going on before her. The warriors had Preston. They were cutting off his clothes with their knives.

"What is happening?" she asked the others, but they all seemed as confused as she was.

Preston was naked. Carrie knew she shouldn't look, but she couldn't help herself. What were they doing?

Paul was standing by the hole he'd dug, only now the piece of wood the warrior had cut was planted in it. The boy tamped the dirt around the edges and tested it to make sure it would not move. He looked up at one of the warriors for approval, and the man nodded and rubbed his head, then gestured to him to move aside.

The end of the stick that stuck from the ground was sharpened to a point. A good two-foot section stuck up.

What were they doing?

The men lashed Preston's knees together with a section of rope, then tied his wrists to his knees.

Then they picked him up.

Preston bucked against them. His face was contorted in horror as they lowered him over the stick.

He screamed as it entered his rectum. They pushed him down and he screamed again.

He screamed, long and loud. Hideously. He tried to push up with his heels, and the dirt around him turned to mud as blood poured out of his body.

Oh, God . . .

Carrie emptied the contents of her stomach on the ground beside her. She wasn't the only one. She realized tears were running down her face as she wiped her mouth on the tattered remnants of her sleeve and retched again.

Oh God . . . are we next?

"I didn't know." Paul was beside her. Tears streamed down his face, streaking the dirt on his cheeks.

"It's not your fault," Carrie said. She raised her arms, and the boy crept beneath them so that her tied wrists circled around him, and he laid his head against her breast.

"We must pray for his soul," she said, and Paul nodded, but whether he prayed or not she did not know.

She prayed. She prayed for Preston, she prayed for Paul and she prayed for the other captives. Then she said a prayer for herself.

They sat and watched as Preston entered his death throes. It took an eternity as the sun seemed to creep across the sky. The mother prayed and sang and the rest of them just sat until the sun was behind them and Preston's movements stopped.

They checked to make sure he was dead. Then they cut away the rope, placed a blanket over his shoulders and laid a rifle in the crook of his arm.

He looked like a sentinel sitting on the bank.

Then they prodded the rest of them to their feet and walked away into the gathering darkness.

Carrie looked over her shoulder before they disappeared into the forest. Preston's body looked toward the east, back the way they came. It was left as a warning to any who dared to follow.

But no one was following. No one would come.

She was lost.

Chapter Twenty-seven

Memories of the last time he'd been in this place washed over Connor. He and Tom had stood in nearly the same place, where the Kanawha flowed into the Ohio, and celebrated like fools because they'd come so far. The Shawnee laughed when they came out of the woods with their guns pointed at their chests. They soon discovered the treasures he and Tom carried, furs from their great adventure, the last they would have before Tom settled down and married. The trip was supposed to provide the money he'd need to purchase a place of his own.

Instead it was his death sentence.

Connor lay on his belly with his spyglass at his eye. They'd been watching the man across the river for nearly an hour, and he still had not moved.

"I think he's dead," Efrem said.

"I think so, too," Connor said as he crawled backward from his spot into the shelter of the trees. He stuffed the spyglass in his pack. "And watching him rot isn't getting us anywhere."

"At least it's a good day for a swim," Efrem said.

"Ye are not to cross the river," Connor said. He placed his hand on his friend's shoulder. " 'Tis hard enough, what I have to do. I couldnae stand it if . . ."

Efrem placed his hand on Connor's shoulder. "I wish to help."

"Then help me by staying behind. If all goes as planned, ye should be waiting to bring her back."

"You should not have to do this."

"But I do." How could he explain his feelings to Efrem, who saw nothing but good in people? "Ever since Tom died, I've felt as if there is a beast inside my soul waiting to be punished. I should have died instead of him. But I didnae. Now is the time to make it right."

"How does your death make his dying right?"

"I could save her. I cannae bring back Tom, but I can make sure she is safe."

"She will not accept your sacrifice," Efrem said. "She loves you."

"She has to. That is why ye have to stay. I trust them to bring her safely to the river. They may be brutal, but they honor their word. Ye must take her back to her father."

"I feel the beast is one of your own making," Efrem said. "One you created from shadows and memories."

"Whatever it is, wherever it came from, I have to defeat it."

Efrem squeezed his shoulder. "I will pray that the beast does not kill you," he said. "And let these words carry you on your way.

The Lord is my shepherd; I shall not want . . ."

Connor bowed his head and recited the Twenty-third Psalm with his friend. If prayer gave Efrem peace, then so be it. And if some rubbed off on him . . .

"Peace be with you, friend," Efrem said when they were done.

Connor nodded in agreement and squeezed Efrem's shoulder in farewell.

He went down to the river and found a log washed up

along the bank. He took off his shirt and his moccasins, placed them in his pack along with his pouch, knives and pistol. He wedged his rifle on top of the log along with his pack and set it afloat. He swam alongside with one arm anchoring his belongings on the log.

The current was fierce. It was difficult to swim straight across, so he let the river wash him downstream a bit.

Connor shook off the water like a big dog when he reached the opposite bank. He quickly dressed, gathered his things and made his way back up river to where the still form sat looking over the water's edge. He circled the clearing and saw no signs of life, so he stepped out toward the bank.

The smell was horrible. Flies covered the blanket and the head of the corpse. Connor wondered what was holding the man erect. The ground around him was stained dark with dried blood, and he had a suspicion as he jerked off the blanket.

It was a horrible way to die. The Shawnee were creative in that respect.

From the look of the body, Connor figured he was three days or so behind the raiding party. Which meant he and Efrem had picked up time on the trail. It also meant he'd never catch up with the Shawnee before they made the village.

The man deserved a burial. But time was something Connor did not have. Efrem would take care of it. Connor said a prayer for the unknown man, crossed himself and covered the corpse with the blanket, this time making sure his head was protected too.

He looked across the river and saw Efrem wave to him in farewell.

Connor waved back and made his way into the woods, knowing his friend would at least cross the river to see about the dead man.

He circled the edge of the forest once again, looking for some sort of sign that Carrie had made it this far.

If only he'd caught up with the raiding party before they'd crossed the river. On the trail he could have taken the chance of sneaking in at night and spiriting her away.

Once the raiders reached the village, it would be another matter. And he didn't even know where the village was. He could go down to the mouth of the Scioto and follow it up. He knew the village would be somewhere along its banks.

But his best bet was to cut crosscountry. If only he could find a sign. A sign that showed she was still alive.

And then he saw it. Just the barest scrap of pink. The same pink as her skirt, a bit of fabric snagged on a tree root.

You will run out of fabric before we get there . . . .

Would she run out of life before he got to her?

He set off at a trot through the forest.

What was she thinking? Did she realize he would come for her? But how could she? Time and time again he'd sent her away. He'd told her he did not want her.

She must realize he'd been lying.

Hadn't he told her the night they kissed that he could not let her go?

Then ye went off and left her, ye fool . . . .

Was there anything he could have done that would have made a difference?

Yes. He could have abandoned her the night of the ball. He could have left her to the ponce.

But he could no more abandon her then than he could now. She was part of his destiny.

He covered the ground at a quick pace as he stuck to a narrow path he found. The broken bits of fern and scattered leaves led him to believe he was on the right trail.

Without thinking he put one foot in front of the other, his main desire to make up time.

As his body settled into the rhythm of his run, his mind wandered back to the path he'd been on years earlier. In a month or so, it would be the same time of year as when he and Tom were taken.

The leaves had not yet turned on the trees when they headed west. Tom was to be married in the spring, and they knew the animals would all be fattening up for the winter, putting on their heaviest coats. They were sure the haul would be plentiful in the western wilderness, and being young and sure of themselves, they set off on an adventure.

They were successful too. A success that the Shawnee took advantage of. The last time Connor had set foot on this ground, he was tied with his hands behind his back and a noose around his neck.

They'd led him and Tom as if they were dogs. They'd had another prisoner with them, an English officer captured from somewhere up on the Monongahela. The prisoners tried to keep each other's spirits up. They were sure they'd be ransomed.

The Shawnee stripped them when they got to the village. The prisoners ran the gauntlet, the women and children hitting them with switches and rocks while the men used their fists.

Later, when he learned the Shawnee language, Connor was told that dying by fire was a trial for the next life. That if a man did it with dignity, then he would have great riches and honor when he passed into the next world. But how could a man die with dignity when the flesh was being burned from his body? How could he face the torture the next day when his tormentors tended to his wounds at night so they could start all over again the next morning?

How was he supposed to stop himself from screaming and crying and begging someone to put a bullet in his brain because the pain was more than he could stand?

Connor had been tied to a tree and he'd watched it all. He'd heard it all. He'd cried because he'd been sure his turn would come next.

And he'd known without a doubt that he would have no honors or riches in the next life. Because he was a coward.

The Shawnee would make Carrie run the gauntlet.

They would strip off her clothes and beat her, marring the perfection of her skin.

Would she be strong enough to stand it? Did she know that she had to stay on her feet, to run through, or they would make her do it again?

Then what would they do? Would some brave want her for his wife? Would some woman claim her as a slave? Would they send her off to one of the northern villages where a French trader could make her into a whore?

Or would they send her to the fires?

He had to get to her. She was only three days ahead. How far was the village?

Would he make it in time?

Be strong, lass . . . I am coming . . . .

Chapter Twenty-eight

There were so many of them. Everywhere she looked there were Indians. From wizened old women to babies in their mothers' arms. From bent old men to strapping young warriors.

And they were all yelling. Screaming. Raising their hands in victory.

But then some of the women looked at the arriving warriors and realized their husbands or brothers or sons were not with them. They wailed their pain. Some of them fell to the ground, their bodies curling up as their grief poured out.

The prisoners were pushed and pulled and jerked and prodded until they arrived at a series of posts set into the ground. There they were tied by their leashes and left as the tribe all moved off together to a long, low structure. They even tied Paul, who had been strangely silent since the episode on the riverbank.

"It's the council house," one of the men said. "It's where they'll decide what to do with us."

"Do they mean to kill us all?" another of the men asked.

"We'll see," the first replied. His name was Jack, and he seemed to have some knowledge of the Shawnee. "Some of us will be kept to replace the ones they lost."

Carrie sank wearily to the ground. She was too exhausted to think. If she were going to die, then let it happen. Just let it be over with.

Time seemed to stop. The sun beat mercilessly upon them, and she was overcome by bone-shattering weariness and the fear that death was imminent. She had no idea whether minutes or hours had passed when they heard shouts and cries coming out of the council house.

Why couldn't time have stopped the night Connor kissed me?

The time with him had been too brief. What would have happened if things had been different? What if she was a shop girl in Williamsburg instead of the governor's niece? Or what if he was a lord who'd attended the ball in hope of finding a wife?

"It wasn't meant to be," she murmured. He was right; fate did not want them together.

"They're coming," Paul said.

"Heaven forbid."

The entire mob poured forth from the council house. They screamed, and most of them brandished sticks and rocks in their hands.

The warriors who'd captured them removed the prisoners' bonds and stripped off their clothes.

Carrie felt many hands upon her. She grabbed at her bodice, but the fabric was weak. Her skirt ripped away, her petticoats, her bodice, until she was down to her shift and her stockings, and they cut those away with her knives.

She tried to cover herself, her face flaming with shame. She pulled her hair around her as best she could.

They were all naked. The men kept their hands in front of their private parts and the women tried to use their hair, but the Shawnee only jeered at their attempts at modesty. The warriors jerked and pulled and prodded them toward the villagers, who formed two lines.

"The gauntlet," Jack said. "We have to run it."

"I don't understand," Carrie cried.

"You have to stay on your feet. If you don't, they will beat you to death," he said.

Already one of the sisters was shoved into the line, and the people swung their fists and their sticks at her bare back and pushed her from one side to the other.

One by one they went through. The first sister made it. The other one fell, and her mother cried out and tried to help her, only to be shoved back with her nose spouting blood. Finally the girl got up and staggered down the line.

Paul's turn came, and they seemed to be gentle with him. Carrie saw them poke him halfheartedly, and some of them laughed as if it were a game.

Then came her turn. Someone shoved her forward and she felt a stinging blow across her cheek. Blood poured out, but all she could do was put her head down and run. She threw her arms up to protect her head as her hair was pulled and she was punched and kicked while blows from sticks rained on her back. Miraculously she stayed on her feet. When she reached the end, a woman smiled approvingly at her and handed her a blanket to wrap up in.

Then she realized the captives were being formed into two groups. She, Paul, one of the daughters, the other two women and four of the men were in one group. They were all given blankets and then led toward the river. The others were still naked and were led to the posts.

What was happening?

The women who surrounded them seemed happy. They smiled as they gently took the blanket away and walked Carrie and the rest of the prisoners into the shallow water and splashed water upon them. Then the women scrubbed at their skin in earnest.

It was impersonal. Carrie tried her best to cover herself, but the women just laughed and smiled and chattered on as they picked up handfuls of sand and rubbed it into her skin, then rinsed it off. She saw that the others in her group were getting the same treatment. The women splashed playfully at Paul and made a production over the men, as if they were being considered for something. There was much whispering behind hands.

Carrie wanted to ask what would happen next. Jack was one of the men in the river, but she was too embarrassed to speak to him while they were both naked.

The women brought forth an earthen jug and used it to pour water over her hair; then they lathered a mixture into her scalp and rinsed away weeks of dirt.

When they were satisfied that she was clean, they dressed her in a hide dress and leggings. One of them placed a poultice on her cheek where it was cut, and she immediately thought of Efrem. Efrem and his healings ways. Healing that was part of his heritage. And part of the Shawnee's too.

But then she remembered what the warriors had done to Preston and Patsy, and her momentary wonder at their kindness was gone.

"What will they do to us?" she asked Jack as they were led back to the village.

"We are safe for now," he said, but he did not seem relieved. "But the rest . . ." His voice trailed off as he motioned with his chin toward the six who were still naked and tied to the posts. The mother sang and prayed with her arms around her daughter while the men pulled at their ropes.

"Pray for their souls," Jack added.

The daughter heard him.

"What will they do?" she asked.

Jack clamped his mouth shut and kept walking with his captors.

"What will they do?" the girl asked again. "Why are we washed and dressed while they are still . . ." Her face changed horribly as realization swept over her. "Noooo," she cried out. She tried to run toward her mother, but the women grabbed her and would not let her go.

"Heaven fobid," Carrie said as she was prodded along. The girl screamed for her mother, who seemed to be praying harder. The women tried to hold her back, and one even slapped her.

"Come here," Carrie said. She broke away from the woman holding her arm and put her arms around the girl. "What is your name?" She knew she'd been told, but it was hard enough to remember her own name under these circumstances.

"Elizabeth," the girl said.

"Elizabeth, you must be strong for their sake."

"Are they going to kill them?" Elizabeth whispered.

"I believe so." Carrie saw no point in lying.

"In the fires." Her voice quavered. "I heard they burn them in the fires."

"It very well could be," Carrie said. "I don't know."

"Why? Why are they doing this?"

Carrie shook her head. She looked at the village, at the women who gently herded them along, at the children who were gathered around Paul, chattering like magpies. The scene reminded her of the small towns that lay between Williamsburg and the wilderness. The houses were different, the clothing was different, but the bustle, the chores, the play were the same.

Except for the prisoners tied to the posts.

"They are evil," one of the women in their group said. "Why can't they just leave us alone?"

"I wonder if they say the same thing about us," Carrie said, more to herself than to her comrades. "You must be brave," she said to Elizabeth. "Your mother would want you to be strong."

Elizabeth nodded before one of the Shawnee women led her away.

If only Carrie understood what was happening. If only she knew what they planned for her. For all of them. They were all separated, all taken to different places, with different people.

The sun dropped behind the treetops and autumn's first chill touched her cheeks as a cold wind blew in from the west. Those left outside would surely be cold. They would be miserable. Did their captors care?

Carrie was guided to a hut. The warrior who'd first captured her was inside, along with a woman close to her age who held a baby in her arms. A little girl peered shyly from around the mother's back. The older woman who'd given her the blanket and bathed her prodded her inside and pointed to a place on a blanket.

Carrie sat and gratefully took the clay bowl that was handed to her. She didn't know what it was, nor did she care. She scooped the food up with her fingers and ate. The family watched her for a moment, then ate also.

The fire was warm and her eyes grew heavy. She watched the family as they watched her. Their images seemed to recede, as if they were shrinking in size. Carrie did not remember lying down, but she knew that someone placed a blanket over her shoulders.

She took it and tucked it up under her chin as a vision of Connor filled her mind. It was the same one she'd seen on the banks of the river.

She saw him running through the trees toward her. His copper hair flew out around him in a blaze. It seemed as if his hair was aflame. Then she realized it was, and the flames ignited the trees, which were bright with the colors of fall. She watched in wonder as he ran through the flames until she realized that Connor himself was the flame.

He was burning. His mouth was opened wide and a scream came forth, only it was not his voice, it was a woman's.

The scream woke her. Carrie blinked against the morning light that poured through the opening in the hut.

I slept through the night . . . .

A horrible smell assailed her nostrils and she fought the impulse to gag.

She heard the scream again, louder and shriller, as it echoed over the yells and calls of the villagers.

The hut was empty. Carrie stumbled to the opening, her feet and mind still tangled up in her dream. The air that greeted her was cool and crisp. Autumn was upon them.

The people of the village were gathered in a circle. Carrie rubbed her eyes as she made her way toward the sounds.

What is that smell?

Then she heard the singing. The words of hymns carried over the cries and screams.

It was the mother. The mother and daughter were being forced into the flames of a fire that roared up nearly as tall as she was. They ran out of the flames only to be shoved back into them by the men of the village.

Carrie watched in horror as the mother sang and the daughter screamed and the men who were still tied to the posts watched, knowing their time would soon come.

And Elizabeth stood in the circle with the woman who'd adopted her and watched. Tears streamed down her face and Carrie saw her mouth move, but she could not hear the words.

All she could hear were the screams.

She stumbled away with her hand over her mouth as her stomach rebelled against the sight. Tears blinded her eyes, but she made her way to the river, only stopping when she reached its edge.

The full impact of Connor's words came back to her.

"Do ye not ken what they do to their prisoners?"

Now she knew. She knew why he'd told her to kill herself before she was captured. He'd been here. He'd seen it. He knew about the fires. He'd watched as someone burned.

How do you watch something like that? How can you stand it? How did Elizabeth stand it, knowing that her mother and sister were dying horrible deaths?

She prayed.

Carrie looked toward the heavens. The morning light that had awoken her was quickly fading away beneath a heavy covering of clouds that blew in from the west. There would be rain soon. Would the rain stop the fires? Would the victims meet a merciful end then?

A dog from the village ran by with a long bone in its mouth. Tall and lean, of indeterminate heritage, it searched for a place to hide its treasure while no one was watching.

No one is watching . . . .

No one was watching her. They thought her asleep, or else they were so caught up in the ritual that they did not care. Did they think that she would stay put? She turned and saw that the entire village was engrossed in the death struggles of the two women.

Could she?

All she had to do was head east. And then follow the river.

But how would she survive? Did it matter? Her chances of surviving here were just as slim.

And just as she made up her mind to run, a tall, striking Shawnee woman walked up to her. Carrie looked at the woman in amazement. She was as tall as most men and looked just as strong.

"You cannot go," she said in English. "Your new family will bring you back."

"They are not my family," Carrie said.

"They are now," the woman said. "They chose you to replace one of their own who died. It is an honor that others would be grateful for."

Carrie knew she was talking about the women in the fire.

"Who are you?"

"My name is Nonhelema. I am sister to Keigh-tugh-qua. He is the leader of the Southwind people."

"You know English?"

Nonhelema smiled at Carrie's question, and she felt her face flush with embarrassment.

"Why are they doing this?"

"As punishment for the sins of your people."

"But they . . . those women . . . what did they do?"

"They were on our sacred land. They abused it."

It was that simple. The Shawnee would do whatever they could to protect the land.

"My people have lost patience with the way of peace," Nonhelema explained. "And they grow weary of the lies told to them. So weary that they do the very thing they accuse the whites of doing. They were not always so bitter."

"You can't replace people," she said.

Nonhelema looked at her in confusion.

"You said I am to replace a lost family member. But you can't replace someone like that. You can't replace a father or a brother or a . . ." What was Connor to her?

Nothing more than a dream.

Carrie wiped the tears from her cheeks. "Who am I supposed to replace?"

"Piaserka was impressed with the patience and fortitude you showed on the trail," Nonhelema said.

"My patience and fortitude?" Carrie asked. "I was terrified."

"He knows that," Nonhelema said. "That is why he was impressed. He thinks you will make a good wife."

"A good wife?" Carrie asked. "I have no desire . . ."

"He lost his wife and son in childbirth last winter," Nonhelema interrupted. "His sister lost her sister. His mother a daughter. It is a great honor they have bestowed upon you."

"I don't want it," Carrie said. "I want to go back."

Back to where? Williamsburg? Fort Savannah? England? *Connor . . . a meadow . . . a dream . . .*

"If you do not accept him, they will sell you to the French, who will not use you as kindly as Piaserka."

"I am to be a slave then?" Carrie asked incredulously. "A whore?"

"Here is your mother now," Nonhelema said, in clever

avoidance of her question. "Do not dwell on the past," she advised. "Look to the future."

The woman who'd cared for her the night before came to Carrie, took her arm and led her away.

This is supposed to be my mother now?

"I want to go back."

Chapter Twenty-nine

The land was much flatter that he was used to. It was hard to find a vantage point to look around himself. But all the signs told him he was close. The land was well used. Game was scarce. The woods were clear of fallen trees and stray branches and most of the nuts and berries had been picked.

Connor was cold and wet from the rain the day before. He ignored his discomfort, but he had to admit that the weather was slowing him down. With each passing day, his hopes of finding Carrie diminished. If they sold her off to another tribe, he would never find her. And if they chose to sacrifice her . . .

He would have to move in closer.

He could not be captured. His plan depended upon his walking into the camp on his own. It was the only way they would accept the trade.

It was the only way to save her.

The air was heavy. The clouds oppressive. Almost suffocating.

Or maybe it was just his fear. He ran along the river and

made sure he had plenty of cover as he moved toward the
northwest. He soon came to a bend in the river, one with
a slight rise, and crept forward on his belly with his spyglass in hand when he noticed a trail of smoke hanging
over the treetops.

There was a village. A big one. The important thing was
to make sure she was there before he did anything drastic.
A blond head among the many dark ones should be easy
to find.

Should be . . .

Connor said a silent prayer as he tried to focus on the
people who moved in and out of his vision.

The fire smoldered. Nothing left but the remnants of
wood and whatever victim had suffered in its flames. He
finally saw five posts in the ground, three of them with
men tied to them.

Men who, even at this great distance, he could see were
full of despair.

How many had died since they'd been brought to this
place?

Was he too late to save her?

He would have to get closer to find out.

He circled the village. Connor made sure he stayed far
enough away that the dogs would not scent him. The
smell from the fires was horrible enough to give him a
sense that the dogs would not be a problem. The problem
was picking Carrie out from the mass of people who stood
around the fire. Even though her golden hair should
stand out, there was too much smoke from the wet wood
for him to see her.

He found a sturdy maple and pulled himself up into its
branches until he was high enough to get a good view of
the village. He pulled his spyglass from his pack.

His heart pounded in his chest as he moved the glass
back and forth around the crowd until he caught a glim-
mer of gold.

She was alive. His hands shook as he tried to keep the

glass focused on Carrie. Connor took a deep breath and tried again.

She wore a Shawnee dress and her hair hung in two braids over her shoulders. There was no doubt in his mind that it was Carrie. He knew her face better than he knew his own. He watched as she moved her hand across her cheek, and saw that one side of her face bore a long gash.

From the gauntlet, no doubt. But she was alive. An old woman held on to her arm. They were forcing her to watch the fire.

She's alive . . . .

A feeling of such intense relief washed over him that he grabbed the trunk of the tree and placed his forehead against the rough bark.

She's alive . . . .

"Lord, give me strength."

There was nothing left now but to do it. He circled back to a wash he found by the river. High waters had carved out a notch in a small hillock and taken a tree down with it. The tree, a thick oak, lay on the bank of the river with its branches curved over the mound of earth. Behind was a cave of sorts, high enough for a man to sit in, and long enough to lie down in.

Connor placed his rifle inside, along with his pack, his knife, his tomahawk and two pistols. He arranged them carefully with the knowledge that this would be the last time he would touch them.

He bent his head in prayer, crossed himself, then removed his shirt and placed it next to his pack.

He had nothing to hide. Nothing to trade. Nothing to sacrifice but his life. The Shawnee would know it when he walked into the village.

Goose bumps covered his flesh as he walked into the river and washed away the dirt, sweat and worry of his days on the trail. He shivered as he moved against the current.

It didn't matter. He would be warm soon enough.

Connor stayed in the water. He knew in his heart that

Efrem was probably a half day behind him. He didn't want to leave a trail that led back to his friend. He also knew that Efrem would watch for Carrie.

For Carrie . . .

One night with her would have been . . .

There was no need to think of what could have been. There was no need for regret. This was his destiny.

How many more days would this last? With the advent of the rain, Carrie had hoped the torture would be over. Instead it was just put off. The man they'd condemned to the fires after the horrid deaths of the mother and daughter was given a reprieve, nothing more. They took him in and tended his burns, and then they brought him out again when the rain stopped. It had not stopped for long. Even now the sky was heavy, threatening. Perhaps it would hasten the death of the current sacrifice.

Her new family always kept an eye on her after that first day. The old woman insisted she stay by her side. She did not go anywhere without Carrie, and Carrie had learned to do what she was told. She wondered how far she would have gotten if she had escaped instead of being stopped by Nonhelema.

Carrie spent most of her time watching the tall, striking warrior woman. Even though she was forced to stand by the fires with her new family as the prisoners were punished, they could not make her watch the slow and agonizing deaths. Instead she studied the people. Nonhelema did not approve of what they did. Several times she saw her pleading with her brother, the chief called Keigh-tugh-qua. And each time she walked away in frustration.

It seemed as if the entire village was consumed with hatred for the whites. Except for a few such as Nonhelema. Yet the family who'd taken her in treated her with some measure of kindness.

Carrie wondered how long the kindness would last. The

warrior, Piaserka, watched her. Even now she saw his dark eyes on her from across the fire. He wanted her for a wife. How long would it be before he decided to take her?

"God help us all," Jack said from his place close by. The man in the fire had been taken from the same settlement as Jack. He did not scream or cry as the others had. He bore the torture well, if such a thing could be done. The assemblage seemed to be impressed. They sang respectfully as he died.

It was horrible.

All of it. No matter what the justification, no one deserved to die in this manner. Not the settlers who tried to carve a home for themselves out of the wilderness, not the traitors to the crown back in England who were sentenced to horrible public executions, or the Christians who were burned and tortured in Rome. From the beginning of time, man had sought horrible ways to punish his enemies, yet wars continued, suffering continued, man's inhumanity to man continued.

When would it stop?

Carrie numbed herself to the horror with her thoughts. When the man in the fire finally succumbed to death, she silently said a prayer as the villagers turned away, their attention suddenly caught by the arrival of two men.

One was white, the other Indian. They were instantly surrounded by the warriors of the village, who quickly let them to Keigh-tugh-qua.

Carrie was amazed to hear the white man speak French and her mind, temporarily confused by her ordeal, whirled in an attempt to understand what was happening.

"The English are coming."

The English were coming. Coming here? Were they even now marching upon the village? Was it possible?

His Indian companion gave details, while the Frenchman's eyes swept the crowd gathered around. His eyes landed on her, and she felt a sudden chill go down her spine as he leered at her. She wanted to hear what he had to say, but also felt the need to escape his greedy stare. She tried to move away, but the old woman grabbed her arm in a tight grip.

Suddenly the villagers broke out into cries of anger.

Carrie felt herself being swept away in a tide of madness. She saw Jack go down among a barrage of punches and kicks. One of the other surviving men was grabbed and stripped and taken to the fire. A warrior grabbed Paul and ran toward the woods.

The woman who held on to her arm chattered rapidly. Carrie did not understand a word she said, but it did not matter. She wrenched her arm free, shoved the woman down and ran as fast as she could toward the trees.

She was free. The villagers were concentrating on the fire. Even now she could hear the screams. She spared a brief thought for Paul, for Elizabeth, for Jack and the others who remained. The cries behind her grew dimmer as she ran as hard as she could between the trees. She could not believe it was so easy. Her heart pounded and she could not breathe, so she stopped, her hand clutching the stitch in her side as she turned to look behind her.

Trees. Nothing but trees. Trees close together with narrow trunks whose lower branches were stunted because of the thickness of the canopy above. The leaves above her head were stunning in their color, especially against the heavy gray of the clouds, which seemed to skim right above the intertwined branches.

In every direction she turned she saw nothing but trees. She was not sure which direction she'd come from.

Then she heard a noise. A thick pop, as if a branch had broken. Carrie took off again, running as hard as she could. Behind her she heard the hard pounding of feet. She heard harsh breathing. She heard a curse . . . in French.

She ran until she thought her lungs would explode. Then she kept on. It wasn't until she felt a hand brush her back, then wrench her hair, that she went down in an explosion of dead leaves. She hit the ground hard and skidded as something heavy landed on top of her.

Carrie twisted. She turned. She bucked, she clawed, she blindly struck out with her fists until her head exploded into a red haze as a fist struck her cheek.

"They will have you for the fires, my sweet," a heavily accented voice said in her ear. "But first I will taste you so your life will not be wasted."

"No." Carrie turned her head away. His breath stank. His body stank. His beard rasped against the skin of her neck. He lay prone over her and she could not move until he lowered his hand to yank up the hide dress she wore.

"You do not have a choice in the matter," he said. He was casual about it. As if he'd done this before. His hand pushed up her dress and Carrie kicked out. She felt the rough grasp of his fingers against the tender skin of her thigh as he found the top of her leggings. She twisted beneath him, but her movements only served to push up her dress further.

"No," she gasped again as he pinned his arm over her chest while he raised himself up to get to the lacing on his breeches.

She bit his arm and he let out a screech. His head bent back, as if someone was pulling on it, and Carrie realized that a Shawnee held him by his hair. She kicked out from beneath the Frenchman as the Shawnee's knife settled against his forehead.

Carrie watched in horror as the Shawnee lifted the Frenchman's scalp. Wasn't he supposed to be the tribe's friend? Hadn't he warned them about the attack? Was she to be next?

The Frenchman screamed his pain but still had the presence of mind to pull his own knife and bury it in the Shawnee's thigh. The Indian quickly slit his throat and then brandished the scalp over his bleeding body.

Carrie watched it all, unable to move. She was paralyzed with fear. The Shawnee pulled the knife from his thigh and flung it aside. Then he took a step toward Carrie.

She looked at the bloody scalp he still held in his hand. She looked at the knife. She looked at the man who lay behind him, his body convulsing as his life's blood coursed out on the ground.

It was raining. Just an easy drizzle, enough to dampen her clothes and give her a chill. Her teeth chattered as she looked up into the eyes of the warrior.

He means to kill me . . . .

She flipped over, and her hands reached out as she forced her legs to raise her, to escape, to run for her very life. Just as she found her feet, the warrior grabbed them and she fell forward. She felt herself being dragged backward.

Once more she was on her back. Once more a man straddled her. Once more she lashed out with her fists and bucked against his weight.

The warrior pulled his tomahawk from his belt and raised it over his head.

This is it. This is my death. I came all the way across the ocean just to die alone in a savage wilderness . . . .

Time stopped for her as her life passed before her eyes. From her childhood up to this very moment, she saw it all unfold in her mind's eye as she watched the sharp edge of the tomahawk swing toward her skull. And in that moment that was too short to measure, she felt only one regret.

"Connor . . ."

Connor had been about to enter the village when the Frenchman and his Indian companion arrived. He'd heard the roar of the villagers at the newcomers' announcement. When he saw Carrie take off, he'd ignored the bedlam that broke out, setting out after her at a dead run. But he'd lost her among the thick trees. The branches of the saplings whipped against his chest as he plunged through the woods.

Now he heard a crashing. He heard the impact of flesh against flesh. And as he burst through a stand of trees into a small hollow he heard his name said as if it were a prayer.

"Connor."

A Shawnee straddled her with his tomahawk raised over his head, ready to strike a death blow. Carrie struggled desperately beneath him.

Connor put his shoulder down and dove toward the warrior with his arms outstretched.

They crashed into the ground, both of them skidding against the rain-slick leaves until they thumped into the trunk of a tree.

Where was the tomahawk? Connor realized he was weaponless, whereas the Shawnee was not. He was also dazed and breathless, but there was no time to recover. He rolled to his feet, his eyes searching, his body poised, his muscles tensed as he tried to spot the weapon.

And Carrie. What about Carrie?

The tomahawk lay on the ground below him. The Shawnee saw it at the same time, and they both dove for it.

Connor's hands came up empty so he rolled toward the Shawnee, who was scrambling to his feet. The Indian raised his arm for the killing blow, and Connor grabbed the forearm that held the weapon as he took the man's feet out from under him. They rolled down into the hollow, and Connor was vaguely aware of Carrie moving around . . . was she kicking the Shawnee?

The lass was trying to help, bless her. He felt the thump of her foot against the Shawnee, who was on top of him; then he heard her fall to the ground in a flurry of leaves.

It was pouring rain now. Pouring as if the heavens were suddenly in a hurry to get rid of all the water held in the clouds above. Rain pounded against his eyes and sluiced

around the head of the Shawnee, who was desperately trying to free his arm.

Connor held on for all he was worth. He did not dare
let go, but he could not get an advantage. Something had
to give. It was the Shawnee. He realized his tomahawk was
not doing him any good, so he reached around behind
him for his knife.

Connor swung his elbow and struck the man in the jaw.
His head snapped back and he lost his grip on Connor's
rain-slick chest. Connor jerked the tomahawk from his
hand as the warrior brought up his knife.

The blade pierced his forearm and tore a path through
the flesh as Connor swung the tomahawk with all his
strength. Connor heard a heavy *thock* as the edge sank
into the Shawnee's neck. Blood spurted forth as the man's
eyes bulged and his head fell over at a strange angle.

Connor had nearly cut it off.

He kicked the man away and wiped the blood from his
eyes.

Carrie crashed into his chest with a sob. He was covered
with rain and blood and her hands slid in all directions as
she wrapped her arms around him. His skin, chilled as it
was, instantly warmed as she filled the place that had felt
so empty for so long.

They might still die, and would most likely if they did
not move, but he had to hold her, just for a moment.

"You came for me," she cried. "You came."

His arms tightened around her. "Did ye think I wouldnae?"

"You're bleeding," she said.

Connor squeezed her tighter. "How can ye tell?"

"I lost my petticoats," she said. "How can I bandage
your wounds?"

"Daftie lass," he said. "If we don't get away from this
place, there won't be enough petticoats in the world to
help us."

He took her hand and jerked the tomahawk from the Shawnee's neck as he pulled her away from the stench of death.

"They're coming," she said as they ran for their lives.

Chapter Thirty

They ran through the trees. Carrie had a vague idea that they were moving in a circle. Connor seemed to know where he was going. They came to a river, shallow and wide, and he led her down the middle of it.

He wasn't worried about the noise, and she realized that it was raining so hard, no one would hear them. The rain would also wash away the signs of their passing.

The water moved quickly, hastened by the rain. They were moving with the current, and several times it nearly swept her off her feet. Only Connor's solid grip kept her from being washed away.

He half carried, half dragged her to an oak tree that lay half in the water. The rest of it rested against a small hillock. He pushed her behind a tangle of branches, dead leaves and vines, and she realized there was a small cave behind. She crawled in and was amazed to see his pack and weapons, along with his shirt, lying inside.

Why? Why hadn't he carried them with him? She'd never seen Connor without his weapons, except at the ball, or the time he was imprisoned. Why had he come for her without his weapons?

She picked up his knife, and the realization of what he'd intended to do washed over her like the cold rain outside. He knew what the Shawnee did to their captives. He'd lived through it. He'd survived it. He'd escaped it. Yet he'd come for her, knowing what his fate would be.

"We cannae outrun them, but I believe we can hide," he said in a whisper as he crawled into the shelter and arranged the branches behind them so they were completely covered.

Carrie shivered. They were both soaking wet and covered with blood, but it was not the wetness or the cold autumn air that chilled her.

She swung her fists at him as he settled in beside her. She realized as they beat against his chest that she might as well be hitting the ground for all the impact she made against his strength. He caught her fists in his hands and folded his arms around her as she collapsed into a trembling mass of emotion. She dared not make a sound for fear of giving away their hiding place.

"You were going to trade your life for mine," she whispered. To think that he would have burned in the fires was more than she could endure at the moment. Too much had happened. Too many had died.

" 'Twas all I had to give," he murmured against her hair. She felt his breath against the top of her head. She felt the beat of his heart against her cheek, and the stickiness of blood. She felt the strength of his arms, yet he shook as he held her.

"Your arm," she said, and pulled away to look at it. A horrible gash stretched from a few inches below his elbow toward the palm of his hand. It poured blood, and she realized that it was a miracle the blade had not sliced open the vein that pulsed in his wrist.

" 'Tis just a scratch," he said.

"No, it's not," she replied. She used his shirt to wipe away the blood. "It needs stitching."

"Then ye will have to do it," he said. " 'Tis the hand that I write with, and I'm afraid the other would not do nearly as well."

She looked up into his eyes. He pushed back the hair that clung to her cheek and she grabbed onto his hand as if he would leave her. "I can."

He dug into his pack and pulled out a small piece of leather that, when unfolded, revealed several needles and different lengths of thread. He laid a pair of silk stockings to the side and held his arm out to her.

The light was dim at best. Carrie moved around until she could see, which put her between his legs, with one knee propped over her lap and his arm atop it. She braced her back against the leg that was against the wall of their shelter.

"This will hurt," she said.

"Compared to what?" he asked, and she saw his lips curve. "Be quick about it, lass, before I bleed to death."

"Don't say that," she said. "Not even in jest."

"I am happy to be alive," he said. "And I'm sure your sewing will remind me how alive I am."

She felt his free hand on her hair as she jabbed the needle into the skin by his hand. He did not make a sound as she sewed. Instead he stroked her hair until he worked the braids free. She concentrated on her stitches and on the rain that pounded even harder now. It was a dull roar as his hand caressed her hair and gently pulled the tangles loose until it hung down her back in a mass of waves. Carrie counted each stitch. When she reached thirty there was a long, jagged line moving up his arm.

"See if Efrem slipped some of his poultice into my pack," he said when she was done.

"Where is Efrem?" she asked as she stuck her hand in his pack and pulled out a piece of lace. She smiled when she saw it. It was her cap.

"Somewhere behind us," he said. "I would not let him come."

"Because you did not want to risk his life?"

"Aye," he said. "I watched one friend die in the fires. I couldnae stand to lose another."

"And now I've watched people die too. Heard the screams . . ." She couldn't go on.

Silently, Carrie found a pot of Efrem's poultice and smoothed it over the wound. Then she slit the stockings with his knife and used them to bind his arm. When she was done, Connor dabbed a bit of the poultice on his finger and spread it over the cut on her cheek.

" 'Twas not your fault," he said, "that you lived and the others died."

"Yet you were going to let me live with the knowledge that you died that way so I could be free?"

He had no answer for her. Instead he stroked her hair.

"If you could not stand it, what makes you think I could?"

He could not seem to keep his hands off her. Even now his other hand caressed her cheek.

" 'Twas my plan to have you long gone from this place before it happened." He took her hand.

Carrie lifted his hand to her mouth and kissed it, then rubbed it against her cheek. "What makes you think I would have gone?"

" 'Twas the only way," he said. "There's no need to dwell on it. Whatever happens between here and the Ohio, it will happen to both of us now."

"As it should," she said. "In the middle of the wilderness, with savages beating down our door, I don't care, Connor. As long as we're together."

"I wouldnae have that for you, lass."

"I choose you. Wherever you go, wherever you live, whatever you do. I want to be with you."

"But you saw what can happen," he said.

"And you knew what would happen. Yet you came for me."

"I couldnae live with myself. I couldnae let you suffer that fate."

"And I cannot live without you." She moved against him. She curled her arms around his neck and placed her cheek next to his. "Let me stay with you, Connor. I love you. I've loved you since the moment I met you. Don't tell me you came all this way just to send me back to Williamsburg."

His arms moved around her. "God help me, Carrie, I love ye."

Joy washed over her. How long had she waited to hear him say those words? His lips found hers, and as he kissed her, she knew that this time he meant it. This time he would not walk away, he would not let her go.

How could he, when she needed him more than air, more than water, more than food, more than life? And he must need her too. She felt it in the way his arms trembled, as if he were afraid he would squeeze her too tight, in the way his breath caught in his throat as she moved against him, in the way his heart thumped against his chest as she pressed up against him and willed her heart to echo his because it was, after all, one heart between them.

She felt his need pressing against her thigh as she tried to move closer and heard his gasp as he pulled his mouth away from hers and squeezed his eyes shut.

"Be careful, lass," he whispered between gritted teeth with his eyes still closed. "Lest I cannae stop myself."

Carrie kissed the hollow in his cheek above the growth of beard where she knew his tick would come. But it would not come today.

"I don't want you to stop," she said.

"I donnae want to take you here." He opened his eyes. They were dark, dangerous, and a shiver went down her spine that had nothing to do with the dampness of their shelter or the hard rain that pounded outside. "Not in the dirt. Not when we're covered with blood and death."

"We could die at any time." Carrie placed her hands on the sides of his face. "And if I die tomorrow, I don't want my one regret to be that we did not make love."

His eyes searched hers and she smiled reassuringly as he kissed her once more.

"Why is it I cannae say nae to ye?" he asked as his lips moved across her cheek.

She had to smile. "You've been saying no ever since I met you."

"Not with my heart." His lips found hers again. *"Mo cridhe. Mo leannon."*

"What does that mean?"

His mouth moved to her neck. "My heart." He pulled loose the ties across her shoulders and the hide dress she wore slipped down as he pushed her hair back and his lips trailed across the hollow of her collarbone. "My love."

Carrie arched her back as his mouth moved to the top of her breast. She gripped his shoulders when her dress slipped down to her waist and his mouth trailed after it.

She wanted more.

Warmth spread through her insides. Her skin felt alive. Her soul threatened to burst out of her body.

The cave was not big enough. Her nails scratched against the dirt of the roof as Connor's mouth moved over her breasts, first one and then the other, then back again, until she was gasping for breath while he held her up against him with the strength of his arms.

There had to be more. She wanted to touch him. She wanted to touch all of him. But if she moved, he would stop the wonderful torment that was driving her insane with pleasure. She buried her hands in his hair and twined the copper strands around her fingers as she sought to hold on to the essence of what was Connor.

"Mo cridhe," he breathed as he twisted both their bodies around until she was lying on the ground and he beside

her. His hand cupped her chin, flattened as it moved down her neck and through the valley between her breasts until he splayed his palm across her stomach, which trembled beneath his touch.

He smiled at her. Gentle, reassuring, and she saw all her life with him stretching out before her: laughter and tears, joy and heartache, and she knew all would be well between them.

If they could stay alive.

"Are ye sure?

"I've never been surer of anything in my life," she said. She reached for him, pulled him close as he shoved up her dress and touched her.

She was overwhelmed by sensation. Her blood boiled. She needed. She wanted. She reached and he pulled away, and she thought she would die of longing, but then she felt him again, pressing against her. She knew it would hurt, but she did not care. She moved her legs up and around his hips and dug her nails into his shoulders as he stopped. She felt him. He was there. She pushed up and he pushed against her. She felt the pain; just a twinge, nothing more, and then he filled her. She cried out, but his mouth silenced her cry.

"Carrie." Her name rolled off his tongue, and she felt as if it were a song. It carried her away from the cave, away from death, away from the horrors she'd seen as they both rose up as if carried on the wind.

Then she burst into a thousand pieces, and she held on for all she was worth because she knew she'd be lost without him.

"Connor," she sighed as she felt the scattered parts of herself float back into the body lying on the dark, damp earth.

He lowered his forehead to hers, holding himself up so as not to crush her. But she wanted to feel all of him, so she wrapped her arms around him and tightened her legs.

"Mo cridhe." He raised himself up to look into her eyes. "Fortis et Fidus."

"Gaelic and Latin?" She smiled. "How am I ever to understand you?"

" 'Tis my clan motto. Brave and faithful. 'Tis you." He moved off her, arranged her dress and then cradled her in his arms.

"I'm not brave, Connor. I was scared to death."

"Yet ye fought. And did I imagine it, or were you helping me today?"

"I was trying to," she said and grinned at the memory. It was easy to laugh at it now that she was safe in his arms. "I tried to kick him, but my dress tripped me up. I wound up flat on my back in the leaves."

He grinned back. "Flat on your back is fine with me," he said. "Perhaps ye should have thrown your shoes at him."

"I lost my shoes and my petticoats and everything else I possess," she said. "I have nothing left. Nothing to give you but me."

" 'Tis more than I deserve," he said. "I donnae understand it and I willnae fight it any longer."

"You can't fight destiny."

"Aye. And I thought it was my destiny to die in the fires. Though it still might be . . ."

"Don't say that, don't even think it," Carrie interrupted.

"It seems as if I've been fighting destiny my entire life."

"Why?"

"My father died at Culloden. Did ye know I was born on the field that same day?"

"Your mother was at the battle?"

"Yes. And your father was also."

"He fought there." Carrie felt a shiver of regret. "My father didn't . . ."

"No. Your father made sure I was born safely. He helped my mother. He recognized my name when we met at Fort Savannah, recognized me. He told me the story of my birth. He is a good man, your father."

Carrie nodded in complete agreement.

"He gave me his blessing to find you."

"What about John?"

"John wasnae so happy about it. We were fighting when you were taken."

"Don't hate him, Connor," she said. "Something happened to him. Something has filled him with hatred."

"Then that is something we have in common," Connor said. "Before you, I hated all the English, especially the ones in red coats."

"Why?"

"When I was ten, my mother took me to Culloden to visit my father's grave."

"It was the anniversary of his death?"

"Aye. After the battle English hatred of the Highlanders was horrible. They took everything we had. My mother was a proud woman. She carried a plaid with her. The clan colors. A patrol saw us." Carrie felt his muscles tighten. She watched as his jaw went rigid. Even in the dim light, she saw the tick appear in the hollow of his cheek. "They raped my mother in front of me and then they hanged her. And they threw me in prison. That's why I was sent to the colonies as a bondservant."

Her heart ached for him. The things he'd experienced. The things he'd seen. And he was only a child. She wanted to hold him. She wanted to comfort him. She wanted to make all the pain go away.

"I know now that we were meant to be together," she said as she kissed the hollow of his cheek.

"Because of your father?"

"No. Because of something that happened when I was six years old. We were at the docks in London. I was in a carriage, and I saw a line of prisoners go by. At the end of the chains was a boy with bright red hair and the bluest eyes I had ever seen."

"Ye were that girl in the carriage?" Connor asked in disbelief. "I remember seeing ye hanging out of the carriage window with your mouth wide open."

"Yes. And I have prayed for you ever since that day. Remember the day of the ball, when I saw you at the palace?"

"I thought you were the daftiest lass I'd ever seen."

"I knew you were the boy."

His hand stroked her cheek. "God's hand has brought us to this place. I can only believe now that He will bring us safely back."

"Would He bring us all this way and let us die?"

"'Tis not our place to question His plan. But I willnae fight it. I will stay with ye as long as ye want me."

"I want you forever."

"Then we'd best get married," he said with a grin. "I have a feeling your father wouldnae have it any other way."

"Neither will I."

Chapter Thirty-one

Connor sat at the front of their shelter and watched the rain pound down as Carrie slept beneath the blanket.

It was a foolish thing he'd done. Foolish because they could have been found in the middle of it. Foolish because they could have died if they were found. Foolish because he'd given in to her, to his desire, to his heart. Foolish because he'd acted impulsively instead of thinking things through.

He always prided himself on being careful. He made his decisions wisely because the wrong decision in this wilderness could cost your life. Not that his life was of any importance to anyone beyond himself.

But Carrie . . .

He seemed to have lost all sense when it came to her.

But he also felt a sense of peace inside his soul. It was twisted up with the want that still pounded inside his gut and the guilt he felt for taking her in the dirt.

She wanted ye just as much . . .

What if Efrem was right? What if the beast inside his soul was of his own making? He'd lived his entire life trying to make up for things that he wasn't responsible for. It wasn't his fault his father chose to stand and fight at Culloden. Yet as a boy he'd tried to live up to the legend of the man. He'd tried his best to be just like his father, but in his mother's memory his father was the perfect man. Brave and strong and true to his word. A man of honor.

Fortis et Fidus.

It was his mother's choice to show the plaid; she'd known the risk involved. There was nothing he could do to stop her or the men who'd killed her. He was just a boy.

And Tom. Connor had been spared his fate because an old woman liked his red hair. He could no more change the color of his hair than he could the color of the sky.

None of those tragedies was of his making. Yet he'd lived his life consumed with guilt.

General Murray thought that perhaps the reason he'd been present when Connor was born was because Connor was destined to save his daughter.

But what if it was actually Carrie who was meant to save him?

Connor looked over his shoulder at her sleeping form. Darkness was nearly upon them; all he saw was shadow. He knew her cheeks to be gaunt. He could count every rib when he touched her. Great shadows haunted her eyes. She'd paid a visit to death's door and still had a long way to go before she'd be safe again.

Yet she loved him. Why did he think he deserved any less than this? Love wasn't something he'd ever planned on. He'd hoped for it at times, wished for it, but never thought it would happen.

Carrie had given him the most precious gift of all. She'd given him herself.

And he would take care of her. He would let no harm befall her. He would protect her even if it meant his death.

The rain had not let up. Steadily, heavily, it drummed on. Nothing moved outside the shelter. The animals had gone to ground and no one disturbed them. Connor let his eyes grow accustomed to the darkness as it turned the dreary afternoon to a desperate evening. Then he turned to wake her.

Gently, he bent and kissed her lips, which were slightly parted in sleep. She sighed, then put her hand against his cheek.

"It wasn't a dream?" she asked.

"Nay, lass." His lips brushed against hers once more, and she wrapped her arms around his neck as he pulled her up. She felt so thin, so fragile. He needed her to be strong. The days ahead would not be easy. "We must be off."

"It's night," she said. She rubbed her eyes. Was she as bone weary as he? She had to be.

"Aye. Just fallen." He felt her shiver. It was cold, and it would only get colder. And wetter. He didn't dare risk a fire.

"Carrie," he said. He saw her eyes move up to his. She was listening. "We've got to get back to the Ohio. It will take us days, and with this weather, 'twill be treacherous. The Shawnee will be on the march. There will be no rest, no fire, no food . . ."

"We have to get there first," she said. "We have to warn my father that they're coming."

She knew. She understood. Now she just had to survive it. "Fortis et Fidus." Connor kissed her forehead.

"As long as you're beside me," she answered.

"We can at least make it a bit easier," he said, and pulled out his knife. He cut the buckskin dress off above her knees. "It will lengthen your stride," he explained.

"So I don't trip while kicking someone?"

"Aye." He grinned. He tied the length he'd cut off around her waist and handed her the tomahawk he'd taken off the Shawnee, along with a pistol that was primed and ready. He rolled up the blanket and put it in his pack as she stuck the weapons in her makeshift belt.

"Ready?" he asked.

"Yes."

He took her hand to help her crawl from their shelter. They were soaked before they took ten steps. And since it did not matter whether they got wet or not, he led her into the river.

As long as the weather didn't turn colder, they would survive the journey. There was no frost yet, but that didn't mean it wouldn't come. At least the rain would cover their tracks. Rain was good.

Connor kept telling himself that as they moved through the shallows. He was used to traveling at night and was able to make out the shadows that were the only visible signs of trees and boulders. But the river bottom was treacherous. There were rocks and hidden holes where one could step in up to one's waist.

"Stay behind me. Put your feet where I put mine," he said. He wanted to hold her arm, but he had to keep his rifle ready. Carrie hung on to his pack. She slipped a few times and caught herself against his back. She did not complain.

He felt her shivering. How long would she be able to fight? How long could she keep up? She needed food. She needed rest. She needed to be kept safe.

How long could she go on?

The rain tapered off by dawn, but heavy clouds to the east kept the sun from drying the earth. They'd left the river hours ago, when it turned south. But the rain still kept them cold and miserable.

It was time for rest. His eyes, which burned from peering through the darkness, scanned the area as he searched for some place that would shelter them for just a few hours. Carrie stood beside him, her face ghastly pale, her eyes sunk into her head, her arms wrapped around her trembling body. The fact that she was still shivering was a good sign.

He finally found what he was looking for: a huge evergreen with branches that dragged against the ground on all sides. It towered above the hardwoods at the bottom of a hill. It should be dry enough for them to sleep for a bit beneath its branches.

"Just a little farther," he said, and took her hand. It felt like ice.

The way down was sloppy and they both slipped. Connor could not decide if it was because of the footing or just because they were both so weary.

He went in first, in case some creature had had the same idea. Luckily, the space beneath was empty, but a doe and her fawn had recently lain there. The needles still bore the imprint of their bodies. Most likely they sensed humans coming and made their escape.

Connor pulled the blanket from his pack. Miraculously, it was dry. He placed it on the ground against the trunk of the tree, where there was enough room beneath the branches for him to sit.

"Take off your clothes," he said. "Ye will warm faster."

She nodded but did not move. Her lips were blue.

Quickly, he undressed her, and then pulled off his shirt and wrapped his arms around her and rolled the blanket over both of them. Her hair was a sodden weight against her back so he flipped it outside the blanket and then set to work rubbing her arms and legs until once again he heard her teeth chattering.

She burrowed against him. She put her icy cold feet in between his legs, and he felt the cold of them through his breeks. She pressed her bare breasts against his chest and her face beneath his neck. And as weary as he felt, he could not help responding.

He wanted her with every fiber of his being. But he would not take her again. Not when she was weak and cold and starving. Not now.

He pulled her against him and rubbed her back, and fought to control the parts of his body that seemed to have a mind of their own. At least his blood was warmed, so much so that he felt it would boil if he did not soon find relief. Thank goodness he'd had the sense to leave on his breeks.

Her shaking stopped and he felt her relax in his arms. "Carrie?"

She slept. He felt her steady breath against his neck. Connor pulled the blanket up tight around her shoulders and fanned her hair out away from her so it would dry. It would be full of pine needles, but there was nothing he could do about that. It would be nice if he could hang out her dress to dry, along with his shirt. The best he could do without waking her was flip them up over a branch.

He needed rest. He couldn't remember the last night he'd slept. But sleep was something he did not dare risk. His eyes burned, his stomach ached from hunger and his legs felt painfully cramped.

It had to be worse for Carrie. She had not been raised to survive in the wild. She was not meant for it. It was not the life for her.

How much longer would it take to get back? How many days were they from the river? Would they find help there if they made it? What about the weather? Could they make it back to the Blue Ridge before the snows came? Carrie had told him that the Frenchman had said the English were coming. Would the English army find them before the Shawnee? How many men marched toward the Ohio from each side? Which side had the advantage?

The worries circled in his head like crows waiting for death to strike. There were too many to count.

Connor wearily closed his eyes. Just for a moment.

He needed a moment to regain his strength.

Something woke him. Connor's mind spun. He hadn't meant to sleep, yet he'd slept for hours. The sun, which filtered down through the inner branches of the evergreen, was directly overhead.

He lay on his back with Carrie slanted across his chest,

his arm securely around her. The blanket covered them both and she slept soundly, her chest rising and falling in unison with his own. Her hair was still damp, but the ends were dry, the golden curls contrasting with the dark blue of the blanket.

What had woken him? His ears strained to hear whatever it was that had roused him. Seconds passed. Seconds when he wondered if someone was sneaking up on them. Moments when he wondered whether he should reach for his rifle or whether his movement would give away their hiding place. An eternity passed, and in that time Carrie opened her eyes and stared into his with questions of her own waiting to be answered.

Then he heard it. And they both grinned wildly. Connor grabbed her face in his hands and kissed her soundly before he whistled an answering call.

Efrem.

He grabbed his rifle and crawled out from under the tree. A few more calls and he saw Efrem coming down the same hillside they had slid down earlier in the day.

"You are a sight for sore eyes, my friend," he said as Efrem reached the tree.

"As are you," Efrem said. "I nearly gave up on finding you."

"How long have you searched?"

"Since this morning. I saw the entire Shawnee nation pass by. Hundreds of warriors."

"How did ye know we were still alive?"

Efrem handed Connor a piece of muddy lace from his shirt.

Carrie's cap.

"I found this caught in the limb of an oak tree that had fallen into the river. Behind it there was a shelter with fresh blood on the ground." Efrem looked pointedly at Connor's arm. "From there it was just a matter of going east. I saw no signs until just a while ago. You must be tired."

Connor ran his hand through his hair. "I am. I was. I sure am glad to see ye."

"Carrie?" Efrem asked.

"I'm here," she said from the shelter. "Can I borrow your comb?"

Chapter Thirty-two

Just one more step, Carrie kept telling herself over and over again. Take another step. Then another. Each step gets you closer to safety. Closer to your father and your brother. Closer to a future with Connor.

How long since she'd enjoyed a bath? A meal? Clean clothes? A full night of sleep? None of that mattered. Nothing mattered but taking another step and staying alive.

Because now there was everything to live for.

They were closer to the river. But the flat land near the Shawnee village had become hills and mountains. They were not as overpowering as the ones she'd traveled through after she was first taken. Then she'd felt as if the earth had swallowed her whole and she would never see daylight again. But the slopes they traveled now were hard and wearisome when you never knew if the next step you took would be your last. She knew she'd passed this way before, but she could not remember it. When she thought of that journey, all she saw was Preston's horrible death on the cliff overlooking the Ohio.

Efrem told them of the eastward movement of the Shawnee warriors. They were marching to meet the English. To surprise them before they could cross the Ohio.

Connor was determined to beat the Shawnee to their goal. Their lives and the lives of her father, brother and all the men marching to war depended upon it.

"How are ye, lass?" He took her hand as they scrambled to the top of another mountain. Dusk would soon be upon them. Even now the sun was behind the trees at their backs and it was hard to see the narrow game trail they traversed.

She nodded her head up and down. She couldn't speak after the hard climb. What breath she had left was taken away by the vista before her. The three of them stood in the shelter of a hemlock and gazed out at the scene before them.

The mountain they'd just climbed was nothing compared to the ones that drifted off to the east. Over and over again they rose and fell into what seemed like eternity. It was hard to imagine that on the other side of those mountains were cities, commerce, families going about their business. An ocean that led to other countries where people lived everyday, ordinary lives. A country she used to call home. She felt as if it were someone else's life. A life out of another time, another place. A fairy tale her mother read to her when she was young.

Below was a river. A river as wide as a lake that snaked through a valley with trees so thick you couldn't see the earth beneath them. As far as she could see the river rolled south.

But to the north . . .

"Can they see us?"

"Nay." Connor was using his spyglass, but even without it, she knew what he saw.

A great gathering of men. Shawnee warriors, along with their allies. A thousand or more. All waiting to cross the great river. They gathered on a plain above the rippling water, looking like an army of ants going about their business.

"We are upstream from the Kanawha," Connor said. "Do ye think the English army will come down from the north?"

"I think a wise general would split his forces," Efrem said. "Send some from the north and others up the Kanawha."

"General Murray is a wise man," Connor said as he put his spyglass away. It was too dark now to see anything but the distant glow of fires from the Indian camp.

"I say we make for Tu-Endie-Wei," Efrem said. "Surely there will be forces there."

" 'Tis still a long way to the river. And we have to make it before daybreak if we are to win the race and warn General Murray of what's to come." He turned to Carrie, who was staring at the dark ribbon of water in the distance. It seemed bottomless, impossibly wide.

We have to swim it at night . . . .

A shiver went down her spine at the thought of navigating the river in the darkness. Connor's arms folded around her, pulled her close against his chest and the steady beat of his heart. " 'Tis normal to fear it," he said. He knew she was frightened even though she had not said a word.

As long as he was by her side, she could do it. As long as they were together, nothing could hurt them. She kept on saying it over and over again in her head. It was the only thing that kept her going, that made her put one foot in front of the other.

They moved down the mountain. Efrem took the lead as he always did, then Carrie, then Connor behind her. His huge body was like a wall, solid and comforting. During the few hours of sleep they snatched just before dawn, he held her and she slept between the two men, drawing what warmth she could from their bodies because they dared not light a fire.

Would she ever look at a fire again and not see the horrible deaths she'd witnessed? Would she ever feel warm again?

Efrem set a quick pace. They were racing now against time. They had to cross first. If not, the Shawnee would be between them and civilization. The weather would turn against them eventually. How much colder could it get before they froze to death? How many more nights could they spend huddled against each other for warmth before they succumbed to illness and eventually death? She did not need a mirror to know how desperate she looked. All she had to do was look into Connor's face.

Carrie felt the chill of evening enter her bones. How much colder would she be before this night was over?

The river lay before them. Was it so immense the first time she'd crossed it? She remembered canoes. She remembered singing. She remembered feeling as if she would never see anyone she loved again. And she remembered Preston's horrible death. Were they close to where he'd died? Was his body still there, sitting sentinel over the river?

The moonlight dappled the water, giving the illusion of creatures of light living just below the surface. But then clouds covered the moon and the water turned black, bottomless. How deep was it?

All this went through her mind as she stood on the bank wrapped in Connor's arms while Efrem went in search of a log to carry their guns over so they could keep their powder dry.

" 'Twill be over soon," Connor said. His voice rumbled against the top of her head.

"Then what?" she asked. "Where will we go? What will we do?"

"We must find a place to spend the winter," he said.

"What about your cabin?"

" 'Tis most likely fallen into disrepair," he said. "And I've no supplies put up for winter."

"I want to go there," she said. "I want to sleep in a bed by a fire under tons of quilts."

"I've no quilts to speak of," he said. "But plenty of furs to keep ye warm. Which are most likely full of wee beasties seeking a warm place to spend the winter."

She had to smile, and her mouth turned up against his chest. She felt the warmth of his skin where his shirt was open.

"We'll go there in the spring," he said. " 'Tis the best time to see it. Can ye wait that long?"

"I can wait," Carrie said. "As long as we're together."

"We'll find a place," Connor said as Efrem dragged up a log and dropped it with a grunt. "We'll most likely have this one hanging around too."

"I just want to be a blessing," Efrem said. "Wherever I hang around."

"Oh, you are," Carrie said. "I'm sure my backside would be frozen without you to shield it at night."

"I do what I can," Efrem said. His teeth flashed white in the darkness. "And I will be happy to bless other parts of your fair form if needed."

"Enough of that," Connor growled as he took off his shirt and moccasins. "We must move. It will be dawn soon enough. Take off your moccasins and leggings," he said to Carrie. "The weight will tire you."

The men stripped down to their breeches and Carrie left on her short dress. Connor bundled up their clothes in the blanket and then lashed their guns and packs to the top of the log with a piece of vine. He placed her hand on the vine. "When we get on, wrap your hand in this and hold on. All ye have to do is kick. We'll do the rest."

The water was icy cold as it lapped around her ankles. A few steps and she was suddenly swimming. It was so dark she couldn't see anything. She struck out with her hand

for something solid. Connor grabbed her arm and placed
her hand on the vine, which she grabbed on to for all she
was worth. Soon they were floating in the current.

She was so cold it was hard to move. Her body shivered
and seemed to want to close in upon itself. If only she
wasn't so cold. If only she could find some warmth.

"Hang on, lassie," Connor said.

She didn't want to hang on. She wanted to let go. She
wanted to let the river take her away to someplace where it
was warm. She tried to move her legs, but they wouldn't
work.

"Carrie?"

She heard his voice, but it sounded so far away. As if she
were in a dream. Was it all a dream? Was it part of the
nightmare? Would she wake up and be back in the village? Or maybe she would wake up and be back in her
bed in the palace, with Patsy standing there holding a pot
of hot chocolate, just waiting for her to open her eyes.

"Carrie, ye must hang on!"

She felt an arm circle her waist.

"Take it, Efrem," he said, but his voice sounded so far
away.

"Carrie, come back to me," he begged. She felt herself
floating. She felt the arm around her, felt the movement.
She felt her legs trailing along as if they weighed nothing.
She weighed nothing. She was without substance. She was
nothing more than one of the lights trapped beneath the
surface.

"We must warm her," the voice said. Who was it? It
sounded desperate. It pulled at her, called to her; it kept
her from slipping away. If only she could slip away.

"Come back to me, *mo cridhe,*" the voice cried out.

Hands rubbed her legs, her feet, her arms. A blanket
was wrapped about her.

"Have her drink this," a voice said, and her mouth was
forced open. something cold and bitter touched her
tongue.

She gagged. She coughed. She opened her eyes.

"Thank God," Connor exclaimed, and crushed her against his chest. Carrie tried to fathom what had happened as he rocked her back and forth. They were in the river. Had she drowned?

"It's better when it's hot," Efrem said apologetically. He pitched the contents of a tin cup onto the ground.

"What happened?" she asked. "Are we across?"

"Shhh," Efrem said.

He stood on the bank with his head cocked. He was listening for something. Carrie felt Connor's breath suck in as the clouds parted once again and the river was revealed in the moonlight.

Hundreds of rafts were on the river. They were covered with men. The Shawnee were crossing, and not far upstream from where they sat.

"God help us," Efrem said. "We must move."

Chapter Thirty-three

Connor jerked on his moccasins and shirt and then helped Carrie with hers. She was trying, but her fingers fumbled, and she was shaking so hard that she could barely hold on to her moccasins. There was no time for her leggings. He stuffed his weapons in his belt. Thank God they were all dry.

When they looked again, they saw that the rafts had reached the bank, which meant that nearly a thousand warriors were already on shore and most likely moving on their way.

Carrie had nearly died, not from drowning but from the cold. He must warm her, but there was no time. He knew she couldn't run. Not fast enough to escape what was coming. Connor slung his rifle over his shoulder and scooped her up in his arms.

"You lead," Efrem said. "If the English see me first, they might shoot me."

"Let's just hope they're here," Connor said as he took off toward the south. The way was almost impassable. The trees and undergrowth were thick, and there were fallen branches and logs everywhere he looked. Running was impossible and haste a necessity.

Connor figured they were somewhere close to a mile or more north of the Kanawha. He'd been this way before, many years ago, with Sir Richard.

Carrie's skin felt like ice against his chest. He felt his shirt flapping behind him and wished he'd had the presence of mind to button it, or at least wrap it around Carrie's body. At least she had the blanket, which she clutched tightly in her hands, but he'd picked her up so fast that it was not wrapped around her.

There was no time to stop. Getting her to safety was more important that how cold she was. It would be dawn soon. Hopefully the sun would bring warmth. The night was already giving way to the dull gray light the hour before of dawn.

The crack of two quick shots broke the quiet. Birds rose from the treetops in a dark mass and flew straight away across the river.

Connor dropped into a crouch behind an uprooted tree with Efrem right beside him. The river was behind them. If need be, they could get in and let it wash them downstream. But would Carrie survive another cold dousing?

With a nod, Efrem snaked off toward the sound of the gunfire.

"G . . . g . . . g . . . g . . . give me a g . . . g . . . gun." Carrie's teeth chattered so hard that he barely understood her until she reached for his belt and pulled out the pistol he kept there. She wrapped her hand around the grip. "Pu . . . put me down so you can fight."

"Can ye walk?" She seemed so small, so frail, as if a stiff wind would blow her away. He doubted if she could stand. He would not leave her. He'd fight to the death to protect her.

"I can run," she said. "Fortis et Fidus," she added with a small smile.

"God, I love ye," he said. His heart swelled with love and pride at her courage.

Efrem reappeared beside them. "The militia is here," he said quietly. "They know. One of the Shawnee who shot at us is dead. The other is on his way downriver."

"Then we're trapped between the militia and the Shawnee?" Connor asked.

Efrem nodded. Both men knew that in the heat of battle, Efrem was a likely target from both sides.

"We must get you behind the lines," Connor said to Carrie. "Efrem, stay close."

As one they rose. Connor took her arm in one hand and held his rifle in the other. Efrem fell in behind her. It would not do to make it this far and have one of the militia shoot him down.

They heard noises behind them. There was no need for the Shawnee to be quiet. The advantage of surprise was gone.

In a matter of moments, they heard drumbeats coming from the south.

The call to arms: The militia was preparing to march.

There was a war cry from behind.

They'd been seen.

"Take her," Connor said to Efrem. "Go!"

"*No!*" Carrie said. But Efrem was already pulling her away. He wrapped his arm around her waist and crouched low. Carrie pulled against him, but Efrem would not let go.

Connor knew his friend would die before he'd let harm befall her. And sending Carrie with Efrem was the only way to save Efrem. The militia would not shoot him if Carrie was with him.

Connor turned and crouched behind a dead fall with his rifle ready.

"God keep her safe," he said. "And let them believe that I'm the entire troop of regulars," he added as a Shawnee warrior came into view.

He fired and immediately rolled toward a tree with a wide trunk. He heard a grunt and a shout. He knew he'd hit his target but did not take time to make sure. Connor lay on his back and reloaded just as a bullet split the trunk of the dead fall. He fired again and heard an answering shot. He slid down on his back behind the tree as splinters flew off the bark.

He reloaded. He shot. Then he took off running toward another tree trunk, firing his pistol over his shoulder as he ran. He dove over the trunk and reached for his ammunition.

Carrie had his other pistol. He prayed she wouldn't have to use it.

Connor reloaded his gun. He heard them coming. Did he have time to reload his pistol? How far away were Efrem and Carrie? Dare he run for it?

The woods around him were dense. Twisted. So thick that it was impossible to determine whether the sun was shining. Was it dawn?

He turned and saw three warriors coming toward him. He shot the one in front and ducked as the other two fired at his position. He slung his rifle over his back and drew his knife in one hand and his tomahawk in the other. He stood to meet the two warriors, who came after him with their own knives and tomahawks drawn.

"*Fortis et Fidus*," Connor roared from deep in his throat. He bellowed so loudly that the first man stopped for a split-second.

That was all he needed. He flung his tomahawk at the man and buried it deep in his chest. That left just one. One who held a weapon in each hand. The Shawnee jumped onto the trunk and then launched his body toward Connor.

Connor went for the hand with the tomahawk. He bent his legs and met the impact of the warrior. He gripped the man's arm and drew in his belly as the Shawnee swiped at his body with the knife. Connor countered with his own blade and felt it tear the flesh of his opponent. He was taller. His arms were longer. He was stronger. As long as he kept hold of the man's tomahawk, he would win.

They danced around, each one slashing and feinting, until Connor was able to force the man up against a tree. He kicked the inside of the warrior's knee, and when he involuntarily bent, he bashed the arm that held the tomahawk against the trunk until it went flying into the leaves at his feet. The man slashed his knife downward toward Connor, but he blocked the blow with his forearm and buried his knife in the warrior's ribs and up into his heart.

There was no time. More were coming. Connor grabbed the tomahawk from the leaves and took off at a run. A bullet struck a tree as he ran behind it.

He needed to reload. There was no place to hide. They would be on him soon. One well-aimed shot would down him

Where were Carrie and Efrem? Had they made it?

He heard movement before him.

"Efrem!" he shouted.

"Show yourself!" someone shouted back.

Another bullet whizzed past his head.

Connor ran flat out as hard as he could toward the voices. He trusted the militia not to shoot him. Surely they'd see his hair and not mistake him for a Shawnee.

He heard a war cry behind him but kept on running.

"Hold your fire!" someone called out. "He's one of us."

"They're right behind me!" Connor yelled as he saw the men behind the trees with their rifles ready.

They fired as he went by. He ducked behind a tree and reloaded his rifle.

"Did ye see her?" he asked the closest man to him. "Is she safe?"

"See who?" the man asked. "A woman? Out here?"

"I sent her this way. She was with a Cherokee."

The man fired his rifle and grinned. "The only Indians

I've seen are the one's I'm shootin' at," he said. "No one's passed this way but you."

Connor's heart jumped into his throat. He looked up and down the line. There were well over a hundred men. Surely someone had seen Carrie and Efrem pass.

He turned and began shooting as more Shawnee than he could count came into sight.

Chapter Thirty-four

"We can't leave him," Carrie cried out as Efrem continued to drag her along.

"We must."

"What if he dies?"

Shots echoed behind them.

Connor . . .

"He has a better chance alone. We all do this way."

Carrie knew he was right. But that didn't make it any easier to leave Connor behind. She tried to keep up. She knew Efrem was doing most of the work. But it seemed as if her legs were cut off from her brain. They were numb.

I almost died . . . .

Her memory of crossing the river was hazy. If only she could get warm again. She was so cold, so cold that her blood felt sluggish in her veins.

She saw the river on her right. It glimmered between the trunks of the trees. The rest of the world was nothing but thick forest. She knew Connor was somewhere behind them. She knew the army was before them. She knew the

Shawnee were marching on them. Yet there was nothing around them but trees.

She heard a noise behind them. Carrie stopped. She turned. "Connor?"

A Shawnee stood before her. Three more came up behind. Water streamed off them. They'd just come from the river.

Efrem fired and one went down. He pushed Carrie behind him as he dropped his rifle and fired his pistol. He missed as the three that remained all moved and fired.

Efrem dove on top of Carrie, but nothing happened. There was no sound of gunfire. Their powder was wet. Efrem rolled to his feet and Carrie staggered up behind him.

The three charged toward Efrem with their rifles raised as clubs.

Efrem pushed Carrie back, and she stumbled up against a tree. He drew his knife and his tomahawk.

You have a pistol.

She looked at the gun in her hand as if she'd never seen it before. Then she fired. The one in front fell, and the other two swung wildly at Efrem with their guns. He knocked one away with his tomahawk, then ducked. The rifle smashed against a tree and fell from its owner's hands.

Efrem now faced two warriors armed with knives. He held a weapon in each hand. They circled him as he kept out the tomahawk. Whichever one came at him first would likely lose an arm.

They both charged together.

Efrem slashed out with his tomahawk. The warrior on his right bent back as the blade sliced through the air and just missed his abdomen. The other came after him with his blade raised. Efrem blocked his blow with his forearm as the other warrior moved in. He slashed out again but was trapped. He couldn't move his left arm or the warrior would strike. He couldn't strike him with his right because he had to keep the other man at bay.

He needed help.

Carrie watched as they circled around, the two locked in combat struggling to get the upper hand, while the other one waited for Efrem to weaken. If only she had a weapon. The pistol was useless now. She had no powder. No shot. Connor had always meant the one shot as her last resort. Efrem's rifle was somewhere beyond them, along with the gun that the Shawnee had dropped. She tried to move toward the weapons, but the fighting men were in the way.

Efrem crashed into a tree. He lost his hold on his tomahawk. It flew into the leaves right before her feet and the second warrior went after him. Somehow Efrem managed to duck and wiggle free, but blood poured from a wound on his arm and across his chest.

They went after him again.

He needed help.

Carrie picked up the tomahawk and swung it over her head as the warriors both rushed Efrem and pinned him against a tree. She felt a thunk, as if she'd split a melon, and a warrior fell at her feet with the tomahawk buried in his skull.

She didn't have time to think about it. Efrem was against the tree with a knife at his throat. Only the strength of his arm kept the blade from slicing his veins.

Carrie tried to pull the tomahawk loose. It was buried too deep. She grabbed it with both hands and jerked upward with all her might.

She fell backward into thin air. She let go of the tomahawk as she swung her arms in a desperate attempt to stop herself from falling into the river.

She caught onto a tree root that jutted out of the bank. She was at least four feet below the top of the bank, and the river was another ten or more feet beneath her.

Efrem.

As she dangled in midair, questions raced through her mind. Was Efrem alive? Was he dead? Would the Shawnee come after her? Should she let go?

One look at the river was enough to let her know she would not survive another swim. The current ripped past. She wasn't strong enough to fight it. She could barely hold on to the root. She tried to pull herself up but hadn't the strength to do it. She managed to get her toes onto another root just as she heard a cry above her.

Efrem and the man he fought flew over her head, locked in combat.

"*Efrem!*" Carrie screamed. She saw the splash. She saw them go under. She watched the water.

Neither one came up.

"Oh, God . . . Efrem . . ."

She stood on the root, her perch precarious at best, keeping a grip on the one over her head. She focused her eyes on the river, searching downstream.

There was nothing. Efrem was gone and she was trapped.

And Connor didn't know where she was. No one knew.

Was Connor alive? Or had he died in his attempt to protect her?

She couldn't even call out for fear the Shawnee, would find her.

Maybe she should let go. Just let the river take her.

Connor . . .

Chapter Thirty-five

The battle raged for hours. After the first few volleys, the line fell back because of the strength of the forces opposing the regulars. They were three hundred in two divisions against a thousand or more. But reinforcements were sent from behind and they were able to drive the enemy back. The commanding officer, Colonel Fleming, was wounded but refused to leave the front, encouraging the men of his regiment to fight before he retired to camp with two shots through his left arm and one through his chest.

The sun was directly overhead when the action abated a bit. The Indians used the heavy undergrowth to cover their retreat and didn't hesitate to throw their dead in the river.

Connor shot. He reloaded. When he ran out of powder and shot he took some from the pouch of a dead man.

Where is she?

What happened to them?

Did they make it to camp?

Each Indian who came into his sights became the

cause of his fears. Each one had taken her. Each one had her. Each one of the Shawnee, Delaware, Mingo, Ottowa, and Wyandot who came into his range became a victim of his rage.

The militia formed a new line. The Indian Nations' retreat gave them the slight advantage of higher ground, but the militia covered over a mile.

It was whispered up and down the line that Colonel Lewis had died, along with several of the other officers.

Charlie . . . He was a good friend. A good man. He would be missed.

Did Andrew know? He was the one in charge. He was the one who'd sent his brother out to lead the men.

The troops finally dislodged the Nations from a long ridge that stretched from the river to the hills. No matter how determined the enemy might be, the militia would not give up the ground that had been so hard won.

Finally, when the sun began its dip into the western sky, the Nations began their retreat. They carried off their dead and fired a few discouraging shots over their shoulders.

The militia had won the day.

Connor did not stop to celebrate. He slung his gun over his shoulder and ran toward the camp.

He saw dead men. He saw men dying. He saw comrades helping comrades. But nowhere did he see Carrie or Efrem. His mind whirled back to the point where they'd separated.

He saw Efrem pulling her away. He saw her reaching out for him. He saw himself turn and shoot as the Indians advanced upon him.

And he saw himself running toward the east while they headed toward the riverbank. Whatever had happened, it had occurred between the line of the militia and the river.

But where? There was so much ground to cover. And it would be dark soon. Where should he start?

The point where the two rivers came together looked much different from the last time he'd visited. The trees were gone, the underbrush cleared, and the building of a fort was in progress. Tents were pitched everywhere.

It suddenly occurred to Connor that there wasn't a red-coat in sight. The army must have divided. Apparently the English had not yet arrived.

Connor knew Cornstalk's ways well enough to be sure that the war chief planned to beat both groups while they were apart. If he had defeated Lewis today, it would have been a simple matter to take the northern division out as the regulars crossed over the Ohio.

But none of that mattered to him. All that mattered was finding Carrie. And all he could think of was that she and Efrem had somehow made it back to the camp. That the men he'd asked as they fought the battle had been mistaken.

In his heart he knew that if they'd seen her, they'd tell him.

The alternative was unthinkable.

"Connor?" Andrew stood in the middle of the camp, surrounded by men who were attempting to give him reports. The big man brushed them away as Connor paced into the clearing. "My God, you're alive."

"Aye," Connor said grimly. "Is it true about Charlie?"

Andrew nodded. "He made it back here. He died . . ." Andrew pinched the bridge of his nose to halt his tears. "He died while talking to me."

"I'm sorry," Connor said, and placed his hand on Andrew's shoulder.

"How did you survive?" Andrew asked as if suddenly realizing why Connor was standing before him. "You must have found Carrie or you wouldn't have returned. Where is she? Does her father know?"

Connor dropped his head to his chest. He had hoped against hope that she would be here. That he would see her golden head pop out of one of the tents, that she would come running into his arms. He had prayed and prayed for her safety since the moment the Indians attacked.

She was lost. He wanted to drop to his knees and howl at the darkening sky.

"I've got to find her," he gasped, as if dying for breath. "I donnae ken where she is."

Andrew's face switched from grief to horror in the blink of an eye.

"We were separated," Connor said. "I sent her ahead with Efrem and stayed behind to cover their escape. I ran right into your troops."

"And no one saw them?"

"Nay."

"We'll form a search party," Andrew said, and Connor nodded. He was afraid to speak. Afraid his fear would show. Afraid to go and search and find her body, cold . . . pale . . . dead . . .

Andrew gave orders and men separated to do his bidding, then stopped just as quickly when a great shout came from the southernmost part of the camp.

Two men dragged a prisoner between them. Beaten and bloody, they pulled the Indian up and dropped him at Andrew's feet. The man pitched forward on his stomach and lay shivering in the dirt as a pack was dropped next to him on the ground.

"We captured this 'un trying to sneak into the camp," one soldier said as he delivered a swift kick to the prisoner's midsection. The Indian grunted in pain.

The other one spit in the direction of the prisoner. "This one speaks English, General. He kept saying your name over'nover agin."

"Efrem!" Connor pushed the men away and turned his friend over. "Where is she? What happened to Carrie?"

Efrem's hands were tied and he attempted to push his hair out of his face. His teeth chattered as he looked up at Connor and managed a weak smile.

"We were attacked by warriors who came from the river," he said weakly. "We fought them . . ."

Efrem was soaking wet and wounded in several places. The cuts and bruises around his face were probably from the men who'd discovered him, but the deep, serious-looking gashes on his arm and chest could only be from a fight to the death. He'd gone into the river. Had Carrie?

"She was hanging on when last I saw her," Efrem said.

"She went over?"

"Yes."

"Where?"

"There would be bodies," Efrem said. "Somewhere along the bank . . ."

There would be bodies. But the Nations were taking their dead with them. Or throwing them in the river. Nowhere on his return had he seen an Indian wounded or dead. And if the Indians did find the men Efrem had killed, would they not find Carrie too?

She was hanging on. . . .

"Help me up," Efrem said. "I will show you."

Connor slashed the bonds that held his friend's wrists as Andrew explained to the circle of men that Efrem was an ally.

"I just thank God that you weren't killed needlessly," he said as he hauled Efrem to his feet.

"The day isn't over yet," Efrem said. It was obvious that he was in a great deal of pain.

"Bring him a horse," Andrew commanded. "And some-one fetch me Charlie's horse."

"They've been stampeded, sir," a voice said.

"Not all of them," Andrew shouted. "Some had sense enough to stay."

A tall, black mare and a smaller sorrel were led up. Andrew handed the reins of the black to Connor. "This is . . . *was* Charlie's mare," he said. "He would have wanted you to have her."

"I cannae . . ."

"Take her. Find your lassie." Andrew turned to Efrem, who was adjusting the strip of linen that someone had just handed him around his middle. He snatched Efrem up around the waist and pitched him onto the back of the sorrel. "Don't come back without her," he said, and slapped the sorrel on the rump.

Efrem doubled over but kept going. "Head toward the river," he told Conner.

Darkness was coming fast. Already the light beneath the trees was dim. The sun seemed to be in a race to hide behind the mountains to the west.

"I'm not sure how far we were from the camp," Efrem said. "I came ashore downriver. It took me the whole day to get back."

"Efrem," Connor said, "no matter what we find, I know ye did your best."

Connor wouldn't blame him. He knew that his friend had done everything in his power to protect her.

Efrem's eyes were not visible in the darkness, but Connor knew they were on him.

"She has a strong spirit," Efrem said. "Her love for you will keep her alive."

Let her be alive . . . .

"It has kept both of you alive," Efrem continued.

Connor kept his eyes on the ground. They should have brought a torch.

The river was to their left. Through the trees they saw the gray ribbon snaking by. Dark masses floated in it.

Bodies.

"They are crossing," Efrem said. "You beat them?"

"I think so," Connor said. "I hope so."

"Look for signs," Efrem said. "We should be close."

Connor's eyes scanned the ground. If the bodies were gone, it would be hard to see blood in the darkness. He wasn't sure if the horses helped or not. Efrem surely couldn't walk, but being mounted made it harder to see.

And it took time for the horses to find a passage through the trees.

He dismounted and handed his reins to Efrem. "I will find her," he said and moved to the riverbank. He stood a good twenty feet above the water as he looked out over its width. Twisted shadows hung about the banks. Tree roots and dead falls from endless floods kept him from seeing his heart's desire. He cupped his hands to his mouth and called out.

"Carrie!"

Birds flew up and squawked angrily. He waited until the flutter quieted and cocked his head toward the river.

All he heard was the sound of the water rushing by.

"Please God," he prayed. "We have come so far . . . please . . ."

"Connor!" Efrem shouted. "This way."

"Let it be her," he said as he ran in the direction of Efrem's voice.

He found Efrem, still astride, with his hand gripped against his side. From the looks of him, Connor was sure he'd broken some ribs. Efrem nodded toward the ground. Even in the darkness Connor could see the dried blood in the leaves and dirt, along with a trail that led to the river-bank.

He ran to the bank, dropped on his stomach and looked. He saw something pale wrapped around a tree root that jutted out from the bank some four feet below him.

"Carrie?" He heard what sounded like a small sigh. She was backed up into the bank where the river undercut the earth with nothing but her hand showing where she gripped the root.

"Come out, lassie . . . Please . . ."

He heard whispering. As if she was saying something over and over again. He couldn't quite grasp what it was.

He heard Efrem make his way up next to him. How was he still standing? "Is she there?"

"Aye. But she willnae come out."

"I'll hold your legs," Efrem said.

Connor shrugged out of his pack and then eased himself out on the bank until he was doubled over at the waist. Efrem lay across his legs to anchor him, so he would not topple into the water.

He touched her hand. It was cold as ice. "Come out, *mo cridhe*," he said gently.

"Fortis et Fidus. Fortis et Fidus. Fortis et Fidus . . ." She said it over and over again. He couldn't see her face, just her legs, bare and ghastly pale against the darkness, and her hand.

"Hang on," he said to Efrem. "I'm pulling her out."

He reached back and felt her body. He was sure he had her upper arm in his hand and pried her fist loose from the tree root and pulled her out by both arms. She felt like a rag doll in his hands.

He braced his arms as he swung her loose.

"Fortis et Fidus. Fortis et Fidus. Fortis et Fidus."

"Pull us up if ye can."

Efrem hauled on Connor's legs until he was once more secure on the bank. Effortlessly, Connor pulled her up until, at long last, he was able to wrap his arms around her.

"Carrie." He kissed the top of her head. " 'Tis safe now." She felt so cold. How was it that she was still alive?

"We need to warm her," Efrem said. He handed Connor his blanket. "We should get her back to camp."

Connor wrapped the blanket around her and held her as tightly as he could. "Shush, *mo cridhe*," he said as she kept repeating the same words over and over.

"Co . . . con . . . Connor?" she mumbled against his chest. "You . . . you . . . ca . . . came." Her voice was weak. As if it were far away.

"I did. Did ye think I wouldnae?"

"I knew you wou . . ." She went limp in his arms.

"Carrie?" Connor felt his heart stop beating and his lungs stop drawing breath as he gently shook her.

Efrem laid his hand on her throat. "She lives," he said. "But we must get back. We must warm her on the inside."

Quickly they went to the horses. With haste they mounted, even though Connor still held Carrie in his arms. He wrapped the blanket around her, made sure every inch was covered, including her face, which he tucked up under his neck.

They had come so far. But they were still in the middle of nowhere with no more shelter than a tent and nothing to warm her but a fire. Would it be enough?

"Please God . . ."

He'd found her.

"Thank you, God . . . Now if it's nae too much to ask, will ye save her?"

Chapter Thirty-six

There were bodies in the water. Everywhere she looked she saw them.

They wanted her to join them.

They even tried to take her with them when they came crashing down right before her. She watched as they came over the bank and bobbed in the water before getting caught up in the current.

Others came after. All day she watched until she lost track of time and warmth and any remembrance of safety.

Connor would come.

Fortis et Fidus. He would come.

Even now she could feel him. She felt the strength of his arms. She felt the warmth of his body. She felt the touch of lips against the top of her head. She heard his voice, coming to her through the cold, through the haze, through the river full of bodies.

"Drink this."

She opened her mouth when she felt the touch of a cup to her lips. Bitter warmth spread down her throat and into her stomach.

"Fortis et Fidus," she said.

"What does that mean?" a voice asked.

" 'Tis my clan motto," he said. "Brave and faithful."

"She is that," Efrem said.

"And a bonny lass besides," a voice rumbled from somewhere above her. "I've sent a message to her father."

"Papa?"

"Shush, *mo cridhe*. Sleep."

Sleep. If only she wasn't so cold. She wanted to sleep. She wanted to sleep forever. Just slide into the river and let it take her away. But she couldn't. Something kept her here. Something made her hold on. Something wouldn't let her go.

"Fortis et Fidus."

"Daftie lass."

She felt warmth. Fire. Blankets. Furs. Skin upon her skin. She reached for it. She grabbed hold. She held on. The warmth was good. The warmth was life.

It wasn't until she felt the bright light of morning against her closed eyelids and heard the sounds of activity outside that she opened her eyes again.

She lay on a pile of furs in a tent. She was naked, lying on her side beneath a pile of blankets with a strong arm thrown over her stomach.

"Connor."

He was instantly awake, looking down at her with eyes so blue she thought her heart would spring forth from her chest. Instead she felt its steady thump, thump, as a wide smile spread over his face.

I'm alive . . . .

"I'm not dreaming?" she asked. In her long hours on the river, the image that she saw now was the very thing that kept her alive, that kept her hanging on, even when she felt her muscles screaming and her resolve weakening. Even when she was so cold, so hungry, so very exhausted, she closed her eyes and thought of Connor.

"If ye are, then 'tis a good one," he said. The look on his face spoke volumes. He was frightened, frightened for her.

"We are safe?"

"Aye." He smile was reassuring, relaxed, confident. "The Indians have gone back across the river. The battle is won for now."

"My father?"

"He is with your uncle, north of here. Andrew sent a courier last night to tell him ye were safe." He pushed her hair away from her face. "I wasnae sure ye were going to make it."

"I held on. I held on for you."

"I never should have left you."

"Efrem . . ." The hollow feeling inside her came back in a rush. Efrem was gone, drowned. He'd tried to save her. "Efrem did his best. I'm so sorry."

"So am I." Connor grinned. "I could hardly sleep for all his snoring." He titled his head toward an empty pallet on the ground beside her. "He slept there last night."

"He's alive?" Joy flooded through her. "I thought he'd drowned. I never saw him come up."

"I nearly did drown," Efrem said. He bent painfully to enter the tent. "It came down to whichever one of us could hold his breath the longest. I won."

Carrie tried to sit up but couldn't until Connor helped her. She clutched a blanket to her neck, reached out her hand and squeezed Efrem's when he took it. "Thank you."

"Yours is a life worth saving," he said as he sat down on the pallet. Carrie settled back against Connor's steady strength. She felt the ridges of his stomach against the bump of her spine. His hand moved over her stomach and pulled her closer. This was where she belonged.

"How did ye wind up going over?" Connor asked. "Did this eejit knock ye over in the fight?"

"No," Carrie said. "I fell over backward when I pulled the tomahawk out."

"The tomahawk out of what?"

I killed a man . . . I killed two men . . . .

She didn't know what to say.

"She fought," Efrem said. "To keep those warriors from killing me. She shot one and buried a tomahawk in the skull of another. She saved my life."

"Yours is a life worth saving," Carrie said. She looked at the Cherokee sitting on the pallet next to her. His arms were bandaged, and beneath his open shirt she saw strips wrapped around his stomach. He was clean, as if he'd just had a bath, and his waist-length hair was damp but neat. His dark eyes glowed with pride and friendship as she smiled at him, then turned to Connor. "There were four of them," she said simply.

Connor looked dumbstruck, but then he shook his head and grinned broadly.

"And to think I was worried about your surviving out here," he said. "I believe ye will survive quite well."

"As long as you are with me," Carrie said.

"Too bad ye didn't have your shoes." He dropped a kiss on top of her head. "You could have used those as weapons."

"I will save those for you."

Efrem looked at them as if they were both insane. "The sutler arrived last night, along with the quartermaster," he said. "His wife has a tub and some clothing, if you are interested."

"I am most interested," Carrie said. She was more than interested. The thought of a bath made her practically giddy. "But only if I can borrow your comb."

Efrem grinned and dug into his pack.

"Is there any food about?" Connor asked as his stomach rumbled. "I am famished."

"I am too," Carrie said. "I cannot remember the last meal I enjoyed."

"There's plenty of beef," Efrem said. "The camp is well supplied." He handed Carrie the comb and slowly rose to his feet. "I'll see what I can find." He paused at the flap of the tent. "I have bad news," he said. "Richard was killed yesterday."

"Richard?" Carrie asked as she turned to face Connor.

"Anne's husband," Connor explained. "Richard Trotter." *Poor Anne . . .*

"I never got to meet him," Carrie said. "Anne was so kind to me."

"She is a good woman," Connor said. "And Will . . ."

"He was your friend?"

"Aye. We lost Charlie too."

"Charles Lewis? I met him. He was so angry when he found out you were locked up."

"Charlie was always good to me," Connor said. "This is his tent. His brother Andrew had been like a father to me. He gave me Charlie's mare." Connor found his breeches and slipped them on beneath the blanket before he stood. "We lost too many good men yesterday. Andrew means to bury them here today."

"What of my father? Did his troops fight also?"

"Nay. This group bore the brunt of the attack. I have a feeling Cornstalk wanted to beat this group, then ambush your father's regiment afterward. He wanted to surprise the English. That's why the warriors left the village as soon as they heard the English were coming."

"It's what saved us," Carrie said. It seemed as if a lifetime had passed since she was in the Shawnee village. "I wonder how many prisoners survived."

"I did see a man carry off a boy when the confusion started." Connor scratched at the growth of beard that covered his chin. "He survived, I'm sure."

"Paul," Carrie said. "I wonder what happened to his family." She looked up at Connor, who raised the flap on the tent to look out. "Your arm," she asked. "How is it healing?"

" 'Tis fine," Connor said. "The surgeon looked at it last night. He said ye were a fair hand with a needle and thread. Then he wanted to know where he could get some of Efrem's poultice."

There was a scar on his back, one she was sure she had not noticed before. Every chance she'd had when they were on the trail to Fort Savannah she'd looked at him, especially when he had his shirt off. She was sure she would have noticed this scar. It was a round puckering of skin that looked fairly fresh.

"How did that happen?" she asked. "The scar on your back. It looks as if you were shot." Who would shoot him in the back? And why? She couldn't imagine Connor running away from a fight.

Connor looked over his shoulder at the scar, then placed his hand on his stomach. Carrie realized there was another smaller scar there.

"I got it the day ye were taken," he said. "'Tis why it took me so long to find ye."

"I don't understand," Carrie said. "Were you attacked too?"

"It doesnae matter," Connor said. "I wish I could have spared ye the hell ye went through. I wish I could have gotten to ye before they took ye across the river. I wish I wasnae so stubborn that ye had to come find me at Anne's."

"Connor, none of this is your fault," Carrie said. "I don't blame you." She looked up into his eyes. She felt as if she were on the edge of a precipice. So much had happened. More than she could possibly recall. Most of it she wanted to forget. But through everything, she'd had only one dream. And he was standing before her. But did he share her love? So many times he had pushed her away. Yet he'd crossed the wilderness to find her. He was willing to trade his life for hers. Still she said, "I have to know. Why did you come for me? Was it guilt?"

He rubbed his hands through his hair as if he needed to find the answer, and suddenly she was very afraid.

"I came because I love ye," he said. "And because I am an eejit."

One answer pretty much contradicted the other, but she realized he wasn't done speaking when he sat down cross-legged before her.

"I have lived with guilt all these years because Tom was killed instead of me," he said. "It kept me from truly living. I always felt as if I should have died because Tom had so much to live for. Then, when you were taken, I realized I was not honoring his memory by throwing your love away. I figured my death would be penance for not appreciating the gift you'd given me." He shrugged. "As I said, I am an eejit. And I truly love you."

Carrie's heart sang. The look on his face spoke volumes. He was scared of losing her again. He was scared she'd turn away. How could she? She loved him with all her heart. All her soul. All her being. "That is all that matters," she said. "That is all we need."

"Will ye marry me?"

"Yes. Now. Today. Is that possible?"

"Would ye not want your father present?"

"I only want you, Connor. And Efrem, I suppose," she added with a grin.

"As long as he doesnae share our bed, he can come."

"I only want you."

The minister who was praying over the dead married them. Carrie wore clothes borrowed from the sutler's wife, with her leggings and moccasins beneath because she had no petticoats. Connor bathed and shaved and put on the white shirt that was stuffed at the bottom of his pack. The shirt he'd worn the night of the ball. It was dusk when they stood in the middle of the camp with the militia gathered around them.

Carrie carried a bouquet of brightly colored autumn leaves tied together with her lace cap around them, courtesy of Efrem.

"What day is it?" Carrie asked when they were pronounced man and wife and Connor kissed her soundly.

Connor shrugged. He wasn't even sure what month it was.

"Tuesday, October the twelfth," Andrew rumbled. "Seventeen seventy-four," he added with a sly grin.

"So much time," Carrie said. "Was it just this spring that we met?"

" 'Tis not the time past that concerns me," Connor said. "But the time we have before us."

"Here's to many years of health and happiness," Andrew exclaimed with a portion of ale that the sutler was more than happy to provide. For a profit.

"Here, here!" the members of the militia agreed.

A fiddle was brought out, and the celebration commenced. Carrie had spent the day in happy anticipation when Connor told her there was a minister in camp and he'd agreed to marry them. But now that it was done, she found she was too weary to stand. She hung heavily on Connor's arm as they were congratulated. She could barely keep her eyes open.

Connor lifted her in his arms to many whoops and calls and carried her to the tent, which had been moved away from the main camp to give them privacy.

" 'Tis not much of a wedding night," he said as he lowered her to her feet. There was a thick pallet of furs covered with a blanket in the middle of the tent, and a lantern hung from one of the posts. His pack and weapons were carefully arranged in a corner by the flap.

"It doesn't matter," Carrie said. "The only thing that matters is that we're together." Her mouth opened in a yawn, and she quickly covered it with her hand and blushed furiously. It was their wedding night. And she was so sleepy she couldn't stand.

Connor grinned. "Off with your clothes then," he said as he bent over to whip his shirt off over his head. He tossed it in the corner next to his pack.

"What?" This wasn't quite what she'd expected as he stood before her.

Connor slowly pulled her bodice loose and down her arms. He undid the ties on her skirt, lifted her off the ground and kicked it away, leaving her wearing nothing but a shift, moccasins and leggings.

He knelt on the ground before her, and Carrie couldn't help touching his hair. It glowed like copper in the light from the lantern and felt silky between her fingers. Connor's hands slid up her leg to the tops of her thighs and a shiver went through her. He unlaced her leggings and slowly slid them down each leg, then removed her moccasins. As he stood, he brought her shift up over her head and tossed it in the direction of her skirt.

Cold air touched her body, but she didn't care this time. She knew she'd be warm soon enough. Connor picked her up and placed her on the furs. He extinguished the lantern, and Carrie watched the silhouette made by the firelight from outside as he stepped out of his moccasins and breeches. He lay down beside her, pulled a blanket over them and kissed her deeply as her arms twined around his neck. Then he flipped her on her side, pulled her against his stomach and whispered in her ear.

"Go to sleep, lassie. I fear I am too tired to please you right now."

Carrie settled against him. The feel of his body against her was comforting. She felt safe, she felt warm, she felt loved.

She felt at home.

Chapter Thirty-seven

She was so beautiful. In the dim light of morning Connor looked at the shadows beneath her eyes and the hollows in her cheeks. The time just passed had been hard on her. It was a miracle she was still alive after all she'd suffered. Yet she still was as breathtakingly beautiful as the first time he'd seen her on the streets of Williamsburg.

Fortis et Fidus . . .

His hand moved over the contour of her stomach. He counted every rib.

"Ye will never go hungry again," he promised.

"Hmmm?"

Carrie snuggled up against him, and Connor felt every part of his body spring to life with an ache that had nothing to do with the trials he'd faced or the battle just fought.

He wanted her.

"Carrie?"

She turned and opened her eyes as he propped himself up on his side and looked down at her. He pushed back her hair, cupped her cheek and kissed her. She warmed to him instantly. Her tongue chased his as he teased her lips, and his hand moved down her neck to her breast.

"Mo cridhe."

Her arms moved around his neck. Her fingers wrapped in his hair as his hand trailed down and his mouth followed, exploring what she generously offered.

"Mo leannon," he whispered against her breast, and her back arched in pleasure.

"My wife," he said as he entered her, and she looked up at him with eyes as blue as the summer sky.

"I love ye," he said when she lay across his chest and he stroked her hair. He felt a peace and comfort spread through his soul that he'd never thought possible. Happiness lay sprawled across his chest with her blue eyes smiling at him. "God, I love ye."

"Whore," a voice snarled. He caught a glimpse of a red coat as the tent flap dropped.

"Who was it?" Carrie asked with trembling lips.

Connor felt his jaw go rigid. Who dared to insult his wife? Who dared to interrupt their privacy? Who dared to judge them? He wrapped a blanket around Carrie.

"Stay here," he said as he jerked on his breeks and picked up his knife.

"Connor?"

"I will take care of it," he said. He saw the fear in her eyes. He'd hoped never to see it again. When would her hell be over? Was it because of who he was? Was it because she chose to be with him?

He stepped outside the tent.

It was her brother. He held the reins of his horse and seemed ready to mount.

"Murray!" Connor roared.

Murray dropped his reins and came for him.

Connor heard Carrie behind him. He heard her gasp as her brother marched toward them with his jaw set and his fists clenched. Murray stopped when he stood chest to chest with him.

"You have defiled my family name," he said.

I should kill him . . . I should kill him and be done with it. . . . He felt the blade in his hand and knew it would only take a moment to bury it in Murray's throat.

Connor saw Efrem standing by the fire watching them. Some of the men of the militia had also noticed the confrontation, and a slight sound of restlessness moved about the camp.

There would be witnesses. But none would blame him. *'Tis her brother . . . she loves him . . .*

Carrie stepped between them, wearing nothing but a blanket clutched firmly beneath her chin. "He is your family now, John. We are married."

Connor could have struck the man and done less damage. A look of horror spread over Murray's face and he stepped back. "How did this happen? Did you consent out of gratitude? Fear? What did he do to you?"

Carrie stepped toward her brother. "I married him because I love him. And he loves me."

Fortis et Fidus. . . .

"How could you do this? Don't you know what he is?"

Connor felt the muscle twitch in his jaw, but he stayed still. For Carrie's sake.

"I do. He is brave and honorable. And for the life of me, I do not understand why you can't see that."

"He's a bloody Scot!"

"He's my husband."

God, he loved her.

"John," Carrie said, "you told me to choose. I choose him. And I choose him for me. Not for you, not for Papa, not for Mama. For me. I choose Connor. I choose to live with a man I love no matter the circumstances. You choose to hate him for reasons of your own. I can't change that. With or without your blessing, I am Connor Duncan's wife."

"What about our father?" John asked incredulously. "Where is he?"

"He's with Lord Dunmore. When we got the message you'd been rescued, he sent me to bring you to him."

"Tell our father that you found me well and happy and with my husband," Carrie said. "He will understand."

John shook his head. "Carrie . . ."

She stepped back until she was braced against Connor's chest. Connor put his hand on her shoulder and she reached up and took it. "I love him, John. I only hope that one day some woman will love you as much. Be safe. You can find us on the Blue Ridge come spring."

Murray opened his mouth to speak and then snapped it shut. He turned briskly and went to his horse. He rode away without a backward glance.

They watched him go. Would they ever see him again? Carrie turned and buried her face in his chest. Connor wrapped his arms around her.

Fortis et Fidus . . . .

"I'm sorry for ye, lass."

"Don't be," she said. She looked up at him with tear-filled eyes. "I'm exactly where I want to be."

"But what of your father?"

"You notice he did not come himself?"

"Aye."

"I know that he loves us. But it's always been this way. Country first. Duty first. He chose to stay where he is, just as I chose to stay to with you. He will understand. He will give us his blessing when he's done fighting this battle."

"Ye are a brave lass." He rubbed away the tears from beneath her eyes.

"And daft?" She smiled up at him.

"Aye, that too," he said as he kissed her.

Spring, 1775

He was nervous. He didn't quite know why except that maybe he'd been too enthusiastic when describing the cabin and his land.

They would arrive soon enough and then she would see for herself.

They had wintered at Fort Savannah. Carrie's father had returned there after the treaty with Cornstalk and the Nations and had given them his blessing, along with Carrie's mother's ring for her to wear. John did not come. He went to a posting in the north. Her father said to let him be for a bit, and Carrie agreed with him.

Connor and Efrem spent the winter trapping, and Carrie learned as much as she could from Anne about making a home.

In her grief, Anne seemed to be grateful for Carrie's presence. Carrie looked after Will quite a bit while Anne went out into the wilderness. She seemed determined to take on the responsibilities of her dead husband. It was sad to watch, but everyone had their own way of grieving. God only knew what he would do if he lost Carrie.

When the spring thaw came, they traded their furs for supplies and made their way down the Shenandoah Valley toward home.

There was a babe on the way. Carrie was determined that it would be born under their own roof, and Connor was determined that roof would be sound before the babe's arrival in late summer.

"Not much farther," he said.

Carrie smiled at him from atop the black mare. Connor and Efrem both led horses heavily laden with supplies. He hoped it would be enough to sustain them through the winter.

"I cannot wait," she said.

The forest on the mountain curved down and away and opened into a wide valley that seemed to hang just below the treetops. A meadow curved over the top, wide, bountiful and covered with fresh spring grass. A creek wound through it close to the woods, and beneath a grove of hemlocks sat a one-room cabin.

Connor stopped and put a hand on the bridle of the black mare.

"This is it," he said as he looked up at his wife.

A look of peace spread over her face. Her eyes swept from one side to the other, seeing the very things that made it such a fine place. There was water. There was pasture. There was shelter beneath the trees.

"It's beautiful," she said.

"I am happy that you think it so," he said.

"It's a fine place," Efrem said.

"You are still sleeping in the shed," Connor reminded him.

They moved out into the meadow and were greeted by a shrill call. A snowy white stallion bolted across the grass. It kicked up its heels and tossed its head at these strangers who had entered his world.

"It's Sultan," Carrie said. "John's stallion. Isn't it?"

Connor was dumbstruck at the sight, but he finally let out a whistle as they watched the horse run around the meadow.

To his delight his whistle was answered with a neigh, and Heather lumbered out of the wood from behind the cabin. She was wide with foal.

Connor laughed.

"It looks like she found her way home after the attack," Efrem said.

"And brought Sultan with her?" Carrie asked.

"Aye," Connor said. "She came home."

He helped Carrie down from her horse and they walked toward the cabin hand in hand.

"It will be a way to make peace with John," she said.

"Do ye think he'd come all this way for his horse?"

"He would," she said. "He loves Sultan. Look at how far you came for me."

Connor stopped and pulled her into his arms. "I think from now on I will keep ye close at hand," he said.

Carrie laid her head on his shoulder. "That's exactly where I want to be."

Don't miss Victoria Morrow's sweeping saga of passion and revenge, set amid the blood, sweat and tears of linking East and West with the transcontinental railway.

Coming in September,

THE EAGLE
AND DOVE
THE

CHAPTER ONE

Sangre de Cristo Mountain Range,
 May 1851

He had been born in the dark of a November night twenty-four years before near the Canadian border. He was a Celt. The stark Highlands of his ancestry were apparent in his pale skin, which contrasted sharply with his dark eyes and hair. He towered over most men and spoke Gaelic fluently, the language his father spoke to him, as well as a curious mixture of French, English and Pigeon Blackfoot. He was a white man raised in a red world and comfortable in his skin.

He came from the high country where Old Man Winter still had a stranglehold on the land and the world was blinding white and his traps were full. He had ridden hard for nearly a week, pushing his big, dun-colored stallion until its powerful body was bathed in lather and its once nimble legs shook from exhaustion.

He slept little and ate less. Pulling a piece of deer jerky from his pack every now and then, he would suck on it until it softened and the smoky juices ran down his parched throat. He was going toward the dunes at the base of the ridge, a mountain man covered in buck-skins and fur with a shock of wild, midnight hair blowing in the wind and piercing, black eyes locked onto the horizon. He wasn't alone.

Above him in the zinc-colored sky, an elegant falcon-hawk circled lazily, easily keeping pace with his relentless speed; traveling beside him loped a lean slant-eyed wolf. The three were companions, a trinity of primitive power; beating wings, talons, fangs, sinew and cunning, bound together by the knowledge that they were of the same clan: predators. Yet, though all were formidable, the mountain man was, by far, the most dangerous of the three. Cresting a bald ridge of rock, he pulled back on the soaking reins, stopping abruptly in a shower of powder-red dust and fragments of nail-thin shale.

"Ease up, horse," he growled as he absently wiped the sweat from his upper lip. "'Tis the blighted camp of the Philistines."

His voice, though companionably soft, was filled with such unmistakable menace that his horse's ears came to attention and began to dance as nervously as its feet. Narrowing his eyes, the man studied the scene below.

Hatred, there was hatred in every breath he took, in every shuddering beat of his heart. And he didn't turn away from it—instead he touched it, breathed it in, owned it until he became it.

Other men might have walked away, trusting God or a badge to fight their battles for them. But not him. His blessing and his curse was the nobility of his soul. He knew right from wrong and took responsibility for every thought, action or deed his mouth uttered or hand performed, expecting others to do the same.

God might show mercy, but Jesse McCallum wouldn't.

Beneath him, nestled as contentedly near the root of the Sangre de Cristo Mountains as an infant to its mother's teat, was a small, crudely built cabin. Massive dunes of rolling sand surrounded it on three sides while on the fourth, a vertical wall of granite effectively sealed the basin from the rest of the range. No one could approach from across the dunes without being seen for miles.

Jesse knew the odds and weighed his options carefully. He knew it was certain suicide for anyone to attempt to approach the cabin on foot or by horse, especially in daylight. Yet he knew that even if he had to go through the front door with his guns blazing, he would do whatever it took to bring his father's killers to justice.

Calmly he noted that behind the house stood a makeshift pen fashioned with posts of thorny mesquite and rails of frayed hemp, spliced now and then with bits of knotted rags that still hinted at some nearly forgotten color. Every few feet, empty cans that were once filled with succulent peaches, tangy stewed tomatoes and other such citified delicacies, were tied to the uppermost rope, clanking noisily like a poor-man's chimes with each passing gust of wind. The "gate"— and it was charity to call it that—was nothing more than the mummified remains of a buckboard, bleached nearly white and laid on its side. Decorating its sagging top were stiff gray blankets, mile-worn saddles, tangled leather traces and rusty bits, one for each of the dozen horses and the odd assortment of New Mexico mules, mingling without prejudice, in the little pen. Just outside the corral and within mere spitting distance from the front door of the house was a pyramid of packs filled to overflowing with stolen booty.

All of this Jesse noted without a hint of surprise, as though he had beheld the scene many times before in the misty landscape of his mind. Yet he knew the picture wasn't complete, so he continued to search, scanning the grounds until he found the missing pieces to the puzzle he had come so far to solve.

"There you are!" he said.

His voice sounded strange. His words were whispered, barely more than a phantom of sound, spoken so gently they seemed less than a sigh. But what a frightful expression colored his eyes! They gleamed like black opals filled with infernal fire, hellish in intensity and intent.

Cursed.

It was as if the tortured soul imprisoned within the massive tower of flesh was slowly dying. A once proud soul ravaged so savagely by the cold hand of guilt that it believed itself lost forever. Beyond hope. Beyond forgiveness. Dead to everything except pain.

He suffered in silence, and he suffered alone.

"And here I am," he said at last.

He announced his arrival in a voice so heartbreakingly soft, so filled with sorrow and regret that the fickle wind seemed to moan in sympathy as it passed.

His journey was over; the circle was about to close....